THE PENANCE WAS DEATH

The
Penance
Was
Death

LENA B. McNAMARA

The Bruce Publishing Company
Milwaukee

Library of Congress Catalog Card Number: 64-21061

To
MARGARET HALEY CARPENTER
Poet, Author, and Invaluable Friend

THE PENANCE WAS DEATH

Chapter One

THERE was silence in the great gloomy room, but not peaceful silence, for a battle was going on: a battle of wits. The flames on the hearth of the black marble mantle added their small quota of light to the one illumined corner, where a shaded lamp showed two figures bent over a checkerboard placed on the table between them. Both were deeply engrossed in the strategy of the next move. Then an old man's arthritic blue-veined hand stretched out from the worn velvet sleeve of his smoking jacket and carefully placed a king into a new position. Very slowly the hand withdrew, and now the silence was broken by triumphant mirth. Hiram Bosch, with rapier-sharp wits at the age of eighty, was goading and baiting his friend, the Rev. John Mark Clemens, pastor of St. Mary's impoverished Catholic parish.

And even before the priest's hand, which suggested those in a drawing by Albrecht Dürer, sensitive and strong and capable, a poet's hand, a workman's, stretched forward to counter his opponent's move, Father John acknowledged his defeat with a smile. Not a very convincing smile, it didn't succeed in suppressing traces of keen disappointment. He watched now as the old man eagerly snatched up his red king and with a lightning move jumped the last three black crowns, the priest's sole remaining men, swiftly sweeping them off the board.

Then he lay back in his spacious chair, a little old figure of unholy glee.

Father John pushed back his chair and was about to rise when, at the far end of the library, the door opened suddenly and the slim young figure of Dale Moncure was silhouetted against the light of the hall.

The door slammed shut again as the girl came forward quickly, reached out, and snapped the wall switch lighting the great crystal chandelier. Dale, vivid and brisk, bringing a gust of fresh moist air from outside, greeted her beloved pastor, and planted a kiss upon the parchment skin of her great-uncle's forehead.

"Uncle Hi," she began enthusiastically, "I've got a surprise for you." Then she paused, seeing the checkerboard, the red king commanding the empty squares. She glanced knowingly at Father John. "Never mind, Father, we'll lick him yet. Listen, Hi — "

"Get off that wet monkey jacket and warm up, gal. I don't like wet fur hugging me. How can I help it if the Reverend Father is off his game?" The mouth snapped open and shut again, and the shoulders shook, then "He that hath patience may compass anything," he quoted. He looked at Dale. "Rabelais, of course."

Dale, slipping out of her damp squirrel jacket, and tossing it carelessly upon the worn brocaded sofa back against the wall, continued to regard her uncle with mock sternness as she spoke to the priest.

"So, the old boy didn't let you win — been bedeviling you again, postponing his donation to The Nursery." Back of the banter there was real disappointment in Dale's voice.

Father John said quickly, his blue eyes placating her: "Yes, and quoting patience to me! Why he's built up in me such a store of patience for so long that I can even hope to save his soul one of these fine days." Father John chuckled. "Never mind, Dale, it was a good game, and as he only lets me win when he's feeling very generous, all my brilliant moves would be wasted anyway, so that's why I never make them."

"If you have done with the smart talk, Monkey," Hi said, cocking a beady eye at Dale, "I'd like to have my toddy. Maggie as usual with her light-headed, absentminded — " He broke off as the door behind him opened and Maggie, bearing a small tray on which one single glass half filled with a pale mixture which might have been whisky and water, came hurrying in and placed it with a flourish on the table in front of Hi, in the center of the checkerboard.

"Light-headed, is it?" she said. "And absentminded?" Maggie was pink-cheeked and plump, with black-lashed Irish blue eyes that still looked round and innocent after fifty-odd years of hard living, most of it spent under the roof of Hiram Bosch, pandering to his capricious temper and rearing his small orphaned great-niece.

"No, don't get up, Father. It's a half hour before dinner and, with Rosina's help, I'm browning the roast which, though light-headed and absentminded I might be, I promise will be worth the staying to enjoy and give the blessing for." Maggie's round sturdy little back turned haughtily away from Hi and made a rapid passage back the way she had come, swinging the door shut behind her. The cook, Rosina, had been recently hired to help Maggie in the kitchen.

Dale sat now on a low stool near the fire, and Father John, looking with affection at the girl's unconscious grace, noted the fine poise of her head and the set of her square, straight shoulders. The firelight threw her face into halftone, but glinted on her short tumbled hair, tinting its blond brightness with an apricot glow, touching into light the high delicate contour of her cheekbone and repeating the accent on her firm, rounded chin. Father John had a very paternal devotion to this child since Maggie had brought her, a little girl of three, to the rectory, and presented herself to him, a much younger Maggie.

"This is little Dale Moncure, Father, the poor little motherless, fatherless girl. Killed in that wreck they were, you read in the papers, Father. And now I'm to bring the poor child up in her great-uncle's home."

"And who is her uncle?" Father John had asked.

"Hiram Bosch, he is, Father, and you must know of him, in the great house on Bermuda Street. He's not of the Faith, or any faith at all, excusing me, Your Reverence; but I made it clear that if I was to raise the child, it's a Catholic she should be and nothing else. So I've come to you, Father, to baptize her, and it should have been done long ago."

So the Reverend John Mark Clemens had become godfather and

3

Margaret Mary Riley, godmother to little Dale Moncure, great-niece of that eccentric old agnostic, a descendant, so he proudly claimed, of Hieronymus Bosch, the fifteenth-century Flemish artist.

Hiram Bosch, though not an artist, had claim to distinction in his own right. His talents had taken a different turn, but there were many who said that Hiram, the stockbroker, and his brother Walter, the banker, had each made an art of his profession. The "Brothers Bosch" had a touch of genius, if success was any proof of it. Each had amassed a fortune. Of the two, Hi's career had, characteristically, been more spectacular.

When Walter, in his prime, died of a heart attack, he left all of his affairs in his brother's hands. Because he had little confidence in women's business ability, and none at all in his two daughters', the ultraconservative banker had created a trust fund, naming Hiram as his administrator.

Marcia, twenty-two, and Dale, seventeen, Walter's two daughters, were each to receive a monthly check — a comfortable amount — but allowing no extravagance — made out by "Uncle Hi." In addition, there was a reserve fund set aside for emergency, to be drawn upon at Hiram's discretion.

Marcia, not surprisingly, resented being treated as a minor, and was outraged at the final clause which provided that in the event of Hiram's death, the bank should carry on with no change of procedure, until both daughters had reached the prudent age of forty, when the estate would be equally divided between them. But as long as Hiram lived, he must handle the funds, as set forth in the first clause of Walter's unique will. It proved a hair shirt for Hi. It was a pure nuisance, he grumbled, and it set a premium on his life. Walter, as president of his own bank, should, Hi felt, have given the bank this job in the first place — the whole job.

But canny Walter knew his two girls, and that Hi was the man to handle them. Dale, his favorite, subjugated everyone by her gaiety and charm, but Marcia, Hi declared, was another bill of goods altogether. Marcia, he claimed, could produce more emergencies than a cat could kittens.

High-spirited Dale, soon after her father's death, had run off and

4

married a very fine young man. And Hi had forgiven her, because he liked the boy, who was the son of an old friend — and because Dale knew exactly how to manage her uncle.

Marcia had married also, and been divorced after a few unhappy years. She had succeeded in obtaining her freedom on the basis of mental cruelty. With Hi's consent she had returned to her father's handsome house, which had never been sold. The old residence had been impressive in its day, and Marcia clinging to the prestige of Walter Bosch's name and fortune, played the grand lady in public, but was an embittered and grasping woman within her own family circle.

No sooner was Marcia settled, than Dale and her husband had both been instantly killed in a car accident. Probably the most genuine act of love in his whole life was his taking Maggie, the young Irish nursemaid, and Dale's little daughter into his home to live with him. Hi had been rewarded. The little girl was very much like her mother, and there had grown up between him and the child of his favorite niece a bond of understanding and affection.

The child of his favorite niece sat now within a few feet of her benefactor, gazing quietly into the fire and furiously plotting to wrench his munificence from him. Direct appeal would fail now, she knew.

The surprise she had eagerly spoken of when she had first come in, and which had been then a purely altruistic desire to give her uncle pleasure, she now turned to account. She'd still let Hi get the picture that her cousin Walter had told her about, but she would handle the deal and extract a commission on the sale, from old Capelli. That would be perfectly legitimate, and good business for the art dealer Capelli, and for The Nursery. She'd give the money to Father John to help with the expenses of running his home for babies, which was always in need of funds. They dreadfully needed a new kitchen stove, and new linoleum for the playroom to match up the color in the Mother Goose pictures which she was painting for it in her studio upstairs. It ought to be enough for both. That picture was a prize!

Delighted with her sudden new plan, Dale turned a glowing face from the warmth of the fire and bestowed her most charming smile

5

upon her great-uncle, breaking the silence which had held since Maggie's exit.

"Hi, darling, don't you want to know about that surprise? It's really *most* stupendous!"

Hi chuckled. "I'll warrant it's something you want yourself. If it's a new car for you to scour around in with my secretary, instead of going to your art classes, the answer is NO. You and Father John may think that Bill's an embryo medical genius, but he can't even get the kinks out of my typewriter."

Dale disdained to rise to this bait. Bill didn't pretend to be a professional secretary or typist either. He would go back to finish at medical school as soon as the emergency created by his father's illness would permit. Hi knew that. Bill was far too good for this job, though he'd been glad to get it, and grateful to Hi for giving it to him. It wasn't all one-sided though. Who else would put up with Hi's temperament — and rummage through stacks and stacks of old books, tracing the Bosch family tree?

She said in a slightly bored tone: "You don't appreciate your blessings, Hi. Some day you'll brag about having a speaking acquaintance with the eminent Dr. William Ballard. I am sure he wouldn't tell you, but Bill was leading his class — an honor student — when he had to come home. But my surprise has nothing to do with Bill. Believe it or not, your nephew, Walter, for once, has thought of someone beside himself — and that someone is YOU."

"Well, well, his mother will approve of his keeping on the good side of the money bags." Hi grimaced with faint amusement. Dale waved him off.

"Do you want to know it or don't you? What would you say if I told you that Walter had found a painting that you will give your eyeteeth for; an Hieronymus Bosch! Right here in Brambleton, in old Capelli's shop."

Father John turned interested, doubtful eyes upon Dale, but she met his questioning look with a straight, clear gaze of undeniable innocence. Father John relaxed. But not Hi. She had her triumph in the old man's reaction. He sat up like a charged wire, drained the the last of his toddy, and smacked the glass down.

6

"A genuine Bosch? Where is it?"

Dale hesitated, she had to be honest. "It isn't signed, Hi. Capelli won't say; it has all the earmarks — it's simply fantastic — no one else ever painted such things, but it's a marvelous copy, done by one of his students, possibly; who knows?" Dale watched for a lessening of interest. "Anyway you'll never come nearer the real thing. I'll venture to bet that Mr. Donald would have snatched it for the museum if he'd seen it first. I will hand it to Walter; he spotted it back in the shop and made old Capelli bring it out. Walter has a flare. If he'd go in for collecting, he might really make a thing of it."

"On a bank teller's salary?" Hi scoffed. "Walter will never be anything more than a clerk. . . ." Hi screwed up his face in a disapproving scowl at the thought of Marcia's son. Dale hastily dropped Walter and entered the play on her own.

"How much does Capelli want for it?" Hi asked. Dale saw the calculating glint in the old man's eyes and decided to squash it then and there.

"It's not a bargain, Hi. If you are going to hagle about it I won't even ask Capelli to let me bring it here for you to see. I don't know what he wants, but it won't be cheap."

"If it's something you approve of, I'll tell the world it won't be cheap," a voice drawled pleasantly from the doorway. Dale jumped up, a deeper color showing in her already pink cheeks.

"Bill, I'm telling Uncle Hi about the picture." She turned to her uncle quickly, "Bill was with me when I went in to look at it. He can tell you it really is a honey — tell him, Bill."

Father John laughed, not ill pleased at the obvious state of affairs between these two young people.

She watched Bill come and greet Father John first. Standing there, the two were just the same height, Bill's hand gripping the priest's for a moment affectionately. Two fine faces; contrast of youth to age; zest and courage in Bill's, experience and strength in the priest's. She was jerked out of her absorption by an angry exclamation from her Uncle Hi. Dale turned quickly.

"Puppy love!" Dale heard her uncle mutter.

"Bill," she said, "if Father won't stay and bless Maggie's roast,

7

you might give him a ride back to the rectory. My car is parked right outside, and the weather is beastly. I would do it myself, but Uncle Hi and I have an important little business to talk over, and we'd like to finish it now. Besides, the painting I showed today in the Museum Portrait Show got a blue ribbon and Uncle Hi is going to be the first to see it."

Dale was grateful for Bill's understanding look; and Father John, of course, fell into line. The priest maintained that he had meant what he said: he had a meeting and couldn't possibly stay. He'd give the roast his blessing from a distance. As the door closed behind them, Dale tucked her arm through the old man's and gave it a little squeeze. "Now we can have a nice quiet talk, all to ourselves."

The old man sat back in the high-winged chair, pulled his pipe from the deep side pocket of his smoking jacket, and Dale pulled her low stool over close beside him. Hi threw back his head, opened his mouth, and snapped it shut again, while his shoulders shook.

"You're a conniving little vixen, but you're a chip off the old block, and I'm going to make an artist out of you. You understand?"

Dale knew better than to argue. "Let out a little line," she told herself. She sighed contentedly and patted his tight, hardfisted old hand.

Chapter Two

LATE the next afternoon Dale stood in line before the teller's window in the Southside Tidewater Bank and watched Walter doing his job. These Friday special banking hours in afternoons and evenings were always crowded, but portrait class had lasted until nearly four.

There was a long queue ahead of her so Dale had plenty of time to observe Walter's technique. Smooth, unhurried, yet lightning-quick, he dispatched each customer with a smile of pleasant assurance. As she watched she wondered if Uncle Hi wasn't wrong about Walter's never being anything more than a clerk. Of course Hi had never seen Walter at work, although he'd wangled this job for him; no not wangled, for all her uncle had to do was raise a finger to get what he wanted at this bank. But Dale, who had never really watched Walter herself, until now, found it hard to believe that this young man, who was so graciously serving each one of the motley crowd of tired people as they edged up to his window, could possibly be her snobbish, supercilious cousin.

She watched Walter take that grimy check from the old man ahead of her and hand him a couple of dollar bills and some small change, with as good grace as if it had been a million-dollar deposit. His manner was quite convincing.

"It's not only his manner," thought Dale, "his ease and suavity, but it's his whole presence." Immaculate, impeccable, from his sleek blond head down as far as she could see, which was about the third button

9

of his well-fitting coat, Walter gave the impression that no less a person than the second vice-president (albeit so youthful) had slipped into the cage to give his personal attention to the clientele.

"How's the big executive, Walter? You do it awfully well." She smiled at him as she slipped her own moderate check beneath the chromium bars of the teller's cage.

Walter nodded in nonchalant acknowledgment of her compliment, picked up her check, held it a moment in manicured fingers, and winked at her.

"Might as well dish it out to them with a smile. Besides you never know who's noticing." He was frankly cynical now. He looked at Dale's check and counted out two tens and a five.

"My prize money for the blue-ribbon portrait." Then she wondered why she'd troubled to explain.

"The family's drawing heavily on its accounts today. Add three goose eggs to that and you'll be matching Uncle Hi." Walter's tone was provocative. He looked at her with a question in his eyes. But Dale didn't notice, she was slipping the money into her wallet and only heard something about goose eggs and didn't bother to ask what he meant. She wanted to talk about the picture, but she didn't think she ought to hold up the people behind her, so she simply said, "This morning I went to see the picture again. Tomorrow I'm to take it for Hi to look at, and since it's Saturday and the shop closes early, I can keep it over the weekend. Come around and see what he thinks of it."

Walter raised skeptical eyebrows. "Did you see old Capelli?" he asked.

"No, only Nick was there — his son, isn't he?"

"His nephew. Capelli's training him. I doubt if Nick will train well. . . ." Walter shrugged. "I knew him at high school." Dale moved away wondering how much commission she could get out of Capelli for the Bosch picture. She had no idea what a copy, even a fine one, was worth, and she hadn't been able to pin Capelli down. She wondered if Walter knew. As she paused, and glanced back, hesitating, Walter looked over the head of the woman who had just moved up to his window and raised his voice for Dale to hear.

10

"I don't think I'll be home for supper tonight. Will you call and tell the Mater that I'm busy? She likes plenty of notice."

"Walter never did anything he could get someone to do for him," Dale thought.

Dale threaded her way through the parking lot to her small sports car with the red leather seat cushions that matched her bright hat. She got in and sat idly for a moment, gazing at the labyrinth of cars around her, seeing none of them. Automatically she dug into her bag for her lipstick.

She was full of hope and plans, of thoughts of all that she could do for St. Mary's Nursery. She pictured Father John's face if she told him that now he could go ahead with the new kitchen equipment, and little Sister Dennis could stop hauling coal for that antiquated old range. She loved Sister Dennis, who looked just exactly like the "Old Woman Who Lived in a Shoe," with her full-skirted gray habit, white linen pinafore and bonnet. Only Sister Dennis was not old; she was just tired and overworked. With those beautiful big eyes and lovely white teeth, she'd be a knockout in an ivory satin strapless evening gown and little silver slippers. Dale tried to picture it, and giggled. All that elegance topped by a shorn head.

"Lady, you're holdin' up this space!" The parking attendant looked pained but accepted her tip ungraciously and Dale apologized, feeling foolish. She maneuvered her car out of the narrow area.

She was in the center of the midtown shopping district and she'd have to go south and then east to get back to the old part of town, which had once been the rich residential section when Brambleton was young. Uncle Hi's house had been built in seventeen hundred and something, then a little later Gothic St. Mary's Church. It was the earliest church in Brambleton except old St. Paul's Episcopal, which had been a neighbor since Brambleton was a borough.

Dale loved this part of town, although it was deteriorating too rapidly for comfort. Hi's house and Aunt Marcia Rowlands were among the few remaining good old landmarks in the section now.

One of the first things that Dale remembered being told when she was a little girl was that she lived in the house where Lafayette had spent a night, and maybe even George Washington, too. All Dale was sure of was that the old brick mansion had been in the family for generations. Maggie wove tales about it all, and Dale knew she was making them up for her entertainment. Still she used to snuggle down under the covers in her large tester bed, until she was only a very small lump in the center of the feather mattress, so that she would not hear strange sounds after Maggie had turned out the light and left her with the creakings of the wide old floorboards, and the mystery behind tall cupboard doors, where she imagined lurked unearthly creatures — such beings as Hieronymus Bosch peopled his canvases with — and, after all, there would be a sort of weird logic in that, in a house belonging to a direct descendant of the fantastic painter.

Now she turned from Granby Street where the bank was, and drove east on Freemason where the Rowlands lived. She would stop at Aunt Marcia's and give her Walter's message instead of phoning after she reached home. It wouldn't take a minute and she could park with impunity here. She ran across the brick walk, up the wide stone steps and lifted the old brass knocker, dropping it lightly against the heavy paneling of the solid black door.

No one came, so she tried the knob, and the door opened. The hall was dimly lighted and smelled stuffy. Aunt Marcia's always did, in spite of the big rooms and high ceilings, smothered with heavy dark portieres at all the doors, and long dull curtains that hung to the floor. Dale thought they must have been here during Great-Uncle Walter's lifetime. Why *did* her aunt cling to these old draperies? Tradition! Damask and brocade, though worn and faded stood for background and culture, even if the wealth was denied her. Aunt Marcia never let anyone in the family forget the unfairness of her father's will.

Dale went through the living room, which was unlighted, and headed for the kitchen, where she could hear voices and a child's shrill laugh.

"I'm gonna sit by Uncle Walter, you can sit by Grandma." The pantry door swung back again and Liza shouted, *"Shut up!"*

Liza Rowland, Marcia's youngest daughter, at fifteen was overgrown and immature, a large ungainly girl whose armor was exaggerated self-assurance and assumed indifference to everyone's opinions,

12

with the exception of those of her brother, Walter. Walter seemed to be her sun and her moon, her alpha and omega. It had always been that way. Dale wondered at it, but she was sure that Liza would gladly go to the stake for Walter, and Aunt Marcia would aid and abet her. It was the one point where mother and daughter saw eye to eye. Dale wandered what magic Walter used. Too bad; she felt sorry for Liza, but not sorry enough to encourage her ill humors, and Liza was certainly in one now. She nodded to Dale, ignored the children who were temporarily silenced, and came forward with the heavy tray she was carrying, precariously balanced, to the table and began unloading it.

"Stay to supper, Dale? My sweet sister Mary left the kids here as usual, while she and Jack go out on the town — cocktails and dinner at Lews — but they can't afford a baby-sitter!" Liza shrugged.

"I'm gonna sit by Uncle Walter, I'm gonna . . ."

"You're *not* going to sit by Uncle Walter, Johnny. Nobody is!" Dale said. "Liza, I just stopped by to tell Aunt Marcia that Walter won't be home to supper."

"Why not?" Marcia Rowland's sharply plaintive voice came from behind her. Dale turned toward her aunt who looked more mournful than usual, in spite of a smart blue tailored wool and carefully waved hair nearly as blue as her dress. Dale noted the silver earrings and matching silver beads. Aunt Marcia certainly did not melt into her environment. "You look very festive, Aunt Marcia. Were you going out tonight?"

"I *thought* I was," Marcia said stiffly. "What's this about Walter's not coming home for supper? I expected him to take me to the Little Theater. Jean Mason couldn't use her tickets, and sent them over. I don't often have a chance to enjoy a play. Why isn't he coming?" Vexation was giving way to anxiety.

"I don't know, Aunt Marcia, but I'm sure he's all right. I just dropped in to the bank to cash a check and Walter asked me to tell you. He seemed in very good form."

Liza brightened up. "Doesn't he look impressive? I go in there sometimes just to see him — not that I have any checks to cash, no such luck."

13

"You can't expect to have what Dale has, my dear," Mrs. Rowland sighed just loud enough, Dale felt sure, to be heard and sound repressed.

"Oh, Mother, come off it," Liza retorted. "You know you think Uncle Hi is an old skinflint. He could do it if he wanted to. He could give us a maid and I could quit being a slavey; and a decent car too."

Marcia ignored her daughter and smiled at Dale. "Pay no attention to her, my dear. Liza is young, and it's a little hard for her to see, but we manage somehow. Of course a maid would make things go smoother; we don't always keep up to our old standards, I fear." She glanced at the table. "You see what I mean." Then she gave a brave little laugh and fixed questioning eyes on Dale. "But what's this Walter has been telling me about a picture that your Uncle Hi is interested in? Is he really going to buy it?" she asked brightly. "How much is he going to pay for it, do you know?"

"Enough to buy you a mink coat, Ma," Liza drawled, "but you can't expect to have . . ."

"I must run," Dale said quickly. She didn't really blame Liza; of the two, she much preferred Liza's open complaints. At least she was honest about them.

Liza followed Dale to the door. "When you went to Capelli's to see the picture, was Nick in there?"

"Yes," said Dale surprised. "I didn't know you knew him, Liza."

"Oh, I don't really," Liza said and added hastily, "I've just heard Walter mention him, and one day he was outside waiting in his car for Walter, and I thought he was right good looking. I guess he's proud of knowing Walter and likes to be seen with him. Walter rides downtown with him once in a while. Walter's always so nice to everybody."

"I never saw him before today," Dale told her. "But Mr. Cappelli wasn't in and Nick knew about the Bosch. It's a wonderful painting, Liza; wait till you see it. Wierd and really amusing. It's called *Death and the Miser*. Are you coming over to my studio to help me tomorrow?"

"May I do some painting on the playroom pictures?"

"Yes, I'm hoping to finish them."

14

"OK, then, I'll come, but I'm fed up with baby-sitting for Mary and I'm not going to start at The Nursery. I want to be an artist, too, Dale."

"I'm not much of an artist, Liza. I'll never make a reputation, in spite of what Hi thinks — or what he *wants* to think."

"Then why don't you marry Bill Ballard and get Uncle Hi to send *me* off to study in New York?"

But Dale was not to be drawn. She ran down the steps leaving Liza standing on the porch. She hadn't the least idea that the girl watching her go was filled with envy and admiration, feeling desperately alone.

Liza had no vanity. She thought that she was ugly and knew that she was awkward, which made it worse. *But why should everyone brush her off until they wanted something?* The girl did not know that most of it was her own fault, nursing resentment, rebuffing kindly impulses, as Dale's suggestion that she help in the studio.

Her blind devotion to Walter, which he'd promoted and made use of when she was a gullible little girl, had grown as she grew. Nurtured by her need to love, it was now, too deep-seated to analyze or root out. She did not know that she was fast becoming a hopeless introvert.

Liza stood on the porch until Dale was out of sight, then, stumbling over the doormat, went back in and closed the door.

Chapter Three

"MARRY Bill Ballard and let Uncle Hi send *me* off to New York to study." Liza's words had persisted in Dale's head as a sort of refrain, ever since the night before, and now, as she looked at Bill coming toward her, she almost said them aloud — at least the first three: *"Marry Bill Ballard."* Magic words, turning her slightly dizzy.

"Darling, what is it?" Bill took her in his arms. Dale turned up a laughing face to his. "Nothing," she said happily. "I was just thinking about Liza."

"Liza?" Bill released her: "I thought you were about to say, 'I've decided to marry you.' Could you possibly tell me what Liza has to do with it?"

Dale laughed, "Nothing, only she was advising me to, just yesterday."

"Well, good for Liza!"

"I think there was an ax to grind, but never mind, Bill, I am thinking seriously of accepting her suggestion."

They were in Hi's study, just off his bedroom, but since Hi was comfortably ensconced in his glassed-in sun porch beyond, with a life of Rabelais and several volumes on fifteenth-century Flemish art, they were in no danger of being overheard or interrupted. Dale turned away, suddenly serious.

"Bill, why do you have to give up everything? You could have

16

gotten through your fourth-year med. I don't think it is fair for your family to let you sacrifice it all."

Bill caught her and swung her around facing him. He held her there, his hands gripping her shoulders, and looked tensely down into her upturned face. Her eyes met his steadily.

"Listen to me, Dale. You know that I love you, don't you?" Dale nodded, then shook her head, and attempted to release herself, but Bill's eyes held her, and if she had ever had a doubt, she had none now. Her own look answered him. Bill grinned and let her go.

"OK. But for gosh sake don't come in here tempting me. You know I don't like this makeshift job. But I've got to do something to help Dad tide over. As soon as he's back at his office things will straighten out. His patients won't desert him. Dad's the best orthodontist in the city, and they know it. But *now* expenses are heavy, especially mine at med school. You wouldn't want me to be a heel about it?"

"No," Dale said with a sigh.

"Good." Bill added, "I'm grateful for this stopgap." He looked over at the desk strewn with papers and stacked with old volumes. "You didn't know I'm learning all your dark family secrets. Well I am. Hi has me tracing it back to the Middle Ages. He's going to write a history — all Bosch, I fear."

Dale laughed. "And nonsense, but spicy, I'll bet. He's a bit hipped on the subject. That's why I hope he'll buy the picture, Bill. I was going to ask you to come with me to Capelli's today, but I'll need you more when I show the painting to Hi. Be sure to come back after supper. The big deal will be on, and he's *got* to buy it, Bill. Twenty babies can eat a lot of pictures."

"I wouldn't worry, I think Hi is going to buy it."

"How do you know?"

"Well, I'll say this much — though I don't suppose I ought to talk about your uncle's business — if my trip to the bank yesterday had any significance — I'd think things look pretty good."

"Why? You've got to tell me, Bill," Dale begged.

"Put two and two together — he was told about the picture Thursday night. Friday — yesterday — he sends me to the bank, and I get quite a big sum for him — in cash. That's as far as I will go, Dale. You'll have to wait until he sees the picture."

"Tonight, after dinner, Father John will be here, and Walter. At least I *asked* him to come. He's a good salesman, Bill, and he found the picture, so I thought I ought to. Be sure to be here, Bill." Dale looked at her wristwatch and started away quickly.

"I'd better go, Capelli closes early Saturdays."

But Dale didn't go to Capelli's shop. As she reached the landing of the broad stairway on her way down, a half hour later, dressed and ready to go, she saw Maggie closing the front door at the far end of the wide hall, and Maggie was holding a long narrow cardboard carton. She was placing it with great care upon the pier table near the door as Dale eagerly ran down the rest of the steps, across the space of highly polished floor, and came to a skidding halt beside Maggie and the box.

"Is it the picture?"

"Now just calm yourself, young lady. Racing down the stairs like a young hoyden! And how should *I* know what is inside it?" Maggie looked aloof and dignified, then an indulgent smile broke her effort at reproof, and curiosity lighted her eyes.

"And it might be the picture, at that. Walter it was, who brought it, only all he said was, 'Give this to Dale, Maggie, it will save her a trip uptown. I'll be around later to witness the unveiling' — whatever that may mean. 'Handle it like a newborn babe,' he said to me, with his high-flown talk."

"Let's take it into the library and open it," Dale urged. "This is the painting, Maggie, that is going to net The Nursery a neat little sum. Come on, we'll unpack it and find the best light to put it in."

"And you're planning to haul him down now — that would be witless, child. Let him come in his own good time."

"Of course," Dale agreed. "We are merely setting the stage now. You must soften Hi up with an epicurean supper. By that time Bill and Father John will be here and we will lead him in and finish the business."

"Providing he doesn't think up some high jinks to torment you," postulated Maggie, with experienced foresight. "I *could* fix the oysters with mushrooms in a cream sauce with sherry, instead of a stew. A bit of rich food will do him no harm just this once, asking the saints to preserve him." Maggie grinned broadly, caught up in Dale's high spirits and the idea of raiding Hi's pocket for charity. "It's worth a risk anyway."

"You'll have to do it yourself, Maggie. Rosina's a good cook but not up to you. And serve it with a glass of Amontillado," Dale added. "That ought to liquidate him."

But when the picture was unwrapped, Maggie was doubtful.

"All those little devils with money bags swarming around that poor old fellow on his deathbed! I don't like it, Dale. It's irreligious, *that's* what it is."

"Now listen, Maggie, don't you go scrupulous on me. This picture is *very fine art,* and points a moral. Don't you see the angel there, guarding him? It just shows what happens to misers when they come to die. They are tempting him to sell his soul, but he'll be OK — his guardian angel will see to that."

"I hope so," Maggie said uncertainly, "but it's fairly outnumbered he is — just look at the varmints."

"Bosch is teaching a good lesson. He's saying: 'Look out this doesn't happen to you!' If you don't believe me, ask Father John," Dale said stoutly, hoping she was right; conscious that there was disagreement among the art critics interpreting the symbolism of this painter's work. "Now you get busy, and put plenty of flavor in that mushroom sauce."

Maggie left still looking doubtful, and Dale, a little discomforted by Maggie's reaction, wondered if Hi would take offense at the implication in the title. No, of course not. He was very generous to her, and she didn't blame him for not giving in to Aunt Marcia, who had her own income, although she called it a "pittance." She and all of them were always trying to ease more out of Hi. "He does a lot for that whole crowd." The big checks at Christmas and on birthdays, were his gifts, Dale knew, not from Uncle Walter's estate. "And look how they spend them! But he *was* mean about Father John." She did condemn Hi for the way he badgered Father John.

19

St. Mary's was no longer the wealthy parish it had been in the early days. The city had grown. The population had shifted and most of the rich had taken their wealth to other parishes. As the neighborhood went down, so did the Sunday collections. Father John always needed money for his poor, but especially for The Nursery, which was a home he had established for little children, orphans and foundlings, and which was largely dependent upon charitable donations. Dale was determined that Hi should make a donation — if not voluntarily — then involuntarily! It would do the babies just as much good either way.

Yet later in the evening, when everyone was assembled in the library, and the painting, unframed but on its stretcher, had been placed upon an easel brought down from her studio, Father John, for whom the whole plan had been devised, was letting her down.

"I don't like it," he said, his rich baritone deepened with quiet conviction. His kindly eyes sought Dale's filled with unspoken regret. "It panders to superstition. Makes death a horror, instead of the blessed release of a soul to God. Those demons are almost obscene. Of course the painting is purely humanistic, and reflects the spirit of his time. It *is* undoubtedly typical of Hieronymus Bosch," he concluded, "brilliant and imaginative."

Dale moaned inwardly. Why did Father John have to be so outspoken? He didn't have to like the picture, but why condemn it so vehemently? She had considered it rather amusing — the little devils, cute. Dale was a bit astonished at the priest's analysis, but not at his impartial judgment. When had her reverend godparent ever been swayed by considerations of material gain? How wrong she had been, prophesying to Maggie, who was looking at her now with an expression of mingled triumph and disappointment.

But Father John's condemnation proved an unexpected ally. Obviously Hi's perversity had immediately taken possession of him and he was delighted at the opportunity to challenge his old friend.

"Ah, yes, Reverend Father," he said. "Here's a fine example of holy religion for you, bargains and threats and bribery!" His head went back, his eyes screwed tight shut, and his mouth opened prodigiously, snapping shut again in a very convulsion of mirth.

20

Dale looked around at Bill and Father John and Maggie, who were here out of interest and loyalty to her, and even Walter, who had just arrived and stood in the doorway, looked amused. She hadn't expected, and was glad, that neither Aunt Marcia or Liza had come. This might be fine entertainment, but it wasn't the kind of show that she had planned, with Uncle Hi riding his high horse!

And now he turned a wicked eye upon her, his beloved niece, after he had moved up closer to the picture and scrutinized it with increasing pleasure.

"Come here, Monkey," he ordered and pointed a knotty finger at the small emaciated figure of the miser. "That might be your Uncle Hi, sitting there in that bed. But I tell you this — if it were, there'd be no argument, me dear, because I'd go with the little devils! I'd take the gold and be damned! They'd be a sight better company than that milksop of an angel."

Dale heard a low shocked murmur from Maggie, which spurred her uncle on. Much to his delight, she never failed, even after all the years under his roof, to protest his irreverence.

"Aye, Maggie, *good* company, I say," He said gleefully. "Death and the Miser. It's a good death, surrounded by his money bags. I'll buy it."

Hiram Bosch stood in their midst, baffling, incredible little man that he was, hugely enjoying the effect of his words. Dale knew this too well, but, for the life of her, she couldn't tell how much of it was an act — sardonic humor or real conviction — and she wondered, too, if he meant that he would buy the picture or only the artist's concept. But in another instant she knew with a thrill that the picture had won, because Hi was looking at it with the calculating eye of an appraiser.

"It's a copy by some unknown," he ruminated aloud. Then he turned and asked directly, "What is Capelli asking for it?"

"Now, Hi," Dale protested, "don't belittle it. I told you I wouldn't bargain."

Walter interrupted, "He wants five thousand for it, and it's worth every cent of that."

No one spoke. Dale was surprised. That was a good deal more

21

than Capelli told her. True, he had only given the amount tentatively. Now she supposed, since he found they were seriously interested, he'd jacked up the price.

"Dale," Walter asked, "did Capelli ever actually say that this is not the original painting?" He sauntered casually into the center of the group, stopping beside his uncle, who regarded him at once uncordially and skeptically. But since Walter had unearthed the picture and taken the trouble to bring it from Capelli's shop for his uncle to see, Hi could hardly question his interest.

Dale answered slowly, "No, he didn't, but he won't say it *is* — and you can bet he would if he knew." She didn't like to stress this point, but she was too honest to sidestep it.

"I don't know so much about that," Walter said, "but it has occurred to me that there might be a good chance of finding out."

Hiram Bosch paid Walter the compliment of silence. Dale noted that he was listening intently. Now he asked sharply, "How do you propose to do that, young man?"

Walter didn't answer. He walked up to the painting and lifted it down from the easel. He took it to the corner table where Father John and Hi played their habitual games of checkers, and laid the painting upon it, face up. Then he snapped on the floor lamp and directed the full flood of light down upon it. Father John, Hi, and Bill came over, while Maggie hovered on the outskirts of the small circle.

"When you were in the bank yesterday, you said you were to get the painting today, so I thought I'd save you the trouble," Walter said, ignoring everyone except Dale, although he raised his voice a little and assumed the manner of a connoisseur delivering an informal lecture as he went on.

"While I was waiting for Nick to find a box for it, I had an opportunity to look more carefully at the painting. It seems to me, Dale, that I can just discern in this lower right-hand corner, where there is still a remnant of dirt and old varnish, the faintest trace of a signature — or what might be at least initials."

Dale leaned closer. "I never noticed that before, Walter. Let me see."

22

"I don't know," she said, straightening up. "The rest of you look. See if you can tell."

Each one took a turn, Bill first. "Darned if I know," he said. "It looks like something beside dirt, though."

Dale looked at him across the table, beginning to feel a stir of excitement. And then she watched Father John who had found Hi's magnifying glass and was looking long and carefully. "I don't see anything that looks like a capital 'B' which should be there. There are some definite strokes which look intentional, but more like an 'A.'"

At this point Hi disclaimed the whole idea and insisted it was a sloppy job of cleaning, and old Capelli would have to finish up that edge, but he'd buy the picture, as it was, for five thousand.

Dale cast a relieved and joyful glance up at Father John, for Dale knew that in spite of her uncle's running battles with "The Cloth" as he often called his lenient friend, Hi had a genuine respect for the priest's opinion. The mere fact that Father John thought a signature might exist would incline Hi to snap up the picture more quickly.

But just as Dale was about to suggest that Hi write out the check, Walter, to her surprise, demurred. "I wouldn't go too fast, Dale, I have one more suggestion to make, and it can't do any harm. It will settle the matter once and for all — at least about the signature. Have you a little of your cleaning solution around?"

"Why yes, I have," Dale said with quick understanding. "If you think Capelli won't mind," she added, hesitating.

"Why should he?" Walter shrugged. "We'd be saving him a little work. It couldn't possibly hurt anything."

"I'll get it in a sec," Dale said and ran quickly out of the room.

Chapter Four

WHEN Dale left, the room was silent. Hi scowled and gazed down at the picture, pulled his pipe out of his deep pocket, and filled it with slow deliberate dips into his plastic pouch, packing the bowl with meticulous care.

Father John sat down, crossed his long legs, and leaned back in the Thomas Jefferson armchair, for which Hi's grandfather had paid a direct descendant — in straitened circumstances — a hundred dollars. The priest's worn black clerical knees were a little shiny, but his white immaculate clerical collar under his freshly shaven chin bravely ignored it.

Maggie fidgeted and smoothed the folds of her best silk print while she fixed slightly faded blue eyes upon the door through which Dale had left.

Bill lighted a cigarette and watched Walter with interest as the latter strolled around the room. He paused before the only painting on the wall, hung in an arched recess over a walnut chest.

"This Breugel, Uncle Hi, will be good company for your Bosch. This *is* no doubt an original? Let's hope for your sake the Bosch will prove to be. You're quite a collector, aren't you?"

Hi's eyebrows went up. "So kind of you." Then sharply, "Don't patronize me, young man!" Walter turned a look of innocent surprise upon the old man and laughed indulgently.

24

Bill repressed a grin. At that moment, Dale came in, carrying a small bottle and a large box of cotton. She went swiftly toward the picture, including them all in her quick smile, communicating her excitement.

Dale explained: "You dampen a small bit of cotton with the cleaning solution, and very lightly, with a circular motion, apply it to the part you're cleaning. Watch it carefully, inspect the cotton frequently, and if, besides the dirty dark brown of the old varnish you see a trace of color, you stop. You're taking off paint. It is a ticklish job, but if the picture is solidly painted, you don't run too much risk. Generally the dirty stuff comes off — at least enough for you to see what's underneath, before you loosen any pigment."

Now with a pile of small cotton puffs on the table and the bottle open, she turned to her uncle.

"OK, here goes. It's all right, Hi."

Her uncle was regarding the proceedings with some concern.

"I wouldn't be doing this if it were dangerous, and I've cleaned whole portraits — helping at the museum — learning to restore. Once from a dark brown background I uncovered a whole lovely landscape."

Hi looked gratified. "You don't have to ask me — you ought to know what you're doing."

After a few moments of work, Dale gave a little squeal. She continued rubbing, daring a little more.

"There *is* a name — it's coming up." She discarded the soiled cotton and grabbed another ball from the table. Bill pushed nearer, pressed his cheek against her soft hair, trying to see, and Dale slanted her head to let him get a better look.

"Durned if it's not!" he declared. "But it isn't 'Bosch' — whatever it is." The lilt left Dale's voice.

"No, it isn't. It's an 'A' and an 'E.' The next is a 'K,' isn't it Walter?" Walter nodded, but did not speak; he was watching tensely.

"The last two look like an 'E' and an 'N,'" Dale said, staring at defeat.

"Well," Walter said philosophically, turning away, "we tried, but I'm still not convinced that this will settle it. There's something about that name that sounds familiar — does it ring a bell with you, Dale?"

25

Bill gazed down at the corner of the picture, where quite visible against the light warm color of the foreground was a signature.

" 'AEKEN' " he read. "Clean a little more to the left of the 'A,' Dale." In a few moments the whole name was visible. "Van Aeken. You know, don't you, whose name that is?"

Dale stared down for a moment, concentrating. Then with a flash of comprehension she asked a little uncertainly.

"You don't mean — *it isn't!*"

"Yes," said Bill, his face glowing with pleasure. "That's one of the family secrets I've been learning. Van Aeken was Bosch's family name — actually the 'Bosch' was derived from the town where he lived."

Dale took it up then. "Most people don't know that. He always signed his paintings 'Bosch'— 'Jerome Bosch' or 'Hieronymus Bosch'!"

"Most people," Hi was bristling, "can't trace their family back to Bosch. *I* knew it, but who said anything about its being signed Van Aeken, until now?"

"And there is no reason to suppose that he didn't sign a few 'Van Aeken,' " Walter interrupted. "Certainly it makes this one very definitely and unquestionably an original. No one else would have signed it that! It would never occur to an imitator or a copyist to put anything except 'Bosch' — or, more honestly, 'after Bosch.' " Walter walked over and put out his hand to his uncle. "So it's your privilege to obtain a genuine Bosch, Uncle Hi. Congratulations. I'm glad I could help." The words were modest, but no one doubted that Walter was assuming full credit for the success of his brilliant suggestion. Automatically his uncle became indebted to him. A very nice coup for Walter.

But Hi was not to be rushed. "That's all very fine, but it isn't guaranteed. Capelli might not back it up. Fact is, he doesn't know a thing about this. He's put his price and I take it — at that. Five thousand."

Dale heard her canny old uncle, but her first disappointment had ended in a rush of delight, and now she was speculating wildly, trying to calculate the huge amount she would be able to claim for her

26

commission. Then, without warning, came a dismaying thought, which stemmed from her innate honesty and Maggie's strict training. It came naturally, logically, and was so obvious to her that although it made her heart sink and her stomach turn over, it was not to be denied — so she faced it.

Knowing she'd be given the bum's rush when the experts took over, nevertheless she said,

"You can't do that, Hi. It wouldn't be fair not to tell Capelli what we've found out. You don't know what it's worth, probably ten times that now."

Walter spoke quickly. "You're right, Dale. It is certainly worth at least twenty-five or thirty thousand, and I'm sure Uncle Hi realizes it's a bargain at that. If he doesn't snap it up, one of the big collectors will, just as soon as it's on the market again."

"On the market? Who's putting it on the market?" Hi came forward, his eyes fixed on Walter's. A fire was building up behind his small black irises, set in deep sockets. Dale hoped that Walter wasn't going to wilt in the heat of Hi's temper which could scorch and sear when it really began to rage. But his temper wasn't raging yet — maybe she could cool him, make him see how five thousand would be just stealing the painting really. Besides the principle involved, a Bosch *original!* It was out of the question to let it go at that — belittling it!

Dale knew that making this point was going to result in her loss. Hi would put her and her conscience out of the deal altogether and settle directly with Capelli, who would consider that he owed her nothing. Perhaps Walter would claim the commission, since he had 'discovered' the picture and even collected it from the shop and brought it here before she could go for it today. If that happened, she'd make Walter come across with half, anyway. Dale perceived a glint of hope for something bigger, and gathered her forces.

"We'll call in an appraiser, Hi, find out what it's worth," she said.

Walter interrupted. "You'd have to be careful there, Dale. You couldn't trust just anyone. Now I do know of a man —"

"You can both just shut up!" Hi said. "Who's buying this picture? *Me!*" he answered himself and continued: "Who's selling it? Capelli.

27

Five thousand is Capelli's price. Did you ever hear that the valuation of a painting is strictly the dealer's responsibility? It's Capelli's job, not mine, to name the price, and he's named it. Ain't that so, Father?" Hi turned to the priest, but didn't wait for confirmation.

"I don't give a continental what name you've raked up from the dirt. It was there for him to find," Hi declared. "If he hadn't been a lazy ignorant moron, he'd have found it himself."

But Dale brushed his arguments aside. There was plenty of Hi's stubbornness in her and they both enjoyed a battle of wits. "If you had bought it in ignorance, Hi, before you found out — then it might be honest —"

Hi stopped her. "I'm not letting a chit of a gal, whose conscience is so warped that she's willing to fleece her old uncle, tell *me* what's honest and what's not!" Hi was fairly prancing now with indignation, and turned suddenly upon innocent Maggie sitting uneasily upon the edge of her chair.

"This is *your* doings, Maggie," he charged. "Yours — do you hear? Dinning your silly scruples into her."

"Holy Michael, defend us!" Maggie cast one imploring glance at Father John. "You'll have to take a hand, Father! And I'm telling you now, scruples or no — it's that evil picture there that's to blame for all this — full of devils it is — and the sooner you get it out of this house the better." With that Maggie bounced up and took the simpler course of leaving herself.

"Light-headed, see?" Hi commented. But Dale felt as if a little imp from somewhere had certainly taken possession of her. She was filled with resentment at them all, and completely outdone with Hi. She would die before she'd let him get the best of her; and flatly refused to carry on the sale until a new price had been fixed.

Bill tried to reason, Father John to reassure. "I don't think you're bound in conscience to go so far, my child," said the priest. "I can understand your reaction, and respect your high motives . . ." Dale had a twinge at this, but continued to steel herself against his kindly admonition.

"You have to be fair to your Uncle Hi, too, my dear, and actually I believe that he is entirely within his rights. Capelli should know the worth of his picture, that is understood by both parties. It is an established accepted fact."

"Better close the deal, Dale," Bill urged in an undertone. "First thing you know he'll call off the whole thing."

Walter was the only one who had agreed with her, who was backing her up.

"Stick it out," he whispered. "Don't let them flummox you. You'll bring the old boy around. He's got the money, Dale, you can count on that."

Was he giving her a tip? Was that what his remark at the bank had meant? But when Hi actually produced his checkbook and his pen hovered over the clean blank surface, Walter lost some of his resistance. And when Hi fixed him with a determined eye and announced his intention of sending the check to Capelli, Walter capitulated completely, and consented to deliver it. Deeply disappointed, Dale remained stubbornly silent.

"All right. You're out of it, gal. Walter can take this tomorrow morning on his way to the bank." Hi handed the check to Walter. "That settles the matter, and I'll hear nothing more from you, young lady. You and your appraiser!"

Hi picked up the picture and, without so much as a nod of good-night, marched angrily out of the room and slammed his study door.

Walter looked cross and squirmed a bit under Dale's accusing eye, and said, "I stood by as long as there was any hope. I *wanted* to help you, Dale, but you were too stubborn. There wouldn't have been any sale at all if I hadn't consented. After all, Capelli is better off with this than with nothing."

"But St. Mary's Nursery isn't." And Dale regarded her godparent with disapproval. "Father, how could you? And even *you*, Bill."

Bill was contrite. "I'm sorry — but you're wrong about it, honey. *I* had to be honest too. I couldn't back you on that one, even Father John . . ." Dale turned coldly away. She didn't want to be convinced, not yet, anyway.

"Listen, child," Father John began, but then there was a thump at the door and it swung open as Liza came bolting in. Father John stopped speaking. They all stared. But Liza saw only Walter.

"Thank gracious, you're here! I've been waiting and waiting! I thought something awful had happened to you."

"My Lord, Liza, don't you think I'm old enough to be out after dark? Did you come all the way over here alone — to protect me?"

"Someone phoned — I couldn't understand what he said — except — 'Walter.'"

"I ought to be sorry for her," Dale told herself, "but I just can't, she's so big and foolish," and her guilty feeling switched to one of irritation. Liza could have come earlier if she'd wanted — she needed no excuse.

Father John stood up and Bill too. "Guess we'd better go," Bill said soberly, regarding Dale with anxious eyes, but making no move to approach her. Father John came over and patted her shoulder.

"Thanks for all your goodwill, my child. I know you were only trying to help me, but we'll get along. Sister Dennis really dotes on that old kitchen range — think of all the scuttles of coal she can offer up for some poor soul!"

But Dale was not to be diverted. "You might as well go, all of you," she said. As she closed the front door behind them, she heard Liza's "Well, Walter, I just wanted to be sure you were safe." And Walter's aggravated answer, "Why didn't you call the Marines?"

Dale giggled. Then, being a naturally fair-minded person, her sympathies switched to Liza. Walter was reaping what he'd sowed. She remembered when they were children, how Walter had traded on Liza's natural affection, making her feel privileged to run his errands, or tell a fib to get him out of a scrape. He'd had her completely bamboozled. Once in a while he'd reward her with a dime or candy or treat her to a movie, but she would have done anything for him without reward. She still would; she'd never outgrown it. Tonight, Dale thought, she really had looked frightened.

30

Chapter Five

NEVER had Dale dreamed of anything so fantastic. Maybe Maggie was right. Maybe the picture had cast a spell over the house. It had come in on Saturday, and now on Monday morning they were all in a preposterous nightmare by Bosch. Her uncle saying that twenty-five thousand dollars had vanished, and expecting Bill to know where the money was. Hi must be possessed.

She and Bill had come at his summons. Only the two of them; all very private. The study doors were closed and her uncle sat slumped down in the cavernous depth of his worn leather chair, facing them calmly. That was part of the unreality. Uncle Hi was *calm*. If anything could make this more of a dream, it was that Hi was saying quite calmly, but with unmistakable conviction and, Dale suspected, even an evil bit of enjoyment,

"Where are they? $25,000 — twenty-five $1,000 bills don't take up legs and walk."

Bill's stricken face was more than she could stand, dazed, bleak. He was a thousand miles away from her.

"Uncle Hi — " Dale's voice sounded strange and off key " — If Bill says he put the money in the safe, he put it there — and you know it! This is too outrageous of you. I won't stand it — do you hear me?"

"Have I said he didn't put it in the safe? All I'm saying is — *the money is not there now*. Is that *my* fault?" Hi asked in a martyred tone. "I gave Bill a job to do, an important one — to get the money from the bank and to put it here in my safe. I hold Bill responsible, that's all. Bill will have to find it! Am I supposed to lose $25,000 and say nothing, for fear of hurting his feelings?"

That didn't deserve an answer, but it served to frustrate Dale. She was quiet for a moment, then she burst out, "You shan't do this to Bill — to us! Uncle Hi — I wasn't ready to tell you — but you might as well know. I'm going to marry Bill."

Hi's face darkened. "So it's got to that, has it? *Us!* I'm not surprised, not being as you presumed me to be, totally blind. I suppose I have some say in the matter, since you are my niece and not yet of age. A young man who is deep in debt can't be planning to marry. Not if he's in Bill's shoes, he can't."

"You needn't think you can keep me from loving Bill. No one can, not even Bill himself," Dale declared. This was quite reckless. She'd better get hold of herself, but she couldn't think.

Bill didn't look at Dale but kept his eyes riveted on Hi's gleaming, beady black ones. Bill stood up, tall and rigid, making Hi more gnomelike, and Dale could only guess at the rage that he was holding in check; except that, knowing Bill and knowing her own fury, she thought she came somewhere near it. He towered over Hi, but even Bill couldn't make Hi look insignificant. A small piece of dynamite isn't insignificant, not to anyone who knows the properties of dynamite.

"All right," Bill was saying, "I'll accept your conditions for the present, and it's not because I'm afraid to have you call in the cops. I wish you would. I don't consider it a favor nor a reprieve. I don't know why you want to play the generous employer, refraining from throwing me out, if you really think I took this money."

"I'm such a kind old man," mocked Hi. "Chickenhearted, ain't I?"

"I don't believe you think I took it."

"I haven't said so, have I? All I'm saying is — find it." Hi stood up now and pointed to the black hole. The steel door was wide open, flat against the wall.

"Yes, I did just as you told me. I came straight up here and put the money in there and hung the picture back over the door, like it always was."

32

"Are you sure of that?" Hi asked, emphasizing each word.

"Certainly I'm sure. You always hang a picture over the safe door." Dale thought of the old faded oil and wondered with one part of her mind, quite apart from that which was following this conversation, if Uncle Hi had finally discarded it. *Death and the Miser* was on its stretcher, sitting on the floor as if it had just been taken from the same place on the wall where the other had hung, concealing the safe.

"I don't know what happened to the money, but you don't think I'm going to let it rest at this, do you?" Bill snapped. "I'll stay on now because it's the only way that I have a Chinaman's chance of finding out where it's gone — if I can't, then I have a right to demand an investigation by the police."

"Cocky, ain't you?" Hi gibed. "Considering you're the only other person besides me who knows the combination of that safe. That's true, ain't it?"

"I thought so up to now . . ." Bill paused. Hi did not seem to notice the implication, and Bill went on quickly. "I intend to stick around until I've found out something about this money, or what *you* did with it — "

"Find it where it's not lost, eh? And give it back to me?" Hi opened his mouth but snapped it shut again, his laugh abortive.

Dale became speechless, but Bill paid no attention. He finished what he was saying as if Hi had not interrupted.

"And until I do, I won't hold Dale; if you could call anything so informal as our understanding an engagement. It's off, honey, until." Bill looked straight at Dale begging for understanding.

"That's not right, Bill! It's silly pride! Father John will tell you so."

Hi jumped at that. "One word of this — one word, mind you — to him or anyone else, and you'll land your fine young man straight behind bars! I'll swear out a warrant before you can say Jack Robinson. You'll tell no one. I'll have no furor. No scandal. It's my money that's gone. I'll handle the loss in my own way, you understand. I mean it." Hi really looked as if he did; though when had Hi ever minded a bit of scandal? Dale was shaken; she knew when to retreat.

33

"All right." She brought her dignity to her rescue. She would not be suppliant to either of them. Her chin went up, her eyes looked away from Bill and met her uncle's squarely. "Bill and I will find this money without any help from anyone, but there is one question I'd like you to answer."

The old man regarded Dale with satisfaction and a little indulgence, now that he had won.

"I'd like to know why you got twenty-five $1,000 bills out of the bank, why you sent Bill for them and had him put them in your safe, if you didn't expect to pay that much for the picture, and you didn't even pay the five thousand out of it — you wrote a check. What were you going to do with all that cash, Uncle Hi?"

Hi shut his mouth in a tight, straight, stubborn line. He turned his back, walked over to the wall, closed the gaping hole, and hung the Bosch painting carefully in place, concealing it and concealing a satisfied grin from Bill. He cocked his head then a little and said, "Curiosity killed the cat, me dear," and settled down into his hollow in the leather chair, like an old fox, snugly in its hole. His bright eyes were watchful, though, fixed upon the two young people standing still — waiting.

"Go on," he said, "get out. And tell Maggie I want my toddy."

Dale turned, her back straight and uncompromising, her head high, poised squarely on her shoulders. It was a pity that she couldn't see the look of possessive pride on Hi's face, as he watched her go. Then quickly came a grin that held a bit of whimsy and sly delight.

"I was thinking of giving it to Father John, me dear, for his babies in The Nursery." The words went dancing after her but there was no sign that Dale had heard. She marched straight out of the door and Bill followed her.

34

Chapter Six

MAGGIE came in to Hi's study a few minutes later bearing a small tray with the toddy. She set it on the table beside Hi's chair. He did not even look at it. He was looking into space with sparkle in his eye and a smirk upon his lips. Maggie regarded him distrustfully.

"You're grinning like a Sleiveen" she said; as near a rebuke as she dared. "You're planning some wickedness. That I'll put my money on," and she handed him the glass. Hi took a long-swallow, smacked his lips, rested his head against the worn spot on his high-backed leather chair, and chuckled.

"And who's to judge what is wicked and what is good sense, Maggie? It all depends on the *whys* and the *wherefores*." Then he leaned forward frowning and pointing a thin gnarled forefinger. "I'll teach 'em a lesson, the young sprigs, billing and cooing behind my back, and defying me to my face. But if I know Bill, there'll be no more of it just now."

Maggie's eyes grew wide with apprehension, "You'll be doing nothing to hurt my Dale — nor Bill either. *Please,*" Maggie quavered, "you wouldn't do that — not with willful intent."

"The end will justify the means — do you understand that, Maggie?"

"I understand nothing," Maggie retorted.

"I'm not surprised," Hi said with meaning, but as Maggie brideled he relented.

"I'll teach that young lady not to try schemes on her old uncle. It will do them no harm to wait a while. That's all it will amount to if they do as I say. Hi looked self-satisfied — "They both know that I've outwitted them, but I'll give them a run for their money." This last seemed particularly to delight him.

Maggie grew bolder. "But *what* are you scheming? Tell me that. Don't you be too hard on my bairn — she's yours too, and you love her, say what you will. The truth of it is — you just don't want to give her up."

Hi sobered. "It's for her own good, Maggie. Too young." There was a short silence. "Her mother ran off — and how did that end? I'll keep Dale safely under this roof a while longer."

For the first time Maggie looked sympathetic, but she said, "Dale's safety is in the hands of the Lord."

"I plan to save Him the trouble," Hi retorted and, at Maggie's expression, became gleeful again. "But that's not the whole of it. I'll stir up the lot of them. This is my pie, Maggie, and don't you put a meddling finger into it."

"And may I ask what the rest of it is — and who the whole lot of them are, that you'll be stirring?" Maggie's cheeks were pink now, but she kept her tone suitably meek.

Hi surprised her then by speaking quietly. "Maggie, I'll tell you this, because in all the years that you've served me, I've never found you trying to squiggle anything out of me. You're honest, Maggie, and you're *not greedy*. That's more than I can say for another soul I have to deal with in or out of this house." Hi's hand came down with a bang on the table rattling the spoon in his glass.

"Dale's not got a greedy bone in her body," Maggie said stoutly.

"Yes she has," Hi answered stubbornly. "She's greedy for love. Let her wait."

"If you go on like this, you'll be having another heart failure." Maggie set her lips. "And I'll be calling in the doctor."

"Call him — the sooner they all get here, the better. Oh, they'll come, Maggie. All snooping, on the theory that findings is havings — to put it delicately."

"I'll hear no more of this. It's riddles you're talking and I'm wasting

36

my time." Maggie was on her dignity. She turned to pick up the tray, and had taken a few steps toward the door when Hi stopped her.

"There's twenty-five thousand dollars gone from my safe." Maggie turned with round eyes and open mouth. "Bill got it from the bank for me. Says he put in the safe as I instructed him. It's not there now, and it's his job to find it. Till this thing is settled there'll be no more lovemaking — *that* he said himself. It will take him some time, I've no doubt."

Maggie, bewildered, continued to stare. Hi was evidently pleased. She couldn't fathom it.

"And is he to have no help?" she asked with unexpected insight. "If burglars it is, you should call the police."

Maggie had surprised him. Hi made a quick riposte.

"And how would that help him — to make a public matter of it? Perhaps land him in jail."

Maggie collapsed into the nearest chair — regardless of her code — which required that she wait to be asked. And Hi followed up his advantage quickly.

"No, Maggie, I'll handle this my own way. No one is to be told of this, but I may, in *strict confidence* — mind you," Hi snickered, "mention it to certain individuals. Simply saying that the money is lost. It will be a very tempting bait. We'll see who swallows it." Hi counted on one hand, finger by finger.

"The Doc — needs money for some junk for his laboratory.

"Marcia — always has and always will want money for the pure love of it. But this time it's a house in a highfalutin neighborhood.

"Walter, the elegant — trims a bit too close to the wind, I suspect *he* has already a few shady deals in his pretty head.

"And even Liza, the poor little nincompoop — I'll not except. God knows what good it would do her."

"But not Dale." Maggie gasped, completely shaken. "Never have I thought I'd live to hear such scandalous talk. You're as good as calling them all thieves!"

"And one of them is," Hi said with finality.

"Who?" Maggie asked scarcely above a whisper.

"Ah, that I don't know." Hi uttered a dramatic sigh.

"Calumny — that's what you're committing — which your catechism would tell you if you were a Christian."

"You're wrong, my good woman. If you know your own catechism," Hi jeered, "you would know that calumny is falsehood. I am speaking the truth. And how do I know it? Because someone has been pilfering from my wallet. Small amounts at first — so I wasn't sure — but a fifty went next, and even then — Christian or no Christian — I said nothing about it, thinking perhaps that memory was slipping and that I'd put less in my wallet than I thought. 'I'll wait,' I said to myself, 'and see what happens next.'"

"And did you see?" Maggie asked, still incredulous.

"Would I be telling you this if I had? No. But this time a hundred — two fifties — are gone, and no mistake about it."

Maggie was stymied. Having no ready answer, she resorted to recrimination. "Many's the time I've told you," she said, "a dresser drawer, under socks and shirts, is no place to be hiding a wallet. If you'd had it in your pocket where it belonged —"

Hi interrupted her. "I'll do what I please with my wallet. If I want to put it in my drawer, who's to stop me? No, Maggie, you can't blame me, it was well concealed. Someone's a thief, and someone who can find a hundred or more with such ease may well hope to find $25,000. Can you deny that, Maggie?"

"And you could be mistaken," Maggie persisted, in her perturbation, becoming quite reckless. "May the saints send you to perdition if you accuse someone wrongly. I'll cut you out of my prayers — Father John notwithstanding!"

Hi let a slow impish grin replace his scowl. "Ah, our holy Father John!" Hi threw back his head, opened his mouth, and was silently convulsed. But when he saw Maggie whirl toward the door like one escaping from the devil himself, even Hi saw that he'd gone too far.

"Maggie!" And there was no brooking the authority in his tone. Maggie stopped and slowly turned.

"One word of this talk outside that door and I'll punish those two youngsters in real truth. It'll be on *your* head, Maggie. We'll keep this between us, and you'll report to me what goes on. Now swear it."

The poor woman, so distressed and befuddled that she no longer knew what to think, except that she could not escape and dared not defy him, said faintly, "I promise."

But Hi was adamant. *"Swear* it, Maggie."

"All right, I swear it." Maggie sniffed and wiped her eyes.

"That's better, and I'll promise you this, Maggie," his good humor restored, "I'm not saying 'No' to the youngsters — I'm only delaying them. That's fair enough. They'll have a lifetime together, and," he added with a rare touch of sentiment, "they can spare me a little time. Maybe," he concluded, "I'll not be here for much longer."

Maggie was touched. It was true. He was an old sick man, and he had been good to her, in his own way. Dale was all that he had. The Rowlands were just a burden to him.

And having got what he wanted, Hi became magnanimous, "There's one more thing, Maggie, that you might as well know." He spoke briskly, once more his impervious self, "I have not told him yet, but that $25,000 was intended as a gift for your dear pastor, the Reverend John Mark Clemens, to pay him for all the suffering hours he's spent giving me entertainment — and," Hi grinned, "losing at checkers. But never mind, Maggie, the money's serving as good a purpose now as it ever will, and Father John shall have it for his little waifs presently, if he has the wits to find it." After this ambiguous statement, with a quick change of mood. Hi dismissed her.

"Now go away and leave me quiet. I have a little verse to compose."

Hi sat quietly, very pleased with himself, for several minutes. He was going to enjoy this — killing many birds with one stone. If anyone found the money, they'd not get away with it. And if no one found it, he could always produce it. He didn't intend to be too hard on Dale and Bill. But let Bill finish his job here, and Dale would benefit by continuing her painting a bit longer.

The big killing would be when he caught the bird who was getting away now with chicken feed, but would surely come back — in hopes of a banquet.

He reached for his pen.

39

Chapter Seven

DALE and Bill kept silent until well away from the study door. Then Dale turned a face full of conflicting emotions to Bill.

"He wasn't going to give all that to The Nursery. . . . Do you suppose he *was,* Bill? And *why* should he treat *you* this way?"

"Well, for one thing," said Bill, "he doesn't think well of me as a future nephew-in-law!"

"Hi doesn't want me to marry anyone yet, Bill. I think he wants to make a sort of Lady Bosch out of me — oh, not painting the same kind of things, but he says I've inherited the talent. Some day I will be a fine artist. Silly, isn't it?"

"And he wants *me* out of the picture."

"You played right into his hands! Do you really mean what you said, Bill? Are you tired of me, or something?"

Bill groaned, "Dale! Don't go temperamental on me now!" Bill looked torn to shreds and Dale relented.

She looked up at him, eyes suddenly full of tears.

"Don't cry," Bill said, "that will be even worse. Come on, let's go where we can have a good talk. I had to agree to his conditions. What else could I do, under the circumstances?"

"That's just what he was counting on," Dale admitted miserably.

"You see," Bill added "he's really got me tied, because Dad's so ill. He just must not be worried by *anything now,* and Hi knows it. You heard him reminding me — 'No furor, no scandal.' He's 'such a kind old man' Bill quoted with bitter sarcasm. He knows I need this job, too. . . . Well it's no use lamenting. We've got to think how to handle it."

"I'll try." But Dale wailed again, "Oh, I wish I hadn't tried to out-smart him about getting a commission for the picture. I ought to have told him exactly what I wanted. He saw through my whole scheme — and that didn't help us a bit. It's uncanny," she added, "the way he can read my mind."

"Could be," Bill agreed, as they started down the stairs. "I'll tell you this — I'm sure he is up to something more than he has told us. There's another string to his bow, Dale. Why should he go to all this trouble simply to frustrate us — he could do that very easily. As he said, you're not of age, and I'm in a very equivocal position, to say the least."

"Bill!" Dale protested.

"There's no denying the fact that I *am* responsible for the money. But I don't believe that Hi's refusal to have the police was entirely altruistic, do you? No, I think it would spoil his plan — whatever it is," Bill surmised, coming much closer to the truth than he knew. "I believe he has hidden the money himself. He's playing a very deep game, unless of course someone *did* really take it — but that seems impossible."

"And who?" asked Dale. "No one in this house last night. Besides, no one but you and Hi knows the combination."

"Your Uncle Hi is devious and inscrutable," Bill observed, "but never irrational. He has a subtle mind, with motives — whether we like them or not. That we must admit. Strong motives, that he believes in, and when he's planning a thing he won't be interfered with."

"Very well," Dale said, accepting Bill's reasoning, "if we can't call in the cops — strip him and search him — we have got to match wits. I suppose all we can do is look for the money — and hope. You never know with Hi, something may change him." Dale was regaining her optimism. Then she drooped again.

"I suppose now, he'll never give the money to Father John, even if he meant to at first."

"No," said Bill, "not until we can find it, anyway."

41

"We haven't got a chance, if he's got it on him. But Bill, you'll have to search his room and his study. You have a better chance for that than I have. Come on," she said, "let's plan."

They had stopped on the landing of the stairway, so absorbed in their talk that they could not actually progress a step farther. Now they started down.

"What are you two so busy about?" A voice came from the hall below. Dale moved toward the banisters and looked down upon Marcia Rowland, who stood in the center of the gleaming floor, looking up at them. How long had she been there, Dale wondered, and felt very impatient and irritated. Marcia, of all people! Liza had been around all morning, and had left just before Hi had sent for her and Bill, thank gracious, because Liza would have been dying of curiosity by now. But Marcia could not be avoided. Dale gave Bill a quick look and said under her breath, "Wait, I'll deal with her," and went down the remaining steps to meet her aunt.

Marcia scrutinized her, as Dale came toward her.

"What's the matter, you're not sick, are you?"

"No," Dale said, "just a little bit tired."

"Then don't look so woebegone. Wait until you have something really to contend with, as I have." Marcia heaved a great sigh. "I'm exhausted! Where's Hi?"

"I'm sorry, Aunt Marcia. Uncle Hi is in his study. Do you want to go up?"

Her aunt didn't look exhausted, she looked fine and smart in a blue cashmere suit and white blouse. Her chic little hat sat becomingly upon a perfect coiffure.

Marcia hesitated. She seemed a little reluctant to go straight up. "I'll just rest a minute first," she said, and sat upon the red velvet settee between the deep recessed windows; fussed a little with her appearance; patting a wave here and there, taking off her gloves, dabbing a bit of powder from her compact on nose and chin.

Dale watched her with growing impatience, wondering what Marcia wanted this time. She was certainly going to promote some extravagance that would require a little "bonus" from Uncle Hi. Everything pointed to it.

42

"You don't need to spruce up, Aunt Marcia, you look very 'Currant,'" Dale said, coining the word on the spur of the moment.

"I don't know what you mean, but I hope something pleasant, and I do hope your uncle is in a better humor than he was the last time I talked to him." Dale saw little anxious lines appearing around Marcia's large brown eyes. "I've found a splendid house for Mary and Jack; they are cramped to death where they are. One bathroom and three children! You can imagine how that is." Dale became suddenly conscious of Bill's presence.

"Where's the house that you want?" she asked.

"Not for *myself,* Dale," Marcia firmly corrected, and then launched into superlatives. "And it's in Westover!"

And cost a fortune, thought Dale, the swankiest section in town.

Marcia must have noted Dale's doubtful expression. "I do all I can to help Mary and Jack. I want this for Mary, though. Jack is a good enough son-in-law, but he's a little touchy. After all, Mary's my own daughter — why shouldn't I have a say? I'm only trying to help. Of course I can't do much — on the money I get. I never buy an unnecessary thing, everything has gone up, and Liza had to have a complete outfit this spring. She's grown some *more!* I should think Hi would want us to have nice things. Mary should be in that young married crowd in Westover and have some fun. Walter's talking about a new car — when I've just gotten the TV. But the house is more important right now — Mary's never had anything but drudgery!"

Drudgery — Mary? Dale had a quick flashback! The Rowland's dining room, Liza looking tired and disheveled getting supper, saying "Mary and Jack always leave the kids here. Cocktails at Lew's. Dinner — "

She interrupted the monologue, "You don't have to sell it to me, Aunt Marcia. You better save all that salesmanship for Uncle Hi. Why don't you bowl him over? Just go in and ask him straight out for $25,000. He drew that much out of the bank the other day. If you don't believe me, ask Walter. But don't tell Hi I told you," Dale added, caution overtaking her.

Marcia Rowland's eyes became several sizes larger. Her mouth opened, though no sound proceeded from it; then she turned around

43

and started up the stairs. Bill came down quickly to join Dale in the hall.

"Golly," he said, "I believe she's taken it on!" They both relaxed, their spirits revived a little. Bill grinned and Dale giggled hysterically.

"Come on, we'd better get into the library. I'd hate to meet her on her way out."

Chapter Eight

"IT WAS all very well to make a plan," Dale thought, "but carrying it out was another thing." Ever since she and Bill had decided how to do it, they had been balked, not by anyone deliberately — just circumstances. It looked as if they weren't intended to find the money. *Find* it? They weren't even intended to *try*. First Uncle Hi getting sick — his blood pressure way up — and no wonder! But it meant that she couldn't search his room. That was to have been her assignment. Bill had taken the study, and he'd done a lot of searching there. But Bill still had his job to do for Hi. Even in bed, Hi was near enough to call Bill in and keep him working. So, after hours was all the time he had. He'd gotten nowhere.

And Dale had accomplished nothing either. Her searching hours were limited too, and were even more subject to interruption than Bill's, because no one would come in just when *he'd* started to take the books off the shelves or ransack a closet and ask *him* what in the world he thought he was doing! That was Liza, with her eternal curiosity, and it seemed to Dale that Maggie had never been so ubiquitous. She'd even taken to sitting with her in the evenings now that Bill didn't. The library, which was hers to search, because Bill would find it more difficult, had become the most popular room in the house. She could never have an hour alone. There was little enough time anyway, with art classes all morning, which could not

45

be skipped — *not* going would bring more questions. She simply hadn't had time to take down more than a half a row of books to look behind them, much less *inside* them!

Now after three days, Dale was desperate. She had made the bad weather an excuse to stay home today. With Hi sick, Maggie ought to be fussing around him, not trailing her. She must get on with it, and the library seemed the most likely place. Hi could have slipped the money between the leaves of a book — even two or three books.

Dale went over to the door and closed it. She didn't lock it because that would arouse suspicion — and immediate demands to be let in. But she put a chair across the jamb, slightly out from the wall; not to look barricaded, just to hear the door knock against it, telling her that one of them was coming in.

If she just didn't have to keep it all so secret! If she could just come out and say that Hi had lost some money, just that much; then Maggie would help. Liza might if she thought it would gain her something. "But it wouldn't," Dale thought dismally. "Hi is offering no reward — Hi doesn't expect the money to be found — he wants to keep us looking for it. How long? — It *has* to be found. If someone really has stolen it, and I can't believe that, then we'll have to find out who, and get it back."

Dale began by climbing up on a chair and reaching for the top shelf. She would be systematic and take row by row. She had stacked two tall dusty piles and was about to settle herself on the floor beside them when it occurred to her that the very dusty ones could be eliminated. She would look for fingerprints or at least for signs of handling. That would simplify matters. But, back up on the chair, she saw that none of the books seemed to have been handled. Maggie's housekeeping had not extended to books. She took down more and more, and stopped in despair, trying to decide how undisturbed they *could* look — to be innocent.

Rain was beating against the windows. Dale had not lighted the great chandelier; Maggie would certainly be attracted by that. She had lighted only the two side wall brackets. The dull illumination was frustrating, and her spirits matched the gloom. She took another last armful and turned to step down, slipped, caught at the shelf; the chair

46

tipped and she came down with a very loud sound of falling and bumping. That did it! The door came crashing against the chair, and Maggie stood and looked at the havoc. No use to try to pretend it was nothing. How could she, with fifty or more of Hi's antiquated volumes piled around her, the chair with its legs in the air.

"You might as well stop all this shenanagin," Maggie said as she stood with a hand on each hip. "And don't tell me it's nothing, that you just took a notion to read all those books in the dark, because I know very well what —" She stopped abruptly, looking scared. She'd nearly slipped. This was driving her daft and breaking her heart — pretending not to know what Dale was about. But she had it to do, she told herself, because of Hi's threats and her own promise. She tried again.

"Bill looks like the witches are riding him — and you, so forlorn." Then slipping again. "Tis a sin and a shame — *he* ought to be ashamed — " but this time Dale saved her by assuming that Bill was being blamed for looking wretched.

"Bill hasn't done a thing!" Dale protested, and, to her own surprise, burst into tears.

Maggie melted instantly. "My pet, my poor bairn." Her arms went around Dale. "Men are all alike, if it's not the young ones, then it's the old. Shake them both up in a bag and I don't know which would come out first." Then reaching the peak of inconsistency, "But I'm thinking it's Bill that has brought you to tears! He's been keeping his distance, I notice. There's a black mood upon him."

"Well, no wonder! If Uncle Hi thought *you* were a thief — how would *you* like it?"

Dale pulled herself out of Maggie's arms, faced her, and then went right on, amazed at herself, and unable to stop.

"All that money Hi sent Bill to get out of the bank — $25,000 — has gone! Hi says Bill has it! Bill put it in the safe. *I* know Hi's got it, hidden somewhere, you've got to help me find it!" Then Dale looked scared. "Hi made me promise not to tell and now I've done it! I can't help it, I had to. I can't go on trying to sneak off and look for it — that way. And until we do find it, Bill's gone high and mighty — and says we won't be engaged, which is exactly what Hi wanted!" Dale was threatened by tears again and had to stop.

"Saints in heaven!" Maggie could think of nothing more to say. Her rigid conscience and fear of Hi's reprisals bound her. She sat down slowly in the Thomas Jefferson chair, which she had never before, in all her years in that house, considered it her privilege to do. Now she was as unaware of it as she was that Dale had suddenly straightened up and was looking toward the door.

Dale just had time to stoop and seem occupied in stacking the books, to whisper fiercely, "Don't you dare to tell a soul! Promise! *Promise!*" Maggie nodded, still without words, and then as she raised her head on the last vigorous affirmative, she saw the reason for the quick change and vehement whispers. Liza had come into the room.

"Is Mother here?" Liza asked before she had got well inside. She looked around at the floor strewn with books, the chair still on its back and Maggie and Dale both helplessly doing nothing at all. They watched her advance.

Liza was a sight. Rain glistened on her hair, which was plastered wet against her temples, and hung uneven and limply around her ears; she never wore a hat. Her only concession to weather, a transparent plastic coat, was sending small rivulets streaming around her feet.

Maggie, who had been struggling to say something light and off-hand, automatically reacted to this.

"And is it too much to expect that you leave the weather outside and not trail it in with you! You're ruining the rug."

Liza wrenched her eyes away from the confusion of books, chair, and Dale, and began to unfasten the metal clasps down the front of her, repeating her inquiry.

"Where is Mother?" she asked, this time with more insistence. "She came in. I saw her ahead of me — on the street. I'd know that purple umbrella anywhere."

"Will you get out of here?" Maggie demanded. "Get out to the back hall and leave off those clodhoppers too!" She pointed at Liza's waterlogged loafers.

Dale, who had decided not to move, to ignore the mess around her, and offer no explanation, contributed a suggestion.

"Maybe she went right up to see Hi. She's been so attentive lately. It's quite touching," and applauded herself for the aptness of her phraseology. She pictured Aunt Marcia marching in on Hi, who would be fairly cornered. In his great four-poster — his back against a wall of pillows, there would be no retreat.

Aunt Marcia would stand at the foot of the bed and bombard him, with words, arguments, pleadings, and recriminations. Hi would sit back, his small body hunched against his pillows and let 'em come. Dale could see his defiant, derisive grin. But Hi was sick, and Aunt Marcia was quite formidable when she was really bent on gaining a point.

"Maggie, she shouldn't be up there. Didn't Dr. Cotten say 'Quiet'?"

Maggie's expression changed quickly to self-reproach. "And me down here, leaving him without protection!" She made a beeline for the door and Dale felt a jealous pang. *She* was the one who always stayed with Hi when he was sick, and now Maggie. Then her stubborn temper asserted itself, and hid the truth from her — the truth was that she didn't like this quarrel with Hi. She missed him.

Maggie's petting was small comfort. She loved Maggie dearly. Maggie was all the mother she had ever known, but Hi was much more. Hi engaged her mind as well as her heart, and deep down under the hurt, she knew that Hi loved her.

There was just enough of the same material woven into the warp and weft of their characters to hold them together in a strong mutual attachment. The same pertinacity — the same strain of whimsicality — they came from the same loom, though the product was so dissimilar. Dale didn't recognize all this, she didn't analyze, but she felt an emptiness, a sense of desertion, that sharpened her pain and resentment, and hardened her determination to win out against him.

She looked up, saw that Liza had returned, and pulled herself up from among the scattered books. She sat down upon the old brocaded sofa back against the wall. Liza came over and sat beside her.

"Dale, I wish you would tell me —" She didn't finish. Liza seemed infected by the virus of misery and nerves that pervaded the atmosphere of the whole house, and she jumped up and began to tramp around the room.

49

"Liza doesn't *wander,* or *pace,* she *lumbers,* when she doesn't stumble," thought Dale.

Liza asked, "Is Uncle Hi very sick, Dale? What's the matter with him?"

"He has high blood pressure. You know that, Liza," Dale answered. "He's always had it. It's just gone up too much. Dr. Cotten puts him to bed when that happens."

"Well, what makes it?" Liza persisted. "Mother says he just uses it as an excuse when he wants to be let alone — she's hell-bent on getting that house for Mary and Jack, and I think she's crazy. There are lots of things much more important; if she wasn't such a nitwit, she'd know it!"

Dale was jerked out of herself by surprise. She really looked at Liza for the first time since she'd come into the room. Liza looked white and strained, and there was almost a tortured expression in her pale gray eyes, a tautness about her mouth, and Dale felt less antagonism, but her sympathy was mixed with curiosity. Of course, Aunt Marcia was hard to take even in small doses. It was no wonder that Liza who had her as a steady diet — as a mother — must reach her limit sometimes.

"She is rather sold on the idea," Dale said, but her understatement was lost on Liza.

"Rather sold? She's plumb nuts — but that's the way she always is when she wants something. It's all she thinks about." Liza pulled down the corners of her mouth. "Mary and Jack! I'm sick of them."

"I have always thought Jack a pretty nice person, with his feet on the ground. *He* never comes begging."

"I should hope not," Liza said. "Mother doesn't call it begging. She thinks Uncle Hi sort of owes it to her, and I think he does too." She held out a protesting hand. "Oh, I don't mean about that crazy house, but the money. She's told me lots of times, Dale, that when Uncle Hi dies, then grandfather's estate will come to her. I don't understand how it is, but she says it's practically hers now — only in trust — and Hi won't let her have it, and that isn't right!"

"He can't, if it's in trust, Liza. Anyone would understand that. What Aunt Marcia wants is *Hi's* money on *her* prospects."

"Well, I hope she doesn't get it for the house, anyway. I don't see why Mary and Jack should have it all. But now she's talking about $25,000 that she says Hi's got in cash. Is that so, Dale? Where does he keep all that money? Gosh!"

"I haven't the slightest idea." Dale's tone was convincing.

Liza moved toward the window and looked out. She gave an exclamation of surprise. "There she goes now! Well, I'll be darned, Maggie must have worked a miracle. It's Mother, and she's halfway up the block."

Liza made a sudden quick movement toward the window again, with the first look of interest lighting her face that Dale had seen on it that morning; then turned away quickly.

"I guess I might as well go too," she said nervously, and hurried across the room toward the door leading to the back. "I'll get my coat." She stumbled over a pile of books before reaching the doorway — which for once Dale thought was excusable, since they were right in her path — and disappeared.

Dale went over to the window then and glanced out. There was a car parked at the corner and, as she watched, Liza came out through the wrought-iron gate at the side entrance of the house, which led from the old basement kitchen, and hurried toward it. A young man opened the car door, stepped out, and gave her the high sign. Liza went quickly — the car door slammed — and they were gone, disappearing around the corner.

Dale burst into a spontaneous laugh, the first she'd indulged in for days.

"Atta girl, Liza! So you had yourself a date, eh? More like a pick-up," Dale thought. "Well — he looked like a nice boy — big and tall — with a thatch of black hair. He looked like somebody . . . of course, that's just who it was! Now how did Liza manage that?" She remembered now that Liza had asked about Nick that day when Dale had stopped by the Rowlands to give Aunt Marcia Walter's message. But Liza had said then that she didn't really know Nick — he was Walter's friend. "So he was Walter's friend, was he? Maybe Liza wasn't so dumb. Nick was good looking. Aunt Marcia would of course have a fit. 'Not in Liza's class at all — just a common dago!' More

51

power to him." She turned away from the window, hearing a step behind her and there stood Bill very close.

With joy she moved toward him, but Bill didn't respond. He was holding himself rigid, his hands dug into his pockets, his face set, his hazel eyes looked at her from under drawn dark brows, and when he began to speak his voice was ragged.

"I feel like a cringing dog, slinking and sniffing into corners!" Dale started to protest, but he stopped her. "I can't find that damn money and neither can you, and I'm going to tell your uncle to send for the cops tomorrow. This can't go on. If he's got it, that will call his bluff, and if he hasn't it's high time the police were notified; too late, really."

"But Bill, what about your dad?" Dale said hesitantly. It was only a conscientious objection, put out reluctantly; she was filled with relief. She closed her eyes for a moment — it was like coming out of a dark hole into sudden light.

"Dad will just have to bear up," Bill answered her. "I'm going over to tell him the whole thing. That's why I said 'tomorrow.' I'll have to explain to him first. It's what I should have done in the beginning, I think."

"But you did what you thought was right then."

"It was a mistake not to have told him. Dad's no coward; I'm the one who was scared."

"Bill! You aren't — you weren't — it was only for your father, and we both thought we'd find the money right away." She said the last of it to his back. Bill was wasting no more time.

Chapter Nine

THE small black car rattled, bumped, and came to a stop. Father John jumped out and made his way rapidly in the dark across the uneven brick sidewalk and up the few stone steps to the door of the historic old house on Bermuda Street. But before he could put his hand upon the bell, Dale whipped open the door, and light flooded out upon him from the hall.

He stepped inside, closed the door with one quick push, and had time for a brief glimpse of her face, white and frightened, before she whirled like a blown feather and raced toward the stairs, beckoning him to follow. He caught up with her and detained her on the landing with a hand on her arm.

"Is the doctor here?" Father John asked. She shook her head, looking up at him with enormous eyes, her cheeks pinched and drawn.

"On his way," she said. "Bill's pinch-hitting. He hadn't left before Maggie yelled to us. But Hi's dying, Father, he's *dying*. You'll have to do something quick — about him. Can you give him absolution — conditional? He can't go like this!" A sob choked her, but she immediately straightened her shoulders and tightened her lips.

The priest gave her a compassionate look. Then he hurried ahead of her up the few remaining steps into the upper hall.

Maggie came down the passageway. When she saw them, her arms went up over her head in one silent gesture of despair. Dale stopped, frozen. It was Father John who spoke.

"Has he gone?"

Maggie came up to him, "No, no, Father. Did you bring the holy water?" Her eyes were great round blue blanks; shock and fear had wiped out all expression. "He's on the brink — God save him! 'It's all purple,' he says, 'and then it's yellow, and then it's both!' 'Tis the flames of purgatory, Father, he's seeing. What else?"

"Don't listen to her!" Dale cried, and in angry relief turned upon Maggie. "I'm glad that at least you're not sending him to hell!"

The priest smiled in spite of himself, and went ahead of them to the bedroom, found the door was ajar, and stepped silently inside.

Bill was leaning over the small still form of Hiram Bosch. He was a very slight mound in the huge old bed, his head sunk into and nearly obscured by the bulging pillow.

At the priest's entrance, Bill straightened up, but did not release his hold upon the thin corded wrist of the sick man. Bill was taking the pulse. Hi lay like the dead, in the dim, shaded light. His face was shrunken, and so pale that it seemed almost blue. Father John approached. Bill released Hi's wrist gently and answered the question in the priest's eyes, forming the words with his lips, without making a sound.

"Down to forty." Bill's coat was off, sleeves rolled up, his forehead damp with sweat. Hi groaned and retched. Bill leaned toward him and put a strong arm around the old man's shoulders, lifting him to a half-sitting position, then as Hi relaxed, eased him back again upon the pillow. Father John moved closer and looked again. Hi's eyes opened and met the priest's with recognition. A faint gleam flickered in one for a moment, as he turned his head on the pillow.

"Come to cheat the devil?" he whispered.

Father John nodded. "Yes, and I want you to join me, Hi — mentally." He made the sign of the cross slowly over the sick man and started to say the "Act of Contrition" in his low clear baritone. Bill dropped to his knees beside the bed, and Dale, who had come silently in, knelt beside him and buried her bright head in the dark silk quilt near Hi's shoulder.

The old man closed his eyes and a look of serenity settled upon his tortured features, for a short moment; then, with another spasm,

54

he twisted and threshed in agony. Bill tried to help him, to support him, but Hi slipped and slithered out of his grasp. Father John continued to pray calmly and silently, and Dale, as if in a trance, raising her head and watching her uncle with suffering eyes and hands clasped, did not move.

A bell sounded faintly, and Maggie, hovering near the door, fled from the room. They heard her scuffling steps upon the stairs. They heard her give a loud ejaculation, quickly hushed by a masculine voice; then quick firm footsteps coming up the stairs, down the hallway, and they all turned as one toward Dr. Cotten as he came into the room.

The doctor nodded to Bill, bowed to Father John, patted Dale's head, and leaned over Hi, almost in one simultaneous move. Father John went over to Dale.

"We'd better get out of the way, my child. Let Dr. Cotten take over now. Bill will stay and help him — he doesn't need us." Dale looked up at the doctor, who nodded agreement. She leaned over and kissed Hi lightly on the forehead.

A black beady eye gleamed at her, and then the lid closed over it, but Dale was comforted.

She turned and followed Father John quietly. Pausing at the door, she looked back and saw Bill beside the doctor as he opened his bag under the lamp on the far side of the room and heard the doctor say, "An intravenous infusion of potassium chloride. Yes — I thought so from what you told me on the phone — a very good diagnosis, Bill."

Then Dale saw Bill move toward the bed and Dr. Cotten was fitting a syringe together. She closed the door; Hi was in good hands.

Father John led the way across the hall into Hi's study, and Dale and Maggie obediently followed him.

"Let's sit here quietly now," said Father John. "If the doctor needs anything we will be right here, near enough to hear him. I'd like you to tell me what happened, what brought on this sudden illness." He turned to Dale. "It *was* sudden, wasn't it?"

Dale sat down in the very same place where she had sat only a few days ago. It seemed months since she and Bill had faced Hi in his old leather chair. Father John sat there now, and Maggie took

Bill's. Dale raised her eyes and saw *Death and the Miser* hanging innocently on the pilaster between the rows of books. Maggie, after one skittish glance at the picture, had turned her chair so that her back was squarely to it. Dale turned her eyes away from it too and looked at the priest who was crowded in Hi's chair.

"All I know, Father," she began, "is that Bill and I had been talking in the library, and Bill was starting home — to see his father. . . . He'd just reached the front door when Maggie came out on the landing of the stairs and yelled for someone to come quickly, Uncle Hi was terribly sick. We followed Maggie to the bathroom.

"Hi — he'd been terribly nauseated, and had collapsed on the floor. His face was blue, I thought he was dead." Dale's voice trembled, she waited a minute and went on. "Bill knelt down and felt his pulse and told me to phone for the doctor. By the look on Bill's face I thought 'It's too late!' I ran downstairs to the phone and called Dr. Cotten, but before I could hang up, there was Bill taking the receiver out of my hands to say something to the doctor. Then I phoned you. When I raced upstairs again I found that Bill had put Hi to bed, and he wasn't dead. Bill sent me back to watch by the door for the doctor and get him upstairs quickly. But you were first, Dr. Cotten had such a long way to come. That's all I know," Dale concluded. They both turned to Maggie and waited. But Maggie sat bolt upright, with her eyes closed, her lips moving. Father John leaned forward and gently touched her on the shoulder. She jumped like a rabbit, her eyes flying open, round and startled.

"Were you listening, Maggie?" Father asked. "We want you to tell us about Hi. What made him sick? Tell us everything you can."

"And that is nothing at all," Maggie said, "but the devil's in it, Father, ever since that picture has come into this house, swarming with demons — things have not been right!"

"Now look, Maggie," Father spoke sternly. "Stop all that foolishness and tell me what happened to Hi this afternoon. When was he taken sick — and how?"

"Can I tell you if I don't know, your Reverence?" The tone was meek but Maggie was on her dignity.

Father John sighed. "Listen, Maggie, you certainly know when you first noticed that something was wrong?" he said patiently.

"Wrong? Certainly, I noticed something was wrong. It's been wrong ever since — well skipping that — since you'll not let me speak of it. I'll only say that humans have also added to the trouble in this house." Maggie clamped her lips shut, and folded her hands tightly in her lap, her fingers clasping and unclasping.

"Maggie, darling," Dale said softly, "I know you've had an awful day, with all of us bothering you — and Aunt Marcia coming. Did she make a fuss?"

"Ah, that one! She did, though I didn't stay to listen to it all. She went in against my better judgment — and she fair ranted at him — and he lying there helpless and sick. It was a house she wanted — and money and then it was the house again — and the world with a fence around it. Ah, she's a one, she is! I went down the stairs, and I thought to fix his medicine. 'It'll give him more strength to withstand her,' I said to myself."

"What was the medicine, something new?" asked Father John, listening intently.

"No, no, Father, just the drops. His blood pressure went up — and breathless, he was as well, which is why he was in bed. Dr. Cotten had increased the dose. 'Fifteen drops in a quarter of glass of water,' he said, 'Maggie, and be careful no more — just once a day.' He's been taking it all along, Father, as you very well know — only ten it was before." Maggie stopped.

"Go on," Father prompted. "Did you give it to him?"

"Not just then, I didn't. I had it all fixed and ready to take up when I heard a great rumpus in the library." Maggie looked at Dale with a question in her eyes, and Dale interrupted her.

"It was just me, Father. I was taking down some books and I fell off the chair."

"It scared me, Father and I left the glass and bottle and went to find out — "

Here Maggie seemed again at a loss and she looked at Dale nervously.

"That has nothing to do with Hi's medicine, Maggie," Dale said firmly. "Father asked you when you gave it."

"It had more than you know to do with it, Dale," Maggie replied, "for after that session with you, I clearly forgot and it was not until long after your aunt had left that I suddenly remembered and went back to the pantry and took it up to him."

"Was he all right then?" asked Father John. Maggie's lips curved upward in a slight semblance of a smile at the question.

"He was that," she said. "He was grinning, laying back against his pillows, and says he, 'Maggie, the general's fair routed. Did you hear her retreat?' *That* tickled, he was."

"Did you give him his medicine then, Maggie?" Father asked.

"I did, Father, and back down I went, as he closed his eyes, I thought, for a wee nap. Both the Rowlands being gone, the house was very still," she added.

"Yes," thought Dale, "it was right about then that Bill and I were talking in the library."

"Before long," said Maggie, "I tip-toed back up the stairs and looked into his room — the bed was empty — then I heard such groans and retchings coming from the bathroom, my heart jerked nearly out of me. I found him there, Father, flat laid out, he was, on the floor. 'Holy Mother,' I prayed, 'watch over him,' and my feet flew to the stairs of their own accord and my voice called for help, though I don't remember opening my mouth — and that's all I can tell you, with a clear conscience, Father."

"I suppose," thought Dale swiftly, "she means she can't break her promise to me about the money; which has nothing to do with it."

But Dale had no more time to wonder about Maggie's confused mental processes. She glanced up and saw Dr. Cotten standing in the doorway. Her heart gave a leap of apprehension.

"He'll pull through," the doctor said and smiled at them. Dale felt weak with relief. She went to him and he put his arm around her.

"You can thank Bill for it," and grinned down at her knowingly. "If he hadn't been smart enough to diagnose the case — I wouldn't have known what to bring with me — as it was, no time was wasted."

Father John came and stood beside Dale. "What was it, doctor?

These girls don't seem to know." Maggie tittered at his little joke.

"It's all right now, we can laugh again," Dale thought gratefully.

But Dr. Cotten was grave once more. "That's a strange thing," he said, not looking at anyone, gazing deliberately at some point across the room. "It was an overdose of digitalis, quite an overdose!"

There was a little silence. "Come back in here. Let's talk a minute," he said easily and went farther into the study. They all grouped around him. He went over toward the window, flanked by Hi's desk, pushed some books and papers, Bill's work, aside, and sat on a corner of it, dangling one foot. "He is being deliberately nonchalant," thought Dale. "Disarming — someone."

"Better close the door," he suggested pleasantly. "Hi has very sharp ears. It's just as well to be careful."

"Now," he said facing them, busy with his fountain pen — sliding it through his fingers and looking thoughtful. "Who gives Hi his daily dose?" he asked innocently.

"He *knows* that Maggie does," Dale thought, "He doesn't want to frighten her. He wants to find out before she gets mad or scared and goes all to pieces."

Maggie spoke up with no suspicion. "You know very well, doctor, that it's my duty to see that he gets it once a day, and it's fifteen drops now, you said, 'and mind you, no more.'"

"Right. And you stuck to that, Maggie, did you?"

"Like the Ten Commandments, doctor," she declared, a trace of defiance in her tone as she sensed the import of his questions.

"Do you think, now, that anyone else could have given it to him before you did, and forgotten to tell you?"

"And that is ridiculous — begging your pardon, doctor. Do you think he would have taken two? He knows as well as myself that one dose a day was all that was allowed."

"Where do you keep the digitalis bottle, Maggie?"

"Always in my little cabinet in the pantry, where it's handy."

Dr. Cotten looked surprised. "Why not in the bathroom upstairs, Maggie. Wouldn't that be safer?"

"Safer?" she asked. "Who's to steal it. And if you mean fewer people to meddle, I'm telling you now that bathroom — and a disgrace it is, only one in this great house, and he'll make no changes. That bathroom is as hard to get into as St. Mary's on a holy day."

Dr. Cotten chuckled. "All right, so you keep the tincture of digitalis in the cabinet in the pantry?"

Maggie nodded. "Where it's convenient to the library where he is of an evening, barring a sickness that takes him to bed; and you know yourself, doctor, that's a rare thing."

The doctor straightened up. "Very well, Maggie, what I was getting at," he said ceasing to be casual, "is this. If you are the only one to give Hi his medicine, how could he have gotten a double dose?"

All this argument was catching at straws, it seemed to Dale, and then, as she thought back over Maggie's statement, fixing the dose for Hi, then going off and coming back much later — a sudden solution sprang into her mind. It was awful — poor Maggie! How she would hate it — but it must be the answer! Maggie had forgotten that the drops were in, and put them in a second time. "When she went back, disturbed and with her mind on me," thought Dale, "and my troubles, she could easily have forgotten. But I could never be so cruel as to ask her," and then Dale heard the doctor doing just that, and Maggie after a stunned silence denying it vociferously.

"Never — never — and me in this house tending to his wants — these thirty years or more! So it's come to this, has it, distrusting *me,* is it?"

"Now hold on, Maggie!" Father John said. "Dr. Cotten just wants everyone to be very careful. From now on."

"And it's careful I am, and I'll have no one doubting it — even you, Father," said Maggie not without dignity, and left them standing there nonplused and feeling a little abashed. In the uncomfortable silence Dale thought of something.

"Did Hi really see purple and yellow, doctor? Maggie said so. She insists he was muttering 'purple and yellow.' "

The doctor nodded. "Oh, yes, it is one of the effects of the drug — an overdose, I mean."

"She thought Hi saw flames," Dale said.

Dr. Cotten looked puzzled.

60

"Yes, she thought so, poor Maggie!" Dale explained. "She said 'flames of purgatory.'"

Dr. Cotten was amused, but resumed his former gravity.

"I've never known Maggie to be careless," he said. "She's more apt to be too scrupulous in carrying out my instructions, but you'd better keep an eye on her, Dale. I'd like to know how this thing happened."

Chapter Ten

DALE opened the Rowlands' front door, which was never locked. She had come quickly, but paused and drew back out of sight when she heard Liza's aggravated tones, and Marcia's martyred ones. She did not wish to get involved in one of their arguments. She could see through the half-open portieres.

Marcia was lying on the sofa in what she termed the "drawing room" and Liza called the "back parlor." A hand-knit throw covered her feet, satin mules lay where she had dropped them on the floor beside her; two cushions propped her nearly upright and she was smoking a cigarette. A newspaper was spread out before her. She pushed it away with an impatient sigh, reached for her coffee cup on the low table at her elbow, where her opened morning mail lay scattered; several letters bearing legends of real-estate firms.

"There isn't a single thing here," she said pushing the paper away impatiently. "The house in Westover is the only possible thing. And it's going on the market tomorrow."

Liza looked over at her mother with a dull, uninterested glance, and shifted her book, which she had not been reading, to the other knee.

"Do they *have* to live in a mansion?" she asked listlessly.

"Why shouldn't they? It's not a mansion, it is merely a comfortable house in good surroundings. It's no more than other young couples do. But *they* have parents who can help them." Marcia's tremulous sigh invited sympathy.

"And poor Mary and Jack only have you — *poor* little poverty-stricken *you!* For heaven's sake, Mother, don't work up to another scene."

Marcia ignored Liza's derisive tone, intent upon her theme. "I tried again yesterday and Hi wouldn't listen to a word I said. Lying there grinning at me, saying he just didn't have the money handy. I didn't like to say outright I knew he had it, for fear it would get Walter in dutch."

"Believe me, Mother, you aren't the only one who'd like to get your hands on that money. Dale's been tearing the house apart — pretends she's cleaning up. Why the sudden interest? Dale never lifts a finger — Maggie does it all. Something funny is going on over there."

"You mean she is looking for it?"

Liza ignored the question, and her voice rose belligerently. "And *why* can't you think of anyone else beside Mary and Jack?" she continued. "There are other things that $25,000 could do. Why shouldn't Walter have some of it?" Then she added almost as an afterthought, "And what about me?"

"You?" Marcia laughed. "Don't be silly! What would you do with all that money?"

"I know what I *could* do with it, and it wouldn't necessarily be all for myself," Liza said coolly, then added defiantly, "And it wouldn't be a house for Mary and Jack! But what do *you* care what happens to *me?*"

"Don't be ridiculous, Liza. I'm planning to make a down payment on a new car for Walter soon — as a surprise."

Liza stood up and dropped the book. "Oh golly," she said. "I wish I'd known. I didn't think you had a cent."

"I haven't," said Marcia. "Not what it would take for a house. I declare, Liza, you don't know a thing about money!"

"I know a lot about *no* money," Liza retorted.

Marcia sighed and lay back upon the cushions. "Please," she said plaintively, "my head is splitting. Have you washed the breakfast dishes?"

63

It was at this point that Dale decided to go into the room. She had not intended to eavesdrop. She felt angry at Liza for her unsavory hints, and dismayed that she was so close to the truth. Dale was tempted to turn and leave. Why bother? They didn't care what happened to Hi; all they wanted was his money — and theirs — if what Marcia claimed was so. But she'd come over to tell them about Hi's illness, because she didn't want to phone; she didn't want to ask them about the medicine on the phone. She could tell better by watching their faces — if they denied it — and they would she feared, after they heard how near a thing it has been for Hi.

"Aunt Marcia never takes the blame for anything. *She* never makes a mistake! But for Maggie's sake I've got to try," Dale thought, and stepped inside the room, almost running into Liza. She looked over at Marcia prone upon the couch.

"Is she sick?" she asked in a lowered tone. "Is that why you aren't going to school? I came early to catch you."

"Oh, no," Liza said. *"I've* got a cold, so Mother's resting." She turned and left the room, without another glance at Dale.

"What's it, Dale? Come over here," Marcia's voice came faintly from the sofa. Dale went over.

"Sit down. I'm sorry, my dear, that Liza's so out of sorts this morning, but that's the way she speaks quite often. I try to be patient, but you know Liza, so I don't need to explain. Why are you so early?" Marcia's eyes betrayed her tired voice; they were quite alive though guarded. "Is there something special?"

"Uncle Hi was desperately sick last night, Aunt Marcia." Dale didn't try a gradual approach, she thought a little shock might break down the affectations which served Marcia's purposes so successfully. Dale wanted spontaneous reaction, but she was disappointed.

"Not really, my dear! How *dreadful!* And how is he now?" The tone was perfect, and if just a suspicion of eagerness flashed out from her eyes, Dale couldn't even be sure she had seen it. Now Marcia's face was full of concern.

"Oh, he'll pull through, but if Bill hadn't been there, he might not have. He's confused — doesn't remember anything. But the doctor says that loss of memory is caused by weakness and poor circulation.

It may clear up as he gets stronger, we hope."

"What happened? He certainly wasn't weak when I was there!" Marcia said bitterly.

"That," said Dale, "is what I came about." She had made up her mind to give her aunt no time to think up an excuse — or an alibi.

"Did you give Uncle Hi his medicine when you came yesterday, Aunt Marcia?"

But Marcia was certainly not trapped into an admission, nor even confused. She looked at Dale a moment, evincing surprise, and then became slightly indignant.

"Why, what a question! Of course *not!* I've never presumed to nurse Hi — I wouldn't *think* of such a thing."

"He got an extra dose. That's what nearly killed him, and we are trying to find out how it happened," Dale said bluntly.

"Well, of all things!" Marcia was now really roused. "I must say, Dale, this is the most preposterous suggestion."

"Oh, I didn't mean did you do it on purpose." Dale gave a forced little laugh.

"How extremely generous of you," Marcia said icily.

"I just thought," Dale continued doggedly, "that you might have seen the bottle and glass out on the pantry shelf and taken it up when you went. He shouldn't have had it but once."

"And are you trying to tell me that Hi had *two* doses instead of one, and you think I am responsible?"

Dale knew that she was not handling this as she had intended. Aunt Marcia's astonishment and injured dignity put her on the defensive.

"I'm not accusing you of anything, Aunt Marcia, please understand that, but naturally we are worried. We'd like to find out — so as to be sure it can't happen again — and we can't ask Hi. Dr. Cotten says positively he must not be questioned."

Marcia seemed a little mollified. Throwing off the coverlet, she sat up, reached down for her mules, slipped them on, and walked swiftly across the room, her robe billowing out behind her. She took her seat in the chair that Liza had been occupying earlier, and faced Dale.

"Now, let's see what you are getting at, Dale," she said crisply, lighting another cigarette, blowing out a stream of smoke and looking coldly at her niece.

"Maggie gives Hi his medicine, doesn't she? She nurses him when he is sick — that's her job, isn't it?" she asked.

"Yes," Dale answered, vouchsafing no more. She could see exactly where Marcia's questions were headed.

"Very well then, find out what Maggie did, pin her down, Dale. She must have made a mistake."

"Maggie insists she didn't — she says she measured the drops into the glass and added the right amount of water."

"Did she take it right up to Hi?"

Aunt Marcia was a witch! How could she know? "Unless, of course," Dale thought quickly, "unless she saw the glass there."

But Marcia spiked that idea too. "Did you say it was on the pantry shelf? In that case, I *couldn't* have seen it. I went right up the front stairs when I came in, and left the same way. I didn't go near the pantry. Maggie didn't give Hi any medicine while I was in his room. When was he supposed to take it?"

"There wasn't any set time, Aunt Marcia, just once a day. That's why I thought possibly he might have had it twice. Although Maggie says that isn't possible, since Hi knows he should take it only once a day. I thought maybe, if he was distracted by something — your talking to him, for example — he might have taken it from you automatically, and forgotten that he had, when Maggie gave it to him again after you left."

"None of that makes any sense, Dale. And why worry about it now? You say Hi is going to be all right. However, I do think you better not let Maggie handle the medicine if it's so dangerous. What is it, anyway?"

"*You* know what. Hi's been taking digitalis right along, but Dr. Cotten had increased the dose, and someone gave him a lot more."

"It was Maggie, of course," Marcia said with conviction, "and she's not going to admit it. She probably doesn't even realize she counted the drops wrong. But she's getting old and she's always been a little batty. Hi ought to have a practical nurse," she concluded,

66

snuffing out Maggie as lightly as she did her cigarette. She was through with them both.

"Hi wouldn't stand it, and Maggie would hate it; she's hurt enough as it is. You needn't worry," Dale said, making it emphatic, "Maggie refuses to pour out another drop of medicine. She's making Bill do it. Bill is there, thank goodnes."

The telephone in the hall rang sharply.

Liza answered it almost immediately.

"She must have been right near; she's probably heard everything I said," thought Dale realizing her mistake in announcing Hi's near-death, before asking her questions. Aunt Marcia was on her guard, and nothing would make her admit it now, if she had caused Hi's illness, no matter how innocently, and neither would Liza.

Liza's voice came clearly in to them, interrupting Dale's self-condemnation.

"Well, *I* can't help it. *I* didn't do any talking. You can tell her yourself!" The phone banged down and Liza appeared at the doorway.

"Jack's just called up — he's in a furor. Says it's all over town that he's buying a fifty thousand dollar house in Westover. He says it's highly embarrassing. He says his boss will think he's crazy! Just when he was hoping for a raise!" Liza was grinning maliciously, "And he says 'Thanks for your interest, but will you please lay off! He and Mary can manage without your help!' I never heard him so mad."

Marcia looked stunned, then she rallied. "That's gratitude for you! But it's none of Jack's business if Mary's uncle chooses to buy her a house."

Liza burst out laughing.

Dale seized the opportunity, while Liza's humor was improved. "Liza, when you went back in the pantry to leave your raincoat yesterday, did you see Hi's medicine and glass on the shelf and take it up to him?"

"Please, Dale, don't imagine I had anything to do with this — I heard all you said to Mother — and I don't believe she did either. Why should Mother give Uncle Hi his medicine?" Then Liza snickered, "She'd never admit now, if she did. Don't you know Mother yet?"

67

"That will do, Liza!" Marcia snapped. "I've had enough of your impertinence for one day. And as for you, Dale, if you think you can make me a scapegoat for Maggie's inefficiency, you're vastly mistaken. I'll speak to Walter about this, you can be sure!"

Liza jumped, "Oh my Lord, Mother, do you have to drag Walter into it?"

One look at Marcia, and Dale said quickly, "I came over here, thinking you two would want to hear what had happened to Hi, and because I felt so sorry for Maggie's being blamed for it. I hoped you'd try to help me." She turned toward the door. "I'm going over to see Sister Dennis and then on to my class. I won't bother you again."

Liza followed her down the hall. She was looking a little more sober now, and she spoke in a lower voice.

"I didn't take any medicine to Hi, Dale. And you don't really believe Mother tried to poison him, do you?"

Dale was shocked. "I never said *anyone* tried to poison Hi. Have some sense, Liza! And I suppose it *was* silly of me to imagine that you would go out of your way to do something for *anyone*. But Aunt Marcia wouldn't hesitate, if she thought it would be to her advantage — and you know it. That's just airs, saying she wouldn't presume! — Oh, what's the use!" Dale turned and left, as disgusted with herself as with her cousin and her aunt.

Liza stepped ahead of her, glancing up and down the street, and then she hurried inside again. "I hope you find the money you're looking for," she said as a parting shot, and closed the door behind her.

"I've certainly played the fool," Dale thought, "antagonizing Aunt Marcia, who thinks I was trying to protect Maggie at her expense; and maybe I was. But Liza was trying to be dramatic — I've never seen her so out of hand. She needn't have talked about 'poisoning.'" It wasn't a nice thought. Last night was still too vivid. A little shiver ran over Dale.

She stood a moment in the warm sunshine, breathing in the fresh spring air, getting the dead stuffiness of Aunt Marcia's house out of her lungs. Then, crossing over to her parked car, she saw a blue Ford coming toward her, and when she drew out from the curb, it slid expertly into her place. In her rear-view mirror she caught a glimpse of the driver — a young man with a thatch of dark hair.

Dale lost some of her depression and smiled, hoping she was right. The idea of Liza carrying on a clandestine affair with Nick, right under Aunt Marcia's nose, was irresistibly funny, and it would explain the sudden self-assertiveness. She wished Liza luck.

Dale didn't stay long at St. Mary's Nursery. She had a look at the pictures, which she had finished and hung there at last. They were gay and well done. Then she left the playroom and ran upstairs looking for Sister Dennis, pausing at the bathroom door to glance in.

She always got a kick out of the rows of miniature basins standing in shining rectitude down the length of the room, each one boasting, like a badge of merit, a small rack on the wall beside it, holding bright plastic baby toothbrushes, making colored exclamation points. And there stood Sister Dennis, a slim gray figure before the cupboard with sliding doors, arranging the children's dresses on hangers. Dozens of them, fresh from the laundry; every little ruffle pressed into perky crispness, every little skirt starched and jaunty.

Haloed by her stiff white bonnet and bib, Sister Dennis greeted Dale with serenity and warmth in her beautiful eyes and the smile of a street gamin.

"Come in, my dear," Sister said, and as Dale stood beside her, "they look nice, don't they?" She ran her hands lightly along the rack, fluffing out a skirt, retying a sash, and admiring her handiwork.

"Yes," Dale agreed, "but Sister, you work too hard over them. Those little imps don't appreciate it. You could get by with half the trouble."

"Don't you believe it, my dear. Mother Alberta teases me, says I'm building up vanity in their little souls, but I'm not. I'm building up love."

When Dale left, she felt renewed. Sister Dennis always made her feel like that. It wasn't anything she said — she never talked about religion. She didn't even look pious — she looked happy.

"People," thought Dale, "who believe that nuns are mournful or mawkish just ought to know Sister Dennis! She looks as frail as a Fra Angelico angel, and is as strong as a horse, and about as senti-

69

mental." But she always seemed to set Dale straight without even trying, just by putting things in their normal perspective again: *How would this look in the light of eternity?* sort of a viewpoint, and *Nothing is too hard to overcome if you're on God's side.*

Dale decided not to go to art class. She was only going because she thought Hi would like her to, but now she wanted to get back to him. She slipped behind the wheel of her car and, for a few blocks, thought about entering a convent; then her thoughts flew to Bill, and she nearly went through a red light.

But when she got inside the house, everything was too quiet, just like a hospital; and it wasn't Bill, but Walter who was waiting for her — with Maggie, who was weeping.

Chapter Eleven

DALE felt instant alarm. "What's the matter? Where's Bill? Is Hi worse?" she asked in one breath.

Walter shrugged helplessly and gestured toward Maggie, who was standing in the center of the hall as if she had been placed there by some power stronger than herself, and could not move of her own volition.

"That's what *I* came to ask," said Walter. "Mother phoned me at the bank, so I'm here on my lunch hour. But Maggie stopped right where she is now, when she saw me." He looked both puzzled and exasperated. "And I can't get a word out of her. She only shakes her head and mops her eyes!"

"What's the matter, Maggie?" Dale asked, trying to be patient. She knew these moods of Maggie's; she went into periods of silent doldrums, and it took hours sometimes to get the reason. They came, usually, from hurt feelings, genuine worry, or an attack of scruples.

"Is Hi worse?" she demanded, hardening her heart against Maggie's misery.

Maggie shook her head and dabbed again at her eyes.

"Is Bill upstairs with Hi? Bill's all right, isn't he? Answer me!" And Dale lifted Maggie's trembling chin with the tips of her fingers, making Maggie look at her. In a moment she was satisfied. "All right, now come sit down, and get whatever it is off your chest."

71

She took Maggie's hand and walked with her through the open doorway to the quiet and comfort of the library.

Walter, obviously very curious, trailed them, and watched Dale push Maggie down into the Thomas Jefferson chair, disregarding her protesting gestures and unyielding body. Then he claimed attention.

"I hope everything is all right now, Dale. Mother sounded terribly upset, but I couldn't tell whether it was because of your coming to tell her about Hi, or Jack's giving her hell about the house in Westover. Then I came in here and Maggie's in a cataleptic fit or something." Walter sounded fed up, and Dale heard his vehemence with slight surprise. This was certainly everybody's bad day. Walter wasn't often ruffled, but he looked a little tarnished at this moment; some of his bright assurance had certainly rubbed off.

It was not surprising, living in the house with Aunt Marcia and Liza, and Dale felt a bit sorry for him.

"Oh, don't worry about Maggie," she said, purposely light and casual. "She'll be all right, won't you, Mag?"

As she had hoped, this broke Maggie's silence. Solemnly and ominously, Maggie spoke.

"So it's 'Don't worry about Maggie,' is it? Little *you* know what I'm holding in my mind; but I'll tell you *this,* to surprise you. It's the other way round entirely. It's myself that's worrying about you — with good reason — and a heavy weight you are!"

"Better start dieting, Dale," Walter murmured facetiously.

But neither Maggie nor Dale thought this was worth notice. Dale, glancing at him uneasily, said quickly, "Oh, I'm sure Maggie's worry is not too important."

"And *when* is money not important, I'd like to know? And *lost* money at that!" Maggie demanded; then, her face turning very red, she shut her lips firmly. "I'll say no more now," she declared with a meaningful look at Walter. "Two's a secret, and three's a crowd."

"You're mixing your axioms, Maggie, but I get you, just the same. I didn't intend to stay, anyway." Walter moving leisurely toward the door looked at Dale, then said, "By the way, old Capelli has another picture he wants to sell. I've told him we aren't in the market, but that's the trouble with the old man — one sale and he's hot on your trail forever. He's even tried to get at Mother, but Liza's headed him off, I think. Now I'll tell him Uncle Hi is ill."

"So *that* was why Nick had been hanging around!" Dale thought, feeling quite disappointed. "It was too bad, if that *was* what it was. It might not be though: selling a picture would be a good cover-up." Dale preferred her own supposition, and she wasn't going to let Walter spoil things.

"I've seen Nick once or twice lately," she replied, "but he hasn't bothered *me*. Don't stop him, Walter, I think he's taken with Liza."

Walter halted at the door to the hall, with an incredulous face toward Dale, and broke into a genuine loud laugh. "Being in love with Bill has addled you for sure! Fixing up a romance for the Ugly Duckling, with the eggshell still on her nose! I'll have to tell that one to Nick!"

"Walter, you wouldn't!" Dale was horrified. "It would be a cruel thing to do to Liza. Besides," she added disarmingly, "I was only joking."

"All right, forget it," Walter said. Then he switched to Maggie. "You can tell the weighty secret now, Maggie. I'll be safely out of the way in a moment." He bowed graciously and left.

But Maggie waited until the front door slammed before she started to speak. "And weighty it is," Maggie sighed, "though he was only making light of me. I said what I did to get rid of him," she added complacently. "I was hoping and praying 'twould be *you,* and then he came. Asking with his lordly airs, and says, 'Tell me, Maggie, what's the matter with *you?*' As if I'd tell the likes of him what your Uncle Hi confides to me. And he so weak he could hardly whisper! But the look in his eyes held me, and I listened, and promised; to my dying day, I promised."

Dale caught her breath; she knew better than to interrupt, but she could barely suppress the question: *"Promised what?"*

And Maggie continued, "'I'm only telling you this,' he says, so low I could scarce hear him, 'in case the farce is over.' And I knew by *that* he meant, should he die. 'You can tell it then, Maggie, and let the devil take the hindmost.' And with that, his mouth came open like he'd have a good laugh if he had the strength for it."

This was *it*. Hi had had that lucid interval — and Bill had missed it. *Oh, Bill, Bill!* Dale lamented.

Maggie's voice quavered, then became more strident. "Then he closed his eyes and slipped off again. When Bill came back in I was smoothing his covers like I'd just been neating things up, and Bill never guessed we'd had any talk at all. 'Go get some rest, Maggie,' he said to me, 'it doesn't take the two of us to watch over him.' So I left quickly."

"But," she declared with firm conviction, "I'll tell you, Dale child, you might as well give up your searching — because you'll not find that money."

"Do you know where it is? Is that what he told you?" Dale exclaimed, jumping up. "How wonderful! We'll get Father John to talk to Hi, and make him tell us, as soon as he's well enough!"

"No, no, not that way!" Maggie protested, horrified. "I've *not* said what I know, have I?" Maggie's silence had melted with unexpected swiftness, but not her distress.

"It's the truth, I've been half out of my wits to know what to do. But at last I said to myself, 'Father John will have to help me and tomorrow is Thursday, and the next day is Friday — the first of the month,' and that settled it!"

"But what has the first of the month got to do with it?" Dale asked, utterly mystified.

"And you know very well. Father will be hearing confessions on Thursday for the First Friday Communions — which is sooner to go than waiting for Saturday — isn't it? With this burden on my mind, the sooner the better! What with worrying over that killing dose, the doctor thinks I gave him, which I'm wondering now, if maybe I did — in a trance — "

"That's silly, Maggie; of course you weren't in a trance," Dale protested.

Maggie went on, disregarding her, "And you and Bill with your young hearts broken because of that money! I'm nearly bereft of my senses — thinking of what to do for the best — and still not to break my solemn vow. I want you to take me to St. Mary's to-

74

morrow, Dale, or else I'll have to walk. It's in the confessional I'll speak about it and nowhere else."

"You know I'm always glad to take you to church, Maggie, but why make it a matter of confession? You've done nothing you have to confess. It would be better to have Father over for supper. I'll ask him over, and you can talk privately and get his advice — ask him anything you wish."

"So she's telling me what's a matter of conscience, and what isn't," said Maggie to the air. "She, that I've taught at my knee the first words of her prayers."

"I'm not," Dale said, hastily contrite. "I'm only trying to help. And you've done nothing bad, I'm sure of *that!*" she maintained stoutly, at the same time sending up a little prayer, "Oh, God, don't let it be Maggie that gave him the overdose."

Then she threw her arms around Maggie's neck. "Oh, it's going to be all right." Hope was singing within her. "Don't you see? If you tell it in confession, Father's lips are sealed, but if you tell him here, Father hasn't promised Hi not to tell." But Maggie didn't waver. "That's as it may be, but I'm under a solemn vow, Dale, which you know nothing about. Your Uncle Hi knew well what he was about when he made me swear." Maggie pushed her away, and said with asperity, "And when he comes to his senses again, he'll be throwing me out of the house for the breaking of my word. No," she continued, "it's not so simple as all that — unless he's to die. And sure, we cannot bear such a thought, can we?"

This sobered Dale. "Of course not, Maggie! Not even for Bill's sake could I wish that. But Hi *is* going to get well. Dr. Cotten hasn't said anything different, has he?"

"No," said Maggie. "He was very pleased when he came this morning — but he's laid down the law. 'There'll be no talking around him — and no bother must he have. Very quiet he must be for I don't know how long.' And it's *that* hard on me," Maggie added, "wishing to ask him about the second dose he took. I cannot remember even giving him the first one now — so mixed in my mind I am by all the doubts and worry," she ended wearily.

75

"But when he is better, couldn't you at least *ask* him to let you tell the secret?" Dale asked gently.

"And what good would that do? He'd just say he'd told me nothing — that it's light-headed I am, he'll say as he always does. . . . No, I'll just walk to St. Mary's if my two old feet will get me there, and that's the end of it."

Dale gave up. "I'll take you to confession, Maggie — Thursday at four; you can be the first one there. I'll cut my class again tomorrow — what difference does it make?" All of her optimism, all of Sister Dennis' good effect, was wiped out.

Then she heard footsteps, and Dr. Cotten followed by Bill came into the room quickly, and Dale, forgetting Maggie ran to meet Bill.

Chapter Twelve

THE Gothic spire of St. Mary's Church rose against heavy rain clouds, which banked up behind it like a theatrical backdrop.

Father John, breviary in hand, stepped out of the back door of the rectory and walked quickly along the flagstone walk that led to the door of the sacristy at the rear of the church. The priest's tall figure was not visible from the street as he crossed the secluded area.

The square, which held the church, the rectory, and the old auditorium, newly painted white to match the other buildings, was enclosed by a high cement wall which gave way at the front and side entrance to a white stone coping surmounted by tall picket fencing. Inside this enclosure Father John followed the curving irregular stones between neat grass plots that fitted like quilting squares between the buildings.

St. Mary's covered a short city block; and as many of the ugly decrepit houses had disappeared with slum clearance, leaving space and empty lots, the beautiful old edifice with its two auxiliary buildings created an oasis of peace and beauty in the midst of the traffic and crowded mediocrity of neighboring streets.

But its peace was being threatened now by an approaching storm. Father John cast a speculative glance up at the mean sky and disappeared inside the church.

About ten blocks away, and ten minutes later, Dale came down

77

the front steps on Bermuda Street and also cast a speculative glance at the sky.

The car was parked at the curb. By the time Maggie had come to join her she was sitting at the wheel studying the sky, feeling an urge to paint it.

The sun was still shining but with less desire, and she could just glimpse St. Mary's spire, pointing up into the dimming light like a pale finger.

But Maggie brought her down to earth by climbing into the car looking like a frogman ready for "Hell Week." Dale suppressed a giggle.

"Why do you need all that? The car doesn't leak."

"And you don't intend to drive straight through the door of the church, do you?" Maggie inquired. "It's common sense I believe in, and self-protection." She looked with disapproval at Dale's light attire.

But Dale's blond head was at that moment concerned with some surprisingly practical thoughts, to wit, the devious method she must invent to extract painlessly Maggie's secret from her. It must be done naturally, and without rousing the least suspicion of self-betrayal on Maggie's part.

But by the time they had arrived at the church, Dale had still not thought out a plan. She'd have to make it a matter of prayer. There was no wrong in begging heaven for aid, because she would not let her knowledge compromise Maggie. Hi must be made to think she'd found the money by pure accident. And surely her cause was righteous! Thus, justifying her intentions, Dale mounted the shallow stone steps to the portal, and pushed open one half of the great arched doors, holding it back for Maggie, following her into the church, into another world, cool and dim and quiet.

Dale raised her eyes to the high pointed arches supported by columns, rhythmically repeated verticals, like giant flower stems, then up to the ribbed, vaulted ceiling which was lost in blue shadows. And as always, here in St. Mary's, a sense of mystery and exaltation took possession of her.

The sanctuary lamp, one small red light, flickered and beckoned before the distant white tabernacle. Like small clusters of sapphires

78

and rubies, the votive lights before the side altars gleamed fitfully, wavering and dancing, almost whimsically.

There was no other light in the church except the last long shafts of a departing sun, shining through the stained-glass windows high up in the west wall, laying ribbons of color upon the backs of the pews.

"We *are* early," Dale thought, coming back to time and material things. "It only seems later because it's going to storm!" She had promised that Maggie should be the first one here, but looking she saw one or two kneeling figures with bent heads, and heard the sound of shuffling feet on the stone flooring. An old man across on the other side of the church was making the Stations of the Cross. His slow progress down the far side aisle, between each scene of Christ's passion, meant that he would not interfere with Maggie's move to the confessional on this side. No one would. Maggie had paused only long enough to divest herself of her tightly fastened waterproof, to fold and store away her plastic hood revealing a small round hat with a neat bouquet of cornflowers in front, and to deposit her umbrella under the kneeling bench of the pew she'd selected. It was toward the front, up the side aisle facing St. Joseph's altar, and so near the confessional that only a step or two would take her through the red drapes covering the entrance of the cubicle nearest her.

A small bulb burned over the center section of the confessional, which indicated that the priest was there, waiting for penitents, who would come to the boxes on either side of him, each in his turn to be heard, and depart with the peace of absolution upon him; and the little wooden sliding door in the partition would close on each as the priest gave his attention to first one side and then the other.

Dale slipped back into a pew much nearer the door. She saw Maggie — for all her desire to get there first — go hesitantly into the confessional. Her own concerns dropped away from her and seemed remote as she imagined the stress and self-inflicted agony of hairsplitting that Maggie would now be enduring. And poor Father John! Dale felt a laugh rising in her. She didn't envy him, either; as much as she would like to hear what the old lady was revealing.

Dropping her head, and clasping her hands, Dale prayed, not for

79

herself and her own desires, but for Maggie, that she should find what she sought: peace and the right solution to her problem.

It was not long before the red curtain was thrust aside and Maggie's short figure emerged and advanced with alacrity up to the very altar rail, stopped before the stand of votive lights, and added another small flame to the lot. Dale watched her extinguish the wax taper in her hand and kneel at the rail to say her penance.

Then Dale rose from her knees. She'd go to confession too, not because her conscience was troubled by any serious sin, but she needed all the grace she could get. Starting toward the aisle, she paused, surprised to see the tall figure of the priest leaving the confessional, walking rapidly away from her, up toward the front of the church. He passed quickly by Maggie kneeling with head bowed low, opened the small bronze gate that led into the sanctuary, and turned, disappearing through the door to the sacristy adjoining it.

Dale stopped and knelt again, waiting for him to return, and waiting for the lights to go on in the church. Father John must have realized how dark it was, that no one could read a prayer; that the old sexton had forgotten. Then she saw Maggie jump up from her place at the rail and follow the priest into the sacristy.

"Now what?" Dale wondered. "What on earth possessed Maggie to go popping in there after Father John?" Searching for reasons, she remembered the St. Christopher medal which Maggie had brought along to be blessed — to be a gift to her, and to be fastened in the car against her reckless driving.

With an exasperated little sigh, Dale waited for Father to come back.

"Why did Maggie have to pick this time? Why delay everyone for this small wish?"

A thin line of people had formed now upon the bench outside the confessional — also waiting. But Father did not return, and neither did Maggie.

A sudden sharp crash of thunder startled her, and Dale realized she'd been hearing distant rumbles for some time. She waited; the lights did not come on. Possibly a burned-out fuse, and Father John was replacing it. He got so little help from feeble old Mark, but he *would* keep the old fellow on, through charity — pure and simple. There was the young assistant of course, but Dale knew he always came for the last half of the confessional hour, to relieve Father John, and it was too soon to expect him yet. So she waited and so did the line of penitents, increasing now to a respectable length.

The deep tones of the clock in the tower, mingling with the grumbling thunder, began striking five. They had been there an hour. It must be at least twenty minutes since Father and Maggie had left.

Had Maggie been taken with another scruple, and was she in the sacristy — rehashing it now — holding Father up? But in that case Maggie would have gone back to confession and, besides, Father John never encouraged scruples. He wouldn't allow her to detain him when he was due in the confessional.

Through the waiting line there was a ripple of impatient movement, of restlessness. Suddenly Dale felt a definite sense of responsibility. She had better go and get Maggie. She couldn't imagine why Father didn't shoo her out, but if he didn't she would do it herself! With firm determination to tell them both where they belonged, Dale squared her straight shoulders, tipped up her chin, and walked resolutely up the aisle. She did not push open the gate in the altar rail following Father's route as Maggie had done, but went conventionally the long way, around the turn to the door of the sacristy which opened on the aisle.

She knocked. There was no response. She grasped the knob firmly to open the door, and found that it was locked. With surprise and a queer uneasiness mounting in her, she turned and went back. This time she opened the small bronze gate and went past St. Joseph's finely wrought statue looking down upon her with strength and fortitude in his benign countenance.

Dale was drawing upon her own store of strength and fortitude now as she stepped through the deep arch and once more laid a hand upon a door, seeking entrance. This time there was no resistance. A touch was all that was needed. As the door swung back she stepped through into the sacristy.

There was no light, but a rush of chilly damp air. She saw no one. The back door leading outside had blown open letting in the rain

81

which was at last coming down in hard driving sheets. The floor was already wet and slippery and she felt the fine spray upon her face before she had advanced a few feet, pushing against the wind, to close it.

If Maggie and Father John had gone over to the rectory in this storm, she certainly wasn't going to follow them! Dale closed the door, her yellow dress spotted dark with rain, her face damp with it.

Feeling bewildered, she stood a moment wondering what to do. Then it occurred to her that they might be over in the room on the other side, behind the Blessed Mother's altar, which was actually only an extension of the sacristy, connected by a curved passageway behind the main altar. Dale's eyes searched for a light switch. Finding it near the door where she was standing, within reach of her hand, she snapped it on.

Light shone down upon the wet floor showing the dark damp smears her shoes had made upon the white stone. Dale stared down at the glistening stains, and her artist's eyes noted the color immediately. They were not just *dirty* smears; they were red, dark red, except where the rain made little wetter spots, brighter when diluted.

She stared down at her shoes; the toes were a little stained and above the thin soles the yellow linen was wet along the sides. She stooped swiftly, snatched off one slipper and examined it, holding it close up to her eyes in the bright light. A thin wire of fear stabbed her. With fingers that were not steady she put the shoe back on her foot.

"Hurt. Which one? Or both?" She never got as far as thinking "How?" or "Why?" only "Where? — Look in the other room!"

Turning, Dale ran into the narrow passage, and midway through, just beyond the curve, where the light behind her no longer penetrated, she tripped on something not very large, and fell forward, saved only from going down upon her face by hands thrust out instinctively. Shaken, she pulled herself up to a sitting position, peering into the darkness, feeling along the floor to see what she'd stumbled over.

Her groping hands received the message but for a second or two her mind rejected it. The cool plastic under her finger tips, and the

82

hard edge of a metal clasp told her nothing. Then a mental picture like a TV close-up formed, enlarged and focused. She saw vividly just two feet, Maggie's feet, stepping into the car — *encased in galoshes.*

Crouching forward, Dale felt frantically, the outstretched leg, the body. "Maggie? In this black tunnel, with no light ahead?" She sprang up, remembering without effort. A bulb on a long dangling wire hanging somewhere along here — between the two rooms.

Miraculously she touched it, swinging just above her head. Light came with the barest flick of her finger, and in the hard bright glare, she looked down upon Maggie humped against the wall.

Her head was sagging sideways. The little black hat clung to it at a crazy angle, covering one eye. The other eye was open in a wide sightless stare. Blood had dripped into it and a thin red thread had trickled down to the corner of her half-open mouth.

Dale didn't scream. Even then, Maggie's early discipline exerted itself. *No noise in church!* Not even here, behind the high altar. Her lips clamped together. She made no effort to touch the body again; she knew that Maggie had gone. All she could do was stand there and stare down at that poor distorted thing that Maggie had left behind.

Shock. She felt nothing; nor could she move. Then, slowly, sensation came back — and fear. Fear broke the paralysis, told her to go — get away quickly — to a safe place — Father John — go to Father John — run!

Dale fled. Back down the passage, away from the dark; through unreassuring light, to the bright empty sacristy, and out, through the back door flinging it open, plunging out into the rain. Stumbling on the flagstone walk, she fell, got up and ran again. "To the rectory," her mind dictated, hovering above her. "Find Father John."

But when she threw herself against the rectory door and banged; then felt the bell under her fingers, and pressed down hard keeping it down, no one came.

With a sudden return of connected thought, Dale realized that Father John had gone — she didn't know where.

Without warning the door jerked open, and she stumbled in.

83

"I want Father John, Nassau. Tell him quickly — is he here?"

The young colored boy stood with open-eyed curiosity, surveying her. Dale had no idea of how she looked. "Don't stand there. Go find him!"

"Father's over at church — hearing confessions. He ain't come back yet —"

"He's *not* in the church, Nassau. I've just come from there. Go look for him! It's urgent — something has happened. Can't you understand?" She pushed past him. "Never mind, I'll do it myself."

But Nassau stood stubbornly in her path, regarding her skeptically. "'T'ain't no use, Miss Dale, to carry on. He ain't here, I tell you. He ain't come in since he left to hear confessions."

"All right, get Father Donahue! Don't just stand there!" Dale yelled at him, beside herself.

"Ain't no use to holler, Miss Dale. Nobody's here. Father Don's gone out someplace. Said he'd be back in time to help out in Church. What's happened?" Nassau asked, curiosity edged now with alarm.

Dale had no more words for the colored boy. Desperately she waved him aside. The phone! Phone to Bill. "And then," she said aloud, her first constructive thought, "the police!" Because Bill would ask, "Did you phone the police?" Yes, she'd better do that first.

Shaking fingers clumsy with nerves, stiff and cold, turned the dial. "O" for Operator — that was quickest. "I want the police! Yes, hurry."

Headquarters answered and Dale's voice was bravely firm as she said,

"This is St. Mary's Catholic Church rectory. Come quickly please — yes, it's an emergency! Someone's in the church — no, no, not thieves — someone's hurt!" *NO,* her mind dictated inexorably, *don't minimize, make it clear!* "Killed!" she added. *Stop dodging — say it! you know it — say it!* "Murdered!" she said with a sob, but quite distinctly, and dropped the receiver quickly, cutting the connection.

Then she took it up at once. Now she could call Bill.

84

Chapter Thirteen

ALMOST at once, after the comfort of Bill's "Wait there, Dale, I'm coming," bolstering her to new courage, Dale heard the distant whine of the police siren. The siren sounded louder and louder, reaching a crescendo immediately outside, and then was abruptly silent. She ran to the door, ignoring Nassau's large frightened eyes and his petrified figure behind her. Before the bell sounded she was holding it open, looking up at the man who took off his hat and came inside without being asked. Out past him, Dale saw, through the slackening rain, a uniformed cop on a motorcycle pull to the curb under the streetlamp and dismount, ready to deal with the crowd already beginning to gather.

"Lieutenant Blackwell. Homicide," he said abruptly. His face was brown and lean; eyes noncommittal. His detached manner, devoid of the sympathy which she was subconsciously seeking, was like a sharp slap. But it was good medicine, just what she needed, and the impersonal academic attitude stiffened her. He hadn't come to condole. This was his job — she had said it was murder — he was here to deal with it.

Then Nassau let in another man who joined them; a short man in a gray suit came and stood at Lt. Blackwell's elbow. Evidently he was one of them on Homicide, but the lieutenant was the boss. Dale knew by the way the gray man looked up at him, waited, and then asked, "Where's the body?"

"The *body?*" Her mind recoiled from the word. But it *was* just a body — no longer Maggie — she had felt that herself. She couldn't bring herself to say the word, though, when she tried to answer.

"It — she's in the church," Dale faltered.

"Tell me what you know, briefly," the lieutenant said.

"She's in the church," Dale repeated. "I'll have to show you. I don't know what happened. This is the best way," she said, turning toward the back of the house. "Not out through the street. We'd better go across the grounds, to the back door of the sacristy." She was explaining and urging. *"I can't talk about it!"* Dale thought desperately. She would lead them there, let them see for themselves.

But she *did* talk — Lt. Blackwell forced her by his questions, short and terse. Then he turned, ready to start, waving her back.

"No, not you. We've got to look around out there first." He turned to the man in gray and snapped, "Get the boys on to it. Cover the square — and inside — through the gate opening on Grace Street."

They nodded and left. Then Lt. Blackwell started going the way she had suggested. Dale protested.

"You don't know that little passageway behind the altar — you'll need me."

The front-door bell stopped her with a loud insistent peal. Nassau jumped to it, and Bill came in. Bill, with his hair roughed up, and a little breathless, but to Dale the whole National Guard could not have been as reassuring. At once he was beside her, holding her hand.

The lieutenant looked back. "Wait!" she called. "Bill's here — *he* knows. It's Lt. Blackwell, Bill," she explained. "He didn't want me to go with him — but I'm going with *you* — hurry!"

"No, Dale, stay here."

"But Father John? We *have* to find him! I'm afraid he's over there, Bill — somewhere." Her voice quavered.

"If he's there, I'll find him, honey. I know the church — every crack and cranny. You stay here and if he comes in, send Nassau to tell us." Bill pushed her back not too gently in his urgency.

"Wait, I'll be back." He followed the lieutenant: "Out," thought Dale, fearfully, "into the dark walled-in courtyard, with its narrow

86

lanes between buildings — where a murderer could hide." She shuddered.

"Wait," Bill had said, not knowing that this was the hardest thing. "No," Dale's honesty corrected, "going back to Maggie lying in that dark little space would be harder." She saw Maggie's face again, with one open eye — and blood in it. Dale shivered, realizing she was cold and wet, her dress still clinging to her.

In the kitchen Nassau was hunched upon a stool in the corner, like an animal, freezing in the face of danger. The percolator was plugged in, with the red glass button shining.

"Nassau, is that hot? Pour me a cup, will you! And one for yourself, too, if you'd like it."

The coffee was hot and it went down quickly. She wasn't shaking so hard now. Nassau, with his eyes like a mournful dog's, gulped his, saying nothing. She knew he was scared and full of questions, but she didn't want to talk about Maggie. He had heard her tell the lieutenant, that was enough. Why wasn't he looking for Father John? If anything awful had happened to Father, too, she didn't think she could bear it. She said, unreasonably angry — suddenly, "What's the matter with you? Why don't you look for Father, Nassau? Don't you care what might be happening to him? He *must* have come here. Where else would he go? Have you searched the rooms, the whole house?"

"He ain't up there, Miss Dale, I told you." Nassau went back to his stool.

Dale turned and left, she might as well look herself. It was better than sitting alone and letting herself think. She was keeping the surface of her mind busy, and not daring to let her thoughts or her feelings go one bit deeper. She knew she would hit bottom later, missing Maggie, grieving for her. It was impossible to picture the house or herself without Maggie, and what in the world would Hi do without her? "You mustn't think," she told herself, and then suddenly wondered who was with Hi now. Bill certainly wouldn't leave him alone in the house. Rosina, the cook, she supposed, who had probably not left for the day, and Bill had made her stay on.

Reaching the top of the stairs, fighting all these scattered anxious

87

thoughts, stifling her emotions, she went into Father John's study. There again she had to take tight hold of herself.

How many long happy hours had she spent here; learning her catechism, receiving instruction for her first Communion, and later, before college, the long heart-to-heart talks about vocations and life and love and marriage. More than a godfather he had certainly been. A parent, wise and gentle, and understanding, filling her needs. Keeping her thinking straight and clear, refuting her doubts, comforting her for failures, applauding her effort, and, above all, instilling into her the pure love of God without fear or poor dear Maggie's niggling scruples.

Dale opened his closet door, feeling a little impertinent, but she *must* look. There was his worn old overcoat hanging limply, his umbrella. Up on the shelf was his Sacra-kit, which meant he had gone on no sick calls. He had not gone out at all. Here were all the things he would have put on, with the storm in full blast.

Dale closed the door quickly. She went through the other rooms, his bedroom and bath. Then she knocked on Father Donahue's door. It was merely a formality, she knew he wasn't there, and she opened it immediately upon a painfully neat and austere interior. There were no cubbyholes here, only an old-fashioned wardrobe.

Crossing the room, Dale considered it. Gingerly turning the key in the lock, she yanked the door open quickly, feeling like a sneak thief.

One clerical vest and a cassock hung there, a dark wool dressing gown. On the floor two neat slippers, and farther back, near the wall, a black suitcase.

She shut the door and hurried out of the room. Across the hall, the bathroom was clearly empty.

Down the stairs again, praying that soon Bill would come, she went to the window. There were people in front, milling around. She could only see them as silhouette in groups, against the diffused glow of the streetlamp. Very little light came through the foggy haze. There was the motorcycle, still at the curb, a good many cars, and she was afraid she saw the ambulance. If they were bringing Maggie out, she didn't want to watch.

She moved away from the hall window and saw the front doorknob move and turn. Dale dashed to the door as Father Donahue entered. He didn't seem to notice her; didn't even pause; but made a dash for the stairs, going up two at a time.

Dale stood for a minute inactive from surprise, and then a terrifying certainty gripped her. She saw it in the priest's white face: insensible to surroundings.

Dale scrambled up the stairs calling, "Father, what is it? Is it Father John? What has happened to him?" Her knees gave way, she sat down halfway up, weak and trembling.

Then she heard him hurrying back. He was coming down now as fast as he'd gone up. This time he had his small box with him, his sick kit. He was going right past her. She reached out and caught at his coat. "Wait, Father, tell me."

He paused and for the first time seemed to see her. "Oh, it's you, Dale? What is it?"

"Father John?" she asked just above a whisper.

"Yes," he said. "They are taking him to the hospital now. I am going with him. They are getting him into the ambulance — pray for him — I don't know how bad it is. I didn't know anything. I'll let you know," he called back, running down the steps and out the front door.

Dale felt faint and sick, carried by will alone she sprang up and raced after him. The young priest must have flown! She only reached the sidewalk and stopped, seeing a black leg and foot disappear inside the ambulance. The attendant slammed the door. The vehicle shot out from the curb led by the motorcycle, with the sirens screaming again, and disappeared around the corner.

Dale stood blinded with tears, then took a stumbling step forward toward the backs of the people, standing in groups a few feet away, watching the ambulance disappear. They were talking loud and fast and interrupting one another. She could not bear to become one of them, asking questions of them. Where was Bill? Had he gone too? She would go back to the church. One of Lt. Blackwell's men must be there and could tell her.

With head down now, not to be stopped by anyone that might recognize her, Dale walked toward the front entrance of the church, following the low stone base of the picket fencing, rows of slender iron spikes pointing up, high above her head.

Why was it there? Protection? What good were fences and high walls if evil was already inside? She hoped Lt. Blackwell and his men would trap it there; would track down the person who might now be cowering in the dark shadows of the wall, back of the church, or the rectory, or the auditorium; there were any number of places.

She welcomed the safety of the sidewalk and people around her. For the second time fear for her own safety entered into her. She stopped. She couldn't go into the church alone.

Turning, she started back toward the rectory and saw Bill coming toward her rapidly. The next instant she felt his arms around her —

"Dale! I couldn't find you."

"Is Father John dead?" Dale's voice was muffled, her face pressed against Bill's chest.

"No, darling."

"Dying?"

"Not badly hurt, hit on the head — a day or two in the hospital will fix him up."

"Where was he?" Dale lifted her face away from Bill, brushing the hair back out of her eyes, straightening up, relieved now and curious.

"We found him locked in the closet in the sacristy — in with the boys' cassocks, tied up and gagged. He'd been knocked out cold, couldn't tell us much."

Chapter Fourteen

Hi's eyes, two small jet-black buttons, were fixed upon hers. Dale's clear and blue, met his gaze. She shoved back the thought that whether he knew it or not, Maggie's death was Hi's fault — making her take that vow! But this was no time to be passing judgment upon him. She must try to help him.

Hi was lucid again, but Dr. Cotten's orders were: "Not a word to Hi. It's only been three days since his attack. He must not be told about Maggie until he's much better. You can't take a chance. No matter how gently you break it to him, it is bound to be a shock. He cannot stand a shock now. It could be fatal."

Dale wasn't taking a chance. She was doing very well, she thought. He hadn't asked for Father John this morning, *that* she was grateful for, but he'd kept asking for Maggie.

"There's nothing to worry about, Hi. Maggie's fine! Never was so happy in her life! You don't begrudge her a little vacation, do you?" she asked brightly, feeling lost and rebellious. What would Hi think, how would he react, if she were to say instead:

"There was an imposter in the church yesterday, Hi. He hit Father John with the brass candlestick in the sacristy, tied him up, and shoved him in the closet. He took Father's place in the confessional, and when he left, Maggie followed him. Now Maggie's dead, Hi. All because you hid that money! She wouldn't have gone to confession Thursday if it hadn't been for that."

"No, no, she *must* not think of it, or she might think aloud. Bury this heavy secret, pretend, pretend. But the weight of it was dragging at her, and her own voice sounded strange and unreal as she answered Hi's querulous question.

"Then why can't she come back here and pay some attention to me?" he asked. "How long is this holiday going to last?"

"How long is eternity?" Dale asked herself, then jerked around and said, "She needs the rest. Hasn't she been slaving over you? Didn't you scare the lights out of all of us? What's the matter with *me?*" Putting on her sweetest smile, "Don't you love me anymore? I'm just as good a nurse as Maggie! And Bill, Dr. Cotten says Bill is going to be the best doctor in this state some day."

"God help this state." Hi rolled his eyes to the ceiling, but his mouth betrayed him, and his shoulders shook just a little, just enough for Dale to notice.

She looked at him hopefully. "He's beginning to soften and he *should* be humiliated when he knows what a job Bill has done on him. She longed to ask him just one question — "What did you tell Maggie?" When he was up and well again she promised herself a showdown. But now she'd have to stick it out a little longer.

If the others would be just as careful, they would get by with this "vacation for Maggie" idea — at least for a time. When Hi had to know, when they could put off telling him no longer, he'd be well enough to take it; Hi was no softy, just let him get over this hump. "I don't worry about the future. Just be careful *now.*" Dale was determined.

She could count on Bill. It was Marcia who made her most uneasy. Impossible to keep Marcia out of Hi's room entirely, without a fuss. She'd come over to nurse him, so she said, "To help poor Dale." Dale suspected the genuineness of that motive, and made it very plain, baldly plain, Dr. Cotten backing her up, that Dale was to nurse Hi with Bill's help. Bill would continue to stay nights for a while. He was on hand during the day anyway — working on Hi's history of the Bosch family.

Marcia could run the house and Rosina could be a help, taking all that off Dale's shoulders, but Dale must take over Hi. *That* Hi

92

would expect, with Maggie gone. Marcia had submitted, secretly glad perhaps; nursing Hi was no bed of roses. But Marcia had been disappointed too. Dale could see that, and wondered if perhaps her aunt had thought that she'd get on the good side of the old man. No one could be sweeter than Aunt Marcia when she chose. Dale strongly suspected, feeling a little mean thinking it, that Aunt Marcia thought she'd profit by this generous loving gesture.

Marcia had been told, Dr. Cotten had told her, told everyone, not to talk too much. He had not said though that Marcia could not just peek in at her sick uncle — he hadn't gone so far as to say what Dale wished she could say: "Don't put your foot inside his bedroom door." But Dr. Cotten didn't know how much Aunt Marcia wanted money from Hi; a gift, a loan, anything just to get her hands on enough to hold that house for Mary.

In spite of all Jack had said, Marcia was still set upon getting the house. She simply ignored Jack's attitude, coolly assuming that what she did for her own daughter was entirely her own business and Mary's. She had won Mary over. It had not been very difficult, Dale thought, but it was a shame. Mary was playing the poor-trod-upon wife, whose husband objects to her having a little ease and comfort.

Marcia was to blame, of course, but Marcia never relinquished her own desires, never admitted defeat. She was going to be defeated this time, Dale was determined. She shouldn't get in here and worry Hi, even if Dale had to lock him in. Of course she couldn't really do that; she and Bill would just have to watch and manage. Thank God for Bill.

Dale looked over at the small figure almost lost in the great bed. She had thought he was dozing, but his bright little eyes were fixed upon her. Reaching out she patted his hand. Plenty of spirit showed in those old eyes, although she could have wept over the poor little shrunken body, not much more than bones when she put her arms around him to help him a bit, when she gave him water or nourishment. She looked again, and Hi's eyes were closed. He was breathing evenly.

She got up quietly from the little low rocker by the bed and went tip-toeing toward the door, and heard as she closed it softly behind her that familiar snort — not a snore — a snort. Dale smiled a tolerant smile, indulging his childish antics. Hi was getting better, he was laughing at her.

But her moment of slight amusement passed and her shoulders, usually so bravely erect, drooped. Everything was awful, really. There was Lt. Blackwell downstairs now waiting for her, with questions, questions!

He had come last night from the hospital, after leaving Father John. She didn't think he had been allowed to question Father John. He hadn't said, of course. If he had anything new, he'd not let on. All that Bill could tell her was what Father had said, still seeming dazed after they had untied and ungagged him, while they were waiting for the ambulance, that he was standing in the sacristy putting on his cassock. He'd heard a little movement behind him, did not turn. That was all.

Later, Bill had called her from the hospital, had said she needn't worry, and Dr. Cotten had been there too, Bill had said. A few stitches, a slight concussion, but not too serious.

Lt. Blackwell had come back last night, when she was too tired to know what she was saying. Couldn't remember now *what* she'd said. He'd asked a great many questions. She did not know what Aunt Marcia and Liza had told him either. Foolish, both of them. Aunt Marcia had stayed, was downstairs now, but Walter had taken Liza home. She hoped Liza had not come over again this morning. She would though, with Walter at the bank, she'd hardly stay alone, and "She won't go to school," Marcia informed Dale. "She says she won't, that everyone will ask her about Maggie's murder."

Going past Maggie's room on her way to the stairs, Dale was surprised to see the door open, the room showing signs of occupancy. She stopped and looked inside, indignation slowly growing in her. Maggie's narrow single bed was carelessly made. An open suitcase partially unpacked was on the low bench at the foot of the bed. From it spilled the pleated lace of a nylon slip and several folded garments still in piles.

Dale's eyes, growing more and more indignant, rested next on Maggie's neat little old-fashioned bureau, with its small mahogany

94

mirror. The shelf was cluttered now with bottles, cream jars, a silver-backed hand mirror, and pin-curl clips dropped everywhere. From the closet door, which was not entirely closed, a pink fold of a night dress protruded.

Her lips compressed, her eyes glinting through lashes almost drawn together in grim scrutiny, Dale's resentment grew at each indication of careless, arrogant intrusion and indifference.

Maggie had been dead only one day and Aunt Marcia had taken over Maggie's room, as casually as if Maggie had never existed!

She remembered now, last night through the fog of sorrow and fatigue, hearing Marcia's voice raised in protest. Now she knew Marcia had been refusing the guest room: "Oh no, I would be terrified — way off there, alone! That's foolish sentiment — of course I don't mind."

"But *I* mind," thought Dale, "and Maggie would, too!" Marcia in Maggie's room, invading Maggie's privacy, shoving Maggie out. A long shuddering sigh escaped her. "If she loved you, Maggie, it would be different. We wouldn't feel this way about it, would we?"

Then she straightened up and closed the door gently upon the disorder. She had to go downstairs and talk to Lt. Blackwell. He was trying to find out who had killed Maggie, and she wanted to help him if she could, but she mustn't let him get wrong ideas. She'd have to have her wits about her.

The girl who went into the library to face the head of the Homicide Squad must be self-possessed and controlled. Sad, yes, naturally, but not frightened; and Dale came pretty near to looking like that when she went in.

They were all there. She saw Bill first, before he saw her. He was turned toward Liza, looking furious, for one brief moment before he heard her come in. Then he smiled, welcoming her; but even as he came quickly forward, she could see anger which had not yet faded from his eyes.

What had Liza said? Had she been up to things, putting Bill or herself on the spot? Dale couldn't see why Liza should; she had no grudge against them. But it was the way she talked — saying things she wouldn't finish — her implications were worse than accusations. Wondering thoughts raced through Dale's mind in the few seconds before Lt. Blackwell turned to greet her.

"Good morning, Miss Moncure. I hope you are feeling rested this morning, and that your uncle is better."

"Thank you, lieutenant. If you want me, Lt. Blackwell, you will have to let Bill go up. Dr. Cotten says that either Bill or I must be with him." That was exaggerating it a bit, but she couldn't risk Aunt Marcia's offering to go.

Her aunt's face wore more than its habitually aggrieved expression. She was painfully tense, sitting erect, blowing smoke through her nostrils in a steady stream, indifferent to the haze through which she watched Lt. Blackwell intently. Aunt Marcia was not putting on the tired invalid act now.

Liza did not look at Dale; Liza's eyes were fixed upon the knot of crumpled Kleenex balled up in one hand, which she had plucked at with the other, making little scattered snowflakes on her dark shirt.

Liza was white and sullen — and scared. Why? Dale wondered for a minute, then quickly changed. "Of course the kid is scared. We forget she looks much older than she is; we're all a bit hard on Liza," Dale thought, "overgrown, but not mature, really just a big kid." And murder wasn't for kids.

Lt. Blackwell nodded at Bill. "OK," he said.

Bill took her hand. "Don't worry, honey," he said, lowering his voice. "Everything is going to be all right." Then he turned and left, but Bill didn't look as if everything was all right; the worried frown came back upon his face as he went out the door and, as he thought, out of her range of vision.

"All right, Dale, you tell him." Liza suddenly looked up. "He thinks I'm making it up about that $25,000 you told Mother to ask Hi for. You told her Hi had it, and it's somewhere in this house. Mother claims she doesn't remember a thing!" Dale reassessed Liza — on the minus side.

Marcia looked thunderstruck. "Liza, what *are* you saying? That I, your mother, was prying into your uncle's affairs? Asking for money! Pay no attention to her, officer, the child is *completely* overwrought.

96

If Dale did make some wild statement about Mr. Bosch having that much cash in the house, it was certainly not my fault. I certainly never asked, and really didn't believe her. It *was* unwise of her to broadcast it — there's no telling who else she told, but, after all, I cannot see what Liza is getting at — why she thinks there is any connection between that and Maggie's being killed in St. Mary's Church."

"I didn't say there was." Liza raised her voice almost to a shout. "I just said something funny was going on — and nobody believes *anything* I say. But I'm not making it up! *He* asked if anybody could think of anything unusual that might have happened — just any odd thing, he'd like to know it. Well, a lot of odd things have happened if you ask me. I just don't want the wrong person to get blamed — when the time comes."

"I'm sure you don't, Miss Rowland. Thank you for trying to help." The lieutenant was very polite, and he smiled at Liza. His smile was quite dazzling. Liza looked completely subjugated.

Dale was herself a little intrigued that Lt. Blackwell could be charming if he wished. It relaxed her a little too. But not Marcia, impatient to be gone.

"Is there anything else, officer?" She ignored a more personal address. "I have a good many duties besides this house. Arrangements must be made for Maggie's funeral." Her voice became a thread — exhausted.

Dale felt a wave of annoyance. Was there no limit to Marcia's presumption? She'd looked down on Maggie most of her life. No one expected her to decide about Maggie's funeral. They had not even reported the result of the autopsy yet. She and Bill were waiting to be told. Dale hoped that Father John would be out and able to say the Mass. Marcia wasn't the one to make these plans.

"I am going to take care of Maggie, Aunt Marcia," Dale said heatedly. "We have to wait until we are notified, though. I want everything that Maggie would wish. There's no reason for you to think of it. Did you imagine we'd have it *here,* with Hi right upstairs?" she asked in amazement.

Marcia shrugged. "I'm sure I don't know what any of you will do, including my own daughter. But if you'll excuse me now, officer, since I'm really no more use to anyone here. . . ."

"Of course," Lt. Blackwell said quickly. "I would like only a few words with Miss Moncure now." He flashed another smile at Liza, who inched herself up from the old sofa and went slowly toward the back hall, following her mother. As she reached the door, she seemed to have reached a final decision.

"Just ask Dale who it is around here that really needs money, Lt. Blackwell. Just ask her that one question!"

Dale was surprised and angry for an instant, then one glance at Liza's frightened face told her that Liza really meant nothing, knew nothing. She wasn't hitting Bill, she was striking out blindly to divert attention from herself.

Chapter Fifteen

THE lieutenant turned to Dale as Liza disappeared. "She seems very much on the defensive, but she's got something there," he remarked conversationally. "Sit down, Miss Moncure. A sum of money as large as that cannot be ignored. Do you mean to say it is lost?"

"No," Dale answered succinctly.

"Stolen then?" The lieutenant was clipping his words again, and not even a ghost of the smile remained.

"No," Dale repeated.

Lt. Blackwell's eyebrows went up. "Not lost, not stolen, but you were searching for it. Do you realize this could be very important — no, no, I don't mean intrinsically — that, of course, but I mean its bearing on this case. Why haven't you or Mr. Ballard, anyone except this young lady, seen fit to mention such a loss? You *were* searching for it, you admit that?"

"It was hidden," Dale felt pushed into the concession.

"Hidden?" Lt. Blackwell looked skeptical. "By whom?"

Dale didn't answer.

"Did Maggie know about this money having — shall we say — disappeared?"

"Yes," Dale answered.

"Did she know where it was?"

"I don't know. She was bothered about it," Dale added with a sickening feeling that everything she said, though actually the truth, was making a completely false and confusing picture to the policeman. But how could she tell him about Hi? He'd never believe it. No, she wouldn't try it; she'd just answer his questions. But the questions were probing deeper and deeper.

"You know, of course, that Maggie Riley was killed by an imposter — someone who carefully planned to take Father John Mark's place in the confessional. Let us suppose that someone believed that Maggie knew where that money was and intended to tell the priest. It at once explains the thing that had seemed up to now so utterly crazy; this masquerade.

"It would have to be someone who knew she was going to do this: someone who knew the ropes — the day and the time — someone who needed information very badly, or the money itself, as Liza Rowland said. And someone" — the lieutenant looked thoughtful, stroking a lean jaw with long brown fingers — "someone about the same size and build as Father John Mark. Can you think of anyone who might fit all those conditions, Miss Moncure?"

"No," Dale said stubbornly looking straight into the keen, no longer noncommittal eyes of the man leaning toward her now. She was terrified that he could read the words that were in her mind. *When Bill stands beside Father John, they are exactly the same height.*

"Let's go back a bit," said the lieutenant. "Your uncle had this money, Miss Rowland said. Did he keep a sum of money like this in the house as a usual thing?"

"No," Dale said.

"Do you know why he had it now?"

"I thought," Dale said slowly, wondering how much to say, "that he was going a buy a picture with it — a painting by Hieronymus Bosch."

Now the lieutenant's expression became completely deadpan. Dale was sure he didn't know. "A fourteenth-century Flemish artist painted it, *Death and the Miser.* My uncle was interested in Bosch's work," she explained. Now she had his interest — a natural, purely academic interest. Dale felt encouraged, and she thought hastily, "Divert him — "

"Wasn't that a large amount to pay for a painting?" Blackwell's tone was incredulous. "Did he pay that for it?"

"No," said Dale, "he didn't pay that much, because old Capelli,

100

the art dealer, thought it was a copy — " She stopped, she mustn't get into that.

"Did your uncle actually buy the picture?"

"Yes," Dale said.

"Then that accounts for some of the $25,000. How much?"

"None of it," Dale explained, not expecting him to understand. "He didn't use any of the $25,000 — he paid by check."

Lt. Blackwell looked puzzled. "Did he have that money in the house when he gave a check for the picture?"

"It was in his safe."

"How do you know that? When did he get the money from the bank?"

Dale thought back, thought of Walter's joking her about the size of her check that day. She remembered Walter's words: "Add three goose eggs to this and you'll match Uncle Hi's — the family's drawing heavily on its credit today." What day? She couldn't remember.

"My cousin, who works in the bank, first mentioned it to me jokingly, about ten days ago," she said. "I don't remember the date," Dale added, knowing that it sounded feeble.

"Did your uncle go to the bank himself and draw this money out?"

"Lt. Blackwell, Uncle Hi is eighty years old. He doesn't do things for himself. He could, up until this illness at least, but he didn't need to. He could get what he wanted anytime. He phoned the bank and then he sent for the money."

"Who went for it?"

There it was, the question she had been dreading, hoping never to bring Bill into it. She must not hesitate now though; that would be worse.

"Bill," she said.

"Bill Ballard?"

"Yes, naturally," Dale said carelessly. "He's Uncle Hi's private secretary."

"Dr. Cotten said he was a very smart medical student. What's he doing here as a private secretary for your uncle?"

"I'd rather you asked Bill about that, Lt. Blackwell. It's his business, not mine."

101

The lieutenant's eyebrows were up again. Dale was beginning to measure the success of her answers by his eyebrows. Up — skepticism; straight — acceptance; drawn together, deeply frowning — refusal. Mostly they'd been up.

"So — you'd rather I asked him. OK. I'll do that too, but now I'm asking you. What was he doing for your Uncle Hi, as private secretary — writing a book or something?"

"Yes," said Dale.

"What sort of a book?"

"A family history." The eyebrows were way up now.

"You interest me extremely, Miss Moncure. Mr. Ballard — a medical student according to Dr. Cotten a very smart one, might even say brilliant — breaking off in the middle of his studies — private secretary for your uncle — writing a family history? Why, may I ask?"

"He was going back to medical school. He only has one more year."

"And he stopped, to write a family history for your uncle?"

"Well that isn't so funny, Lt. Blackwell! Bill's father has been ill, and Bill had to stay home this year — to help out."

"I see," said Lt. Blackwell pausing deliberately, significantly. "He needed money!"

Dale was sick with fury. But she must be calm — she must make Lt. Blackwell understand.

She dug down into her pocket, found her cigarettes, pulled one out. Lt. Blackwell leaned forward with the match folder ready, snapped a match, furnished her with the light — graciously, easily.

The lieutenant was an antagonist now; she was on guard.

Then he disarmed her. "I can understand that, Miss Moncure. It isn't of course criminal to help one's father out."

She looked at him, he wasn't being sarcastic.

"You said the money was hidden, Miss Moncure?"

"I'm sure it was, lieutenant."

"By whom?"

"My Uncle Hi himself. I don't expect you to believe me."

"Are you telling me that your uncle sent Mr. Ballard to the bank and drew out $25,000 and then hid the money. Oh, I don't

102

mean put it away secretly — that would be expected. You imply
something else. Where did Bill Ballard put this money when he came
from the bank? Did he give it to your uncle?"

"No, Uncle Hi told Bill to put it in his wall safe. Bill put it there."

"And it's not there now?"

"No."

"Tell me about this — stop answering me in monosyllables. It just
takes longer. Olives out of a bottle."

She didn't want to volunteer anything, that was tricky, and that
was how she'd messed it up already. She'd say as little as she could.

"Uncle Hi called us, Bill and me, in to his study and said the
money wasn't in the safe. That was the morning after Bill had put
it there. Bill said he'd put the money in the safe, just as Uncle Hi had
told him. It was in $1,000 bills, twenty-five of them, and the safe
was empty."

"Who knew about that safe in this house, the combination of that
safe?"

"Only Uncle Hi and Bill."

"What did your uncle say when he called you two in?"

He told us that the money was gone and asked Bill where it was.
"He wouldn't send for the police, lieutenant. Bill wanted him to, but
he wouldn't hear of it. He simply said that Bill was responsible. We
both think that there is more to it than that. We don't believe that
Hi would go so far, just to stymie us. He wouldn't have to — it
just doesn't make sense. Bill believes he's playing a deep game. You
don't know my uncle, lieutenant. No one can predict what Uncle Hi
is going to do. He's a law unto himself. I am sure he knows where
that money is."

"He wanted to make his private secretary, whom he had engaged
to write a book for him, look like a thief?"

"He never actually called Bill that," said Dale doggedly.

"Miss Moncure, is your uncle sane?"

"Uncle Hi is smart, smart as a whip. He knows how to get what
he wants, by hook or by crook," Dale explained. "Uncle Hi is an
individualist; ordinary standards don't count for him. I mean conventions. He does as he chooses. He wanted to handle this himself.

103

He wouldn't let us tell anyone, and threatened to swear out a warrant for Bill the minute we did."

"Well?" Lt. Blackwell's eyebrows were again highly arched. But Dale could not tell whether Hi's behavior or her attitude had sent them up.

"I told you you wouldn't understand. All Uncle Hi wanted was to make Bill and me break our engagement — but quietly — he wasn't going to let it go any further than that."

"Did you break it?"

"Bill did, until the money is found. We didn't call Uncle Hi's bluff and make a lot of fuss, because of Bill's father, who'd been ill. Bill couldn't — so we decided to try to find the money ourselves."

"But you didn't?"

"No."

"But you thought Maggie knew. Knew something, anyway," he said, as Dale started to protest. "You took her to church, didn't you, Miss Moncure?"

Dale stood up. "If you think that this was a put-up job by Bill and me, you're crazy. That's all, *crazy!*" Dale gulped. She wouldn't cry — damn it. "You can't possibly think Bill would murder anyone — or that I'd help. Maggie was like a mother to me. I loved Maggie. Do you understand? And Bill did too — Bill was home nursing Hi — Bill saved Hi's life! Does that sound like a murderer to you?"

Dale turned away. She was through. She was going. Dr. Cotten was standing in the doorway.

"Doctor," she said, trying to keep her voice steady. "Tell him that Bill saved Uncle Hi's life! That neither of us are murderers!"

Dr. Cotten went in to Lt. Blackwell. He stood quietly and regarded the police lieutenant with a long calculating look. Then he said quietly,

"That girl's been through a lot in the past few days, lieutenant. I wouldn't push her too hard; high strung. Takes a light hand to gentle 'em."

"Am I supposed to carry a lump of sugar in my pocket?" the lieutenant snapped.

Dr. Cotten grinned. "Maybe. What's the matter?"

104

"This Bill Ballard of hers," he said, after a moment's pause. "She says Bill Ballard saved her uncle's life, doctor. How was that?"

"The old gentleman had a very sharp attack. Bill diagnosed the case to me on the phone — saved a lot of time and Hi's life, I should say — yes."

"What was the matter with the old man — screwy? Isn't he a bit balmy?"

"Not a bit of it! Eccentric, yes."

"And Ballard saved his life? How was that?"

"Well," said Dr. Cotten, "he's eighty years old, and his heart's not all it should be. I've been prescribing a dose — five or six drops of digitalis — once a day over a period of time. I increased the dose recently to fifteen drops once a day. Unfortunately he got too big a dose. I'm afraid it was poor Maggie Riley's mistake — I don't know — but there was some mix-up and he got a lot more than that. Bill sized up the situation to me on the phone. Poor old Maggie went all to pieces. I felt very sorry for her."

"Did she say she'd made the mistake?"

"As a matter of fact, she didn't. No. Naturally she swore she didn't."

"Did you let it go at that?"

"Why not?" Dr. Cotten looked surprised. "I put Bill in charge. It wouldn't happen again. Maggie refused to give Mr. Bosch another drop of anything — even plain water. I'm afraid I hurt her feelings — sorry about that — tragic death — I can't imagine who would want to kill that poor woman. I don't believe anyone did. Some horrible accident. Hope you get to the bottom of it, but it sounds crazy as hell to me."

"You say Bill Ballard knew right away what was wrong with the old man? Would a medical student be able to do that — generally speaking?" Lt. Blackwell asked casually, examining the point of his pencil with deep absorption. Then he threw the pencil on the table, stood, thrust his hands deep in his pockets, and looked squarely at the doctor.

"Yes, lieutenant, a student of Bill's ability would indeed be able to do that."

105

"I see," said Lt. Blackwell. "He'd know about digitalis — normal dose — and overdose — how much would be fatal, too, of course. Thank you, Dr. Cotten. Don't let me keep you."

Dr. Cotten stood very still for a moment, looking at the younger man.

"In the medical profession, a man is trained to think and act with caution. Snap judgments are sometimes required, but those decisions are based on knowledge and experience, not guesswork. I hope the police department training works on those same principles, Lt. Blackwell," Dr. Cotten said. "I'm sure it does. I will go up to my patient now. Good luck, lieutenant."

"I'm anxious to talk to Mr. Bosch, Dr. Cotten. It's important not to wait."

Dr. Cotten frowned. "Not yet — not until I give you word. Mr. Bosch is still very sick, Lt. Blackwell. He must not be interviewed — yet."

Granite gray eyes watched Dr. Cotten go. "Wise old owl! Think you've got me hog-tied, eh? But you're hog-tied yourself, Doc, by an octogenarian and two youngsters!"

Chapter Sixteen

FRIDAY morning, after leaving Blackwell, Liza went home — and about an hour later, she walked slowly down Granby Street looking into shop windows. She paused at the drugstore and contemplated a display of electric pads, thermos bottles, and Kleenex, and then moved on, dawdling before the book shop, absorbed apparently in the *Life of Thomas Edison, Travel in Space,* and *Prehistoric Animals.*

When she straightened her back and peeled herself from the glass front of the shop, she saw her reflection in it. A tall bulky figure, the narrow skirt of her dress reaching just below the knees, did nothing to help the pattern of her mirrored silhouette. Fortunately the stout, serviceable legs were out of the picture, just at the point where the calves began to bulge they were cut off from view by the marbelized base of the window frame.

Liza raised her eyes to the upper half of herself. The piled-up hair, in a sophisticated do, carefully copied from Sunday's fashion ads, was a little strange above the square of her face, and revealed her ears too prominently. She slumped her shoulders, curved in her back, and her stomach came forward proportionately. The effect was more reminiscent of a vamp in the silent movies than a modern screen siren, but the rather blurred reflection of herself seemed to afford satisfaction.

She seemed quite pleased, and affectedly indifferent to the world and her surroundings, she stepped gingerly on pinpoint heels toward the next store front.

The sign above this door, "The Gaiety," looked a bit worn, but the theatrical display in the window should certainly have intrigued the imagination and tickled the fancy of any embryonic thespian.

The assortment was varied and unrelated — but if a donkey's head next to a bright red wig and scores of rubber masks with horribly distorted features seemed surprising company for a suit of synthetic armor, and a helmet with a limp pink plume, the ensemble was at least entertaining.

Liza stood regarding the display for a long time. Then she turned her head away from the shop window with a slow, cautious movement, making a swift survey of the street, which was almost empty. She took a step forward, stumped her toe on an uneven spot in the pavement, lurched unsteadily, then regaining her balance hurried into the shop, and almost knocked over a stack of boxes piled on the floor at the entrance.

The place was chaotic, but the confusion and disorder seemed to be its normal state. No one stood behind the small counter which was cluttered with an array of large and small pasteboard boxes, affording glimpses of miscellaneous objects and rainbow colors through cracks and breaks in their tops.

No one appeared from the maze of piled-up crates and grotesque half figures on pedestals. The clowns' heads and the witches' hats, the slightly soiled tarlatan and tinseled Titania, all in one motley crew, were left, an unsupervised and ill-assorted company.

Liza raised her voice and called, "Is anyone here?"

Slowly, from the mystery of the back area, came a woman, more drab and uninteresting perhaps in the midst of all the fanciful display; but her face would have been dull in any setting, and her apathy irritating to any prospective customer.

She registered a faint surprise, however, as she regarded the young face with the erratic makeup confronting her. Black hairline brows penciled in high twin arches gave Liza a ludicrous expression of astonishment that the cynical slash of scarlet mouth could not nullify. But the woman was used to seeing funny faces. She listened phlegmatically to Liza's impatient and detailed description of the desired purchase. Finally, slow comprehension dawned and, reaching up to the shelf behind her, she pulled down a small box and took out one single article, which left the box empty. At Liza's sign of relief and nod of acceptance, she slipped it into a small brown paper bag, and handed it across the counter.

"This is the last one," she said in a detached voice. "I sold one just like it a few days ago."

Liza's face lighted up. "I thought so," she exclaimed, her incredible mouth stretched to a gratified smile. "To a tall young man with brown hair and kind of hazel eyes?"

"Well, I don't know as I can say *that*. I don't remember what he looked like; just like I told that police fellow, when he came in here asking. There was a fancy dress ball on that day and I sold a lot of things. I just know I sold it — that's all!"

"What policeman?" Liza asked eagerly. "Lt. Blackwell?"

"I don't know, something like that," the woman answered indifferently. "He left me a phone number to call in case I remembered, but I don't know what I did with it."

"Well, don't strain yourself," Liza advised patronizingly. "These detectives can get you into a lot of trouble. And please don't mention that I came in here. You have a right to sell something without telling Blackwell about it, don't you?"

The woman nodded agreement. "I don't hold with dealings with the cops," she volunteered with more conviction than she had evinced up to now. "This is my business — not theirs."

Liza heartily endorsed this sentiment. "How right you are," she agreed, as she extracted a coin purse from her blouse pocket, counted out her two last dollars in small change and hurried to the door. There she paused for a cautious glance through the glass top of the door, then assuming the attitude of a person with no particular mission, she sauntered leisurely out; her precarious balance on unaccustomed heels somewhat marred the attempt at nonchalance.

From the obscurity of a deep doorway a dozen yards behind her, Walter moved out and followed her. He'd been following this strange phenomenon for several blocks: Liza, trailing down the street in a freakish getup, dodging furtively into a theatrical store which sold second-rate, shopworn stuff, and coming out now, looking elated and in spite of her obvious efforts at disguise, more conspicuous than a neon light.

Walter now crossed over to the parking lot, retrieved his car, tipped the man a dime, and, avoiding the late traffic by cutting through side streets, arrived at home well in advance of Liza.

While waiting for her, he went into the dining room and mixed a stiff highball. The house was silent, with Marcia over at Dale's doing her duty.

"How sweet of you," Liza had said to her mother, "and how convenient! It'll give you a swell chance to poke around and locate the mystery money that everyone is itching to get their hands on."

Walter had chuckled and Marcia had been indignant.

There were stealthy sounds in the front hall. The door opened so quietly that a slight draft along the floor was all that betrayed it. Then uncertain footsteps, a faint bump, and Walter called with the voice of the bank official, "You needn't be pussyfooting around. Come in here and give an account of yourself."

Liza sounded startled and hurried. "Wait until I come back, Walter, I have to go upstairs first."

There was a rush, heels clacking quickly down the long upper hall, and a door slammed. Walter waited. Then he got up frowning and went upstairs. Going to Liza's door, he tried and found she'd bolted it.

"Open this door, Liza! I want to talk to you!" Sounding fierce and looking uncertain, he stood with his hand on the knob. The bolt slid back and Liza opened the door reluctantly, her eyes filled with tears as she regarded him uneasily.

Walter walked in and stood scrutinizing her as if she were an army private standing inspection.

She had taken off her shoes and most of her makeup. There were black streaks still across her forehead, and the shape of her mouth was uncertain. Her face was so camouflaged that only her eyes revealed the anxiety amounting to near-frenzy with which she regarded him.

"Walter, are you all right? No one has said anything to you —
yet? You're safe — so far —" Liza's voice quavered and halted.

Walter regarded her coldly. "What are you talking about? Are you
completely crazy? What do you think is going to happen to me?
What's the matter with you, anyway?" he asked roughly. "Can't you
see I'm all right?"

Liza sat down on the side of the bed, with a deep sigh. "You
don't know how scared I've been. I'd do anything for you, Walter.
You know that, don't you? I would die for you, Walter, I would
really if I thought it would help — but I've got a plan."

Walter's dignity and self-assurance seemed about to fall away, leaving only his fury and alarm. But he recovered himself, and his eyes,
icy blue, probed her agonized face coldly, and his voice was unsteady
as he lashed out at her.

"Look here, Liza, I don't know what you're talking about, but if
you don't quit all this play-acting you're going to get me into trouble
sure enough. The very way you look at me would make anyone think
that I'm condemned to die. What are you scared of? What do you
think you know?" Walter waited, scanning her face. Liza's eyes im-
plored him, but she remained silent. "If you think I killed Maggie,
you're just plain nuts," he continued. "I wasn't anywhere near the
church — I was in the bank all day Thursday — everyone knows
that, so what's eating you?"

"Oh, no, Walter, I didn't mean —" Liza's mouth dropped open;
she caught her breath. "You know I couldn't think *that* — but someone might — if —" she faltered, "if they find out —"

"Find out *what?*" Walter demanded.

"Nothing," Liza whispered.

"Well, you'll damn well make that lieutenant think *that* — trying
so hard to protect me. Making all those fool suggestions about people
who need money! Don't we all? You keep out of my affairs, Liza. Do
you understand? I can take care of myself, and," Walter concluded,
"what were you sneaking into that lousy 'Gaiety' for, looking like
some doll from a cheap nightclub?"

"I just thought I'd be less noticeable, I mean no one would ask
me what I was doing, if they didn't recognize me — which is what

everyone always does ask — I only put on a little makeup and did my hair differently, that's all."

"*What* were you doing?" Walter persisted. "Did you have an assignment with Nick? A little bird told me something like that," he added slyly. It was a punch below the belt, and he could have counted ten before Liza moved or spoke.

She flushed a dull, painful red; then she said vehemently, "No, you know I didn't — but I would if he asked me. Nick is wonderful! He's kind and he's your friend, Walter."

"Let me tell you something, kid. Don't get any ideas about Nick's altruism. Nick is looking after himself, first, last, and all the time!"

"But, Walter —" Liza turned very red again, found it difficult to speak, and then finally, with a desperate recklessness, blurted, "But, Walter, he says you need money — badly — that — that — if Lt. Blackwell finds that out —"

Walter paled, his eyes scorched into Liza's miserable ones. He made a tremendous effort at control, and attained a certain degree of calm. "I don't know what hogwash Nick has been feeding you, Liza. If you *must* know, I happen to owe Nick a small poker debt, which he ought to be ashamed to mention even, after all I have done for him. But let me tell you this. *I don't need your help.* When I do, I'll ask for it. Nick isn't worrying about me — he's working for himself and no one else. You are just a little fool to listen to him: you don't know what you are doing. And," he warned her, "don't try any tricks, Liza. Just lay off me."

The door slammed behind him and Liza flung herself upon the bed face down to smother her sobs. Walter's footsteps, clattering down the stairs, melted into silence.

After a time she pulled herself up. "I'm going to help you whether you want me to or not, Walter," she said aloud, and added in a choked voice, "I wish I didn't care, I wish I didn't care what happens to you! So Nick is lying — is he? A little poker debt!"

She went into the bedroom and scrubbed her face hard with soap and water, combed her hair again into its usual unflattering lines straight back from each temple, and viciously dug the white plastic

112

barrettes against her skull, pulling every strand mercilessly tight. Then she surveyed herself in the mirror, with dislike, and with eyes full of bitterness far beyond her years. What she saw gave her no inkling, no hope or prophetic vision that in the structure of her large bones there was a certain splendid sculptural quality, which some day might transform her into a very handsome woman; when the ugly-duckling awkwardness might become stateliness, with poise and maturity.

All she saw was a large-featured girl with dull suffering eyes and a wide mouth which she did not recognize as generous or sensitive.

"An assignment with Nick," she murmured dreamily. Then she made a hideous face at herself. "Don't kid yourself, Liza. All he wants is to be Walter's friend — not yours. But that's enough, if you save Walter. And that's what you are going to do —"

She reached down inside her blouse and drew forth the small brown paper bag where she had hastily secreted it. "After Lt. Blackwell finds this," she said, "he won't be prying into your business, Walter; he'll never even wonder if *you* needed that money." She replaced the small package inside her blouse, and managed to make very little noise going down the stairs, although she knew the house was empty — that Walter had left. In a few minutes she was letting herself out the front door, and on her way to Bermuda Street. It was late afternoon, but she would still have time; the coast would be clear — she hoped. Lt. Blackwell would surely be gone after being there all morning.

And in the house on Bermuda Street, at about the same time, Dale flung herself upon the old sofa in the library, back in the shadows, not lighting the lamps, hoping no one would see her — waiting for Bill. Bill was taking care of Hi and refused to leave him. She was very nearly at the end of her rope. If he didn't come soon she'd just go up and bang on Hi's door! Hi would just have to behave. He was being very difficult, and Bill had only shaken his head at her, with a rueful grin, when she had tried to get him out of the room after her dash away from Lt. Blackwell's frightening insinuations. And now it was late afternoon and the lieutenant might be coming back. Bill ought to know. She must warn him, so that he'd be prepared.

113

But Bill hadn't seemed to catch the urgency in her. She'd tried to make him listen, standing there at Hi's door. He had only come outside a minute, and taken her in his arms and kissed her and told her he'd talk later, but that now he was giving Hi a sponge bath — he couldn't leave him like that. And shut the door firmly in her face; then softened the act by opening it again and saying in tender cajoling tones, "Relax, Dale — the money's not on him — that's for sure! No use getting panicky though, Blackwell hasn't got a thing, actually. He's just trying to scare you. Take your car and go somewhere — but get out of the house — go see Sister Dennis or Father John, if he's back. Dr. Cotten seemed to think he'd be — today."

She'd done as he said. She'd taken the car and gone. She'd seen Father John, who looked only a little pale and was wearing a modest bandage behind his right ear.

But her godfather had been very grave and troubled, had made no attempt to minimize the situation — nor the vulnerability of Bill's position, nor hers, when Dale had told the priest the whole story. Hi's accusation of Bill, Maggie's overwrought state of mind, her determination to go to confession to unburden herself and receive advice — and also, Dale felt quite sure, to reveal to Father John the whereabouts of the vanished money. And that was the danger point, Lt. Blackwell was sure of that too, and knew just how important that information would be to Bill Ballard — and to Dale.

But Dale had come away with a certain comfort in her heart, not because things seemed less precarious, but because the priest was prepared to fight their battles, and didn't pretend it would be merely tilting at windmills.

That was why she'd always trusted Father John so completely. He never tried to put her off lightly, never sugarcoated things. And it was a satisfaction to have him admit frankly that things could be very bad — that she was not exaggerating her problem. They might as well face this thing squarely, fully aware of all the implications and dangers. Bill's innocence — and hers — would have to be proved. The two of them certainly would be Lt. Blackwell's choice — they had so much to gain. The police were apt to discount love and loyalty and even ordinary decency.

114

"Remember, Dale, they see so much of greed and ruthlessness. Crime is their daily diet, so they get to be skeptics about the Beatitudes playing a part in real life. I think we will have to find something very definite and factual to wipe you two out of their calculations."

"The obvious thing," Dale thought, "was to get the truth. But how? Where to begin in this fantastic, incredible nightmare?"

It was at this point, when Dale had come to a blank wall in her speculations, that Marcia and Walter came into the room, and after their first words, she lay perfectly still praying that they would not discover her presence.

Chapter Seventeen

THEY did not notice her in their preoccupation with each other. Marcia had pushed the door open and entered with Walter at her heels, quite confident that they were alone. Walter, talking in discreetly lowered tones, was repeating his question, "Where did you get the money, Mother?" each time a little louder, and was receiving no answer from Marcia. She did not even glance toward the end of the room where Dale lay, small and unhappy, on the old brocaded sofa back in the shadows of the alcove.

Marcia went straight to the other end of the room, switched on the reading lamp near Hi's chair and stood in the small circle of light, taking the spotlight, as it were, as she turned and faced Walter. Dale could not analyze her aunt's expression at that distance: from the tone of her voice, she was sure that Marcia's face had her cat-with-the-cream look upon it.

"My dear boy, just because you work in a bank, you cannot claim to be the only member of the family who can handle a financial transaction."

Walter halted in front of his mother, checked abruptly by her quick turn and her airy gesture of finality, waving him off.

"Mother, have you lost your mind? You can't mean to do this?"

Marcia dropped her affectation and reverted to her natural tone. "Don't be silly, Walter! I've already done it."

There was a moment's silence while Walter absorbed this blow, then —

"Where did you get the money?" he demanded again, in much the same tone that he had used to Liza, but without the same results. Marcia didn't answer. She ignored his question; in fact, she was ignoring Walter entirely, as she had never before been known to do.

Taking her seat in Hi's red chair, she deposited her large handbag upon the checker table, pulled off her gloves, and removed her hat, fluffing out her hair and putting it back into place again. Then with elaborate indifference to Walter's silent unwavering scrutiny, calculated, Dale supposed, to break down his mother's defenses, Marcia began unpacking her handbag: her compact, her lipstick, her cigarettes, the long amber holder, and her small silver lighter.

She took up her compact and quietly went about the business of making up her face. Casually snapping it shut after a satisfied inspection, she opened her cigarette case. Watching, fascinated, as the small flickering flame of the lighter made unerring contact with the end of the cigarette in the long holder jutting from Marcia's mouth, Dale applauded silently, "Right on the nose!" She was astonished at Marcia's dexterity and aplomb with which she was maintaining this wordless pantomime: quite sure, too, that it was really a play for time; that Marcia was trying hard for a good plausible lie. Dale waited as tensely as Walter for her aunt to speak.

Now there were no properties left to devise a new act, and Marcia would surely *have* to say something. But she didn't. She merely leaned back wearily, draped her arms upon the leather arms of Hi's chair, and, dangling loosely between her fingers, the long amber holder with the burning cigarette seemed about to slip to the floor. Smoke curled upward in a thin spiral and spread into cobweb patterns, about her face.

"Creating a smoke screen isn't good enough, Mother —. Where did you get the money to close this deal with Boman's Real Estate? *If* you've really closed it. You swore you didn't have a plugged nickel just two days ago."

Marcia merely shrugged her shoulders and Walter's agitation increased.

117

"Wait a minute," Marcia interrupted, "Blame your grandfather for his crazy unjust will and Hi for his miserly ways — not me!"

"That's your usual alibi. 'Hi should break the trust fund,'" Walter quoted wearily. "But," becoming emphatic again, "you seem to manage when you want to. Magically, you come up with a bag of gold; and the fairies didn't give it to you. Did you sell your soul to the devil?"

"That will do, Walter." Marcia sounded tearful. "I don't expect you to believe me or credit me with any business sense." Her voice steadied and self-satisfaction was clearly evident as she went on. "This time I've succeeded and I don't intend to tell you about it, but to settle your doubts you can look at these papers." She dug into the handbag again.

"I never said I'd *bought* the house. I only said I'd made the required down payment. Jack can pay the rest as rent. Young people are all buying that way. I think he should congratulate me on managing so well, but I never get appreciation from one of you."

"Why should Jack appreciate your saddling him with a couple of hundred dollars a month more than he can afford to pay?" asked Walter, taking the papers. He scanned the real-estate forms with grudging acceptance of plain facts.

"You've got it sewed up all right. But how in hell did you get $1,500 in cash?"

"I told you it was a small business transaction. I managed without your help, Walter, and that's all I intend to say. I really can't see that it concerns you."

"Well the Lord help you if Lt. Blackwell gets on to it. Anyone who has two extra dimes to jingle comes under his microscope."

"I hope you have loyalty enough to keep this to yourself, son," Marcia answered sweetly.

"How long do you think buying Mary a house in Westover is going to be a secret?" Walter asked. "I'll find out about this deal sooner or later, Mother. You're as bad as Liza, who fixes herself up like a circus queen and thinks she's invisible!" His tone changed, became ominous. "You'll have to take that kid in hand, Mother. I came here to tell you. You *must* come back home. You ought to be

118

there," he urged. "You are just getting into Dale's hair over here, anyway. Better come back before we have an elopement in the family. How'd you like Nick Sartoni for a son-in-law?"

Dale was so shocked at this statement that she barely escaped a sharp exclamation of denial. Walter was not playing fair, and Marcia had swallowed the bait.

"You don't mean to tell me you've let her go about with Nick! Taking advantage of my absence! I certainly thought you'd look after your little sister while I am slaving myself to death for your Uncle Hi."

Marcia swept up her real estate papers.

She was picking up her hat and gloves, saying, "I'll go have a talk with Liza this minute," when Walter stooped and retrieved a small white envelope from the rug at her feet.

"You dropped this," he said, and then quickly held it under the light for closer inspection, looking puzzled. "It says in pencil here, 'For Father John' — it looks like Maggie's scrawl."

"Oh, it is," Marcia said without interest. "I found it among Maggie's things when I was cleaning out her chest of drawers. It is just some silly verse, a bit of doggerel inside. It doesn't make any sense. But you know Maggie always was stupid. I was going to give it to Dale, but you can."

"I'll take it to Father John, instead," Walter volunteered. "After all, Maggie meant it for him, poor old girl." He slipped the small envelope carefully into an inside pocket and Dale came very near to revealing her presence then, in protest. But Walter was hurrying after Marcia who had been revitalized by her fear of Liza's indiscretions.

Dale comforted herself with the thought that she could ask Father to show her the verse. He'd understand Maggie's little puzzle. She felt a new ache at this typical reminder of Maggie, and unhappy that Walter should be the one to take it to Father, and that Marcia should have been the one to find it, "among Maggie's things." She had no business "among Maggie's things!"

Marcia was dreadful; she *had* to manage everything — her own way. How awful to have bought that house! Dale had not had time to assimilate this new bit of Marcia's strategy, nor perceive the possible implications; it had all come so suddenly, so unexpectedly. She

119

saw it only as another example of Marcia's determination to have her own way. And that decided her. She'd go and put away Maggie's things before her aunt did any more rummaging. Tomorrow Father John had said he'd come over and talk to her, and they'd make arrangements for Maggie's funeral.

The police were through. The lieutenant had come and told Father John Maggie had been hit with the same heavy candlestick that had been used on him, the nearest weapon at hand.

"Lt. Blackwell wouldn't say, but *that*," said Father John, "makes me sure that the murder had not been planned. I think that Maggie was killed because she followed the imposter out into the sacristy, saw him clearly for the first time, and recognized him, or could have given a good description to the police. He had already knocked me out, and that too seems something not planned. He must have been terribly surprised to see me there — I should have been on sick call. There *was* a telephone call, you know, Dale, a very urgent one, for me to come to the hospital. If I had gone it would have given my impersonator a clear field and plenty of time. He engineered that sick call to keep me out of the confessional, of course. He must have known that Father Don was away on vacation for a week, but he could not have known that Father Donahue had come back unexpectedly and had taken that sick call for me. No one at the hospital knew anything about that call when Father Donahue got there, and the police have not yet traced it."

"When poor Maggie came and stood before him with the St. Christopher medal in her hand, he had hit to kill. He probably thought that he'd killed once, anyway. I might be dead in that closet, and he couldn't take a chance with Maggie. And he took time to wipe all the fingerprints off the candlestick."

"She took that medal to be blessed for me." The thought had haunted Dale ever since Father had told her this, and that the police had found it under the table. She had been right, she had guessed why Maggie had gone scurrying back to the sacristy after confession. "If she just *hadn't*," Dale agonized again. "And now Lt. Blackwell has it — *Exhibit A in Maggie Riley's murder!*"

Suddenly the gloom of the library became unbearable. Dale jerked herself up quickly from the low sofa, shuddering, and walked mechanically toward the back hall.

As she mounted the stairway, which curved narrowly between the walls, Walter's question came unbidden. "Where did you get the money, Mother?"

She reached the top and pushed open the door leading into the upper hall. Now came light. She'd been in almost complete darkness, and hardly noticed it. But now with the light came normality and relief.

Where *had* Marcia gotten the money? The question was accompanied for the first time with sudden and clear penetration. Could Marcia have found Hi's twenty-five $1,000 bills? She knew now that that was what Walter thought. Engrossed by this startling idea, she stepped through the doorway and started toward Maggie's room.

"But she *wouldn't*," Dale's own conscience protested. "How could she — just *take* it?"

Arguing this point, Dale reached Hi's study. His bedroom door was right there across the hall, and she turned toward it, tempted to knock. She thought Bill would still be there, he never left if he could help it. Hi *might* say something and give him a clue about the money. Besides, this was an excellent chance to search Hi's room, when he was asleep. Then with a stab of pride, she withdrew her hand. "No you don't — you'll wait." And turning away, whirling quickly, she bumped squarely into Liza. Liza! She had not seen or heard a thing. Liza was just there, suddenly obstructing the way. And then as suddenly, with one dismayed exclamation — "Oh! I thought you were Mother" — Liza left by the door that Dale had just come through. Dale heard her stumbling down the dark back stairs.

Where had Liza come from? The study door was closed. Maggie's door was closed. Was she hiding from Marcia? Had she heard her mother? Did she know her mother was looking for her?

Dale thought. "I hope she gets away. She needn't be afraid *I'll* tell on her." Had she been hiding in Hi's study? Dale opened the door and went it. Everything looked the same. There was really

121

nowhere to hide. Liza could hardly squeeze into the small cupboard under the book shelves.

The picture, *Death and the Miser,* still hung upon the pilaster over the wall safe. Dale turned her eyes away from it. It no longer interested her. It only brought unhappy memories. It was, as Maggie had said, the center — the beginning and not yet the end — of all her troubles. She wished she'd never seen it, never brought it into this house. There it hung smugly mocking her. Yes, it was full of little devils, laughing at her.

Dale went over and sat with her back to it, as Maggie had done, the night that Hi had been so ill. She faced Hi's desk where Bill worked now, when Hi let him out of his sight. The filing case stood behind it with its drawers half open. She got up, automatically, to close them — then it came to her that Bill never left them this way — not when he'd finished for the day. Maybe he was coming in, maybe he had just left and was coming back. "Bill, darling," she murmured, "please come."

She had her hand on the drawer — a glance in the files would tell her — and she looked inside. There was something stuffed between the orderly spaced folders. She pulled up a small brown paper bag, badly crumpled.

"What in the world has Bill got here?" she said aloud. She thrust her hand into the bag and jerked it out again dropping it to the floor. She stood and looked at it for a full minute without moving. Then she stooped and picked it up. The thing felt slippery but prickly too. Curiosity conquered, gingerly she stuck her hand back in the bag and quickly drew it out.

Slowly her eyes widened. She held it out before her — a wig, made on a rubber foundation. An old man's wig — but not so old — the small flesh-colored bald spot was surrounded by a fringe of mottled gray hair — like Father John's — sparse and graying. This was very odd. And what was it doing in Bill's files? She couldn't think now; but it was wrong, all wrong! "Get rid of it!" She slipped the limp thing back into the bag, and raised her eyes then, because she felt someone was there at the door.

Dr. Cotten was standing on the threshold. She couldn't read his

122

expression, but his eyes were on the bag in her hand. She deliberately turned away from him and seemed intent upon closing the filing-case drawers. She managed to slip the bag between the folders, without visible movement she hoped; back, very far back, and shut the drawer. Then she casually closed the other drawers, and turned to smile at Dr. Cotten. It was then that she saw the lieutenant and a dreadful hand seized her heart.

Lt. Robert Blackwell was also there, just behind the doctor. Had he just come? Had he been there all the time? What had he seen? Had either of them seen anything? Only a small brown paper bag. Why should that interest them? She had to gamble — she could not possibly tell.

With a smile, she greeted the two men. "Come in. Why don't you come in?" she asked. "I was just tidying up after Bill."

She turned playfully to the dark and inscrutable face up behind the doctor's shoulder. "It's my go first, lieutenant. I've been waiting for a word with Bill. But maybe you've already talked to him. Or — did you come for me?"

Chapter Eighteen

BUT the lieutenant was in no playful mood, he was smoldering with suppressed anger.

"No! Not you! I want Ballard again. And how long," he snapped, turning belligerently upon Dr. Cotten, "do I have to wait to question your patient? This whole setup smacks too much of collusion! 'You cannot talk to my patient, he is a very sick man,'" mimicked the lieutenant. "Who says he's a very sick man? You! But you leave him with a young medical student all day long. You haven't even looked in since this morning. You can't claim calls have prevented you — you haven't made any. Since your hospital rounds, you have been shut up in your offices."

Dale had been watching Dr. Cotten for signs of interest in the filing cabinet and had detected none. Not once had his eyes turned toward the drawer. She breathed more easily. If Dr. Cotten hadn't seen her put the bag back, neither had Lt. Blackwell, who had been behind him.

The doctor was standing now gazing up at the Bosch painting seemingly fascinated, but at the lieutenant's surprising attack, Dale saw him become alert, and transfer his attention to the police officer.

"I am under no obligation to offer you an explanation, Blackwell, but since you seem so disordered in your thinking, misconstruing simple truth, I will try to straighten you out."

Dale was glad to see that Dr. Cotten was justly angry.

124

"First let me say that Bill Ballard is fully capable of caring for Mr. Bosch, under my direction. He is far more acceptable to the patient than someone from the registry, who would necessarily be a stranger.

"I think you will have to rely upon my judgment there. As for myself, when I am not actually out on required sick calls, and have completed my office appointments, I spend every available moment in my laboratory. I have a laboratory, Lt. Blackwell, in my quarters, which I shall be glad to show you, if you think you could understand the nature of my work, the study of capillaries — that is, blood vessels."

The doctor paused, thoughtfully considering the man facing him, and not flatteringly, as was apparent when he added, "I hardly expect that you would." Nevertheless, he quickly reverted to his subject again.

"I have been engaged in this research for years — but now with the aid of more modern facilities, newer methods, I anticipate great strides! Great strides," he repeated with relish, a gourmet gloating over a promised feast. "For instance," he said, advancing upon Blackwell, who instinctively stepped back to avoid being stabbed by the long index finger. "Recently" — and the finger still threatened — "with the use of radioactive isotopes, the possibilities of advancement in this field have been much increased. I hope to make valuable contributions. You have heard, no doubt, of the *American Society for the Study of Capillaries?*"

Dale suppressed a grin. The doc was riding his hobby! In spite of her perturbation, she could enjoy this. The lieutenant was going to be carried off willy-nilly, into the mysteries of medical science, and Cotten's pet theories.

But she had underestimated the lieutenant, who brought Dr. Cotten to a sudden halt by the simple means of raising his voice and drowning the doctor's out, in peremptory tones, with this startling statement: "I am bringing my medical examiner here in the morning, Cotten, to examine Mr. Bosch. If we find you've been deliberately delaying our investigation by keeping him behind locked doors, when he could throw some light on the mystery of this missing money, then I promise you, it will not be good for *you,* doctor."

125

Dale could see the angry red stain his cheeks, as the doctor answered, with sharp rebuke!

"Look out, young man! Your badge gives you no license for such ill-founded suppositions." Then, more quietly but somewhat loftily, he continued, "My reputation, my years of practice in this city, will fully establish my integrity. You may bring your medical examiner, of course, but you will do so on your own responsibility. Ordinarily I would welcome him. I have no fear of being discredited, but I have a very strong fear for the welfare of my patient. I know that he will be endangered, and perhaps fatally, if at this point in his convalescence he is subjected to excitement or unpleasantness."

Lt. Blackwell cut him short, "Calm down, doctor; no doubt, by tomorrow morning, you'll find that your patient is fully able to answer a few questions."

Dale could not tell whether the lieutenant was backtracking or maintaining his skepticism.

"Understand, Blackwell, my interest is solely bound up in my patient, who is not an easy person to handle. What possible motive could I have for thwarting the investigation of this case? And let me say for these two young people: it is only because of my strict injunction that they have exercised great restraint and have not asked Mr. Bosch the questions, which more than you, lieutenant, they wish him to answer."

The officer was unimpressed. He looked at Dr. Cotten with the noncommittal eyes that Dale disliked, and said, as if there had been no previous discussion, "Now I am ready to talk to Ballard."

His cool imperviousness to all that had been said roused Dale's stubborn resistance. "But you talked to him this morning, before you talked to me!" she protested. "What more do you want? Bill and I are going to have supper now. He has to go to see his dad, too."

Lt. Blackwell just looked at her, and she trailed off, feeling the weakness of her objections, feeling childish and foolish.

"Go get him, Dale," said the doctor. "You can stay with your uncle for a while."

"I don't anticipate a sudden relapse, Blackwell. It is likely only if the patient should become overexcited."

Dale was grateful. Dr. Cotten, bless him, was giving her a chance. She hurried across the hall and now her knock upon Hi's door had the assurance of authority behind it.

Bill came promptly this time, looking tired and glad to be released. But Dale said nothing. She slipped in quickly and closed the door behind her, with a finger upon her lips. He looked at her in puzzled surprise as she tripped across the room, saw that Hi was lying with eyes closed, and beckoned imperiously for Bill to follow her out to the sun porch leading off the sickroom.

Bill reached her quickly and silently, and stood waiting, his eyes upon her troubled upturned face. Indignation and very real fear widened her eyes and deepened their blue to a dazzling intensity. She looked up at Bill with cheeks flaming and lips trying to form the first words of warning. How to begin. She must be quick and effective. Bill was so apt to brush off her apprehensions. But he must know now. She must make them real to him.

"Lt. Blackwell is out there, raising such a fuss! Says we are ganging up on him. He has pitched into Dr. Cotten. The doctor is furious, but he sent me for you — he had to, Bill — before you go out there, you *must* know what your are up against."

"I know," Bill nodded. "Calm down, Dale."

"But you don't! *Listen* to me! That man thinks that you and I — that we — that we —" She could not put it into bald words, so Bill did it for her.

"Killed Maggie, eh?" He was serious enough now. "So that we could skip out with the dough?"

"Yes, and Father John says we're in an awful spot. It's all my fault, everything I said made it worse. Blackwell twisted it when I tried to make him see that Hi wanted to make *you* call off our engagement — and why you were writing our family history — and about your father's illness — and that you needed money." Dale stopped aghast at the incriminating list.

And Bill pursed his lips for a low whistle. "So I killed Maggie to clear my fair name! That's better than just to hijack the money — such a low grasping motive that would have been!"

"Shut up!" Dale said crossly. "You'd laugh in the electric chair!"

127

She gulped, as Bill grinned. "Someone *is* trying to send you there. Someone *wants* you to be suspected! I found a horrible thing in your file case — put there just for that reason! But I don't think either of them saw me looking at it — though I can't be sure. We'll have to get it out again, Bill, and destroy it." Dale shivered. She was very near to tears now.

"What?" Bill asked, all amusement gone. "And *who* saw you? Pull yourself together, Dale. Tell me what you found."

"A wig — with a bald spot just like Father John's." Then at Bill's utter disbelief: "It looks real. Don't you see?" Dale explained desperately. "If you'd put it on, you'd have looked just like Father John — in a dim light — in the confessional. You're exactly his size — do you know that, Bill? If Lt. Blackwell finds that thing in your file case, he'll think you wore it."

Bill interrupted. "Is it still there? Why did you put it back?" he asked bewildered.

"I *had* to. He and Dr. Cotten were coming into the study just as I found it — I don't think he saw it, but I'm not sure. I slipped it back, way back into the third drawer. Get him out of the study, Bill, and I'll go and get it as soon as you're gone. You *must* go now!" Dale exclaimed. "He'll think it's funny if we are so long. Dr. Cotten sent me instead of coming himself to give me this chance to talk to you, because I said I'd been waiting all day. Hurry now, but be careful, please, and don't tell Blackwell anything else."

"I can't think of anything else," Bill said. "Can you?"

But Dale didn't smile. "Hurry, Bill, he's so suspicious."

"I can't say I blame him. He's got plenty of grounds for it, hasn't he?" Then at her stricken look, added hastily, "Not from anything *you* told him, honey, he got a lot out of me too. I'm just made to order for him! A handpicked murderer! Some guys have all the luck!"

They'd reached the door. Bill turned and looked over at the large bed, with the small figure lying so still, so peacefully. He gave Dale a final admonition. "Handle with care, honey," Bill whispered, "he still has enormous potential! He's a nice innocent little package of TNT, on the point of exploding if we don't produce Maggie. I've given him a mild sedative."

128

Bill closed the door behind himself, quickly and quietly. And immediately Dale was startled by Hi's voice from the bed.

"Going to explode, am I? Right about that! Where's Maggie?"

Dale walked slowly toward the two small black dots in the white expanse of pillows. Hi's eyes, undoubtedly clear and intelligent, remained fixed unwaveringly upon her until she stood, without an answer, close beside his bed.

"Sit down, gal. You little hardheaded minx. You love that guy, don't you? Sure? How do you know?" He shot the questions at her rapidly.

"How do I know when the sun is out? How do I know I'm alive?" Dale shot back.

There was a short silence after that, which she made no effort to break. Hi's eyes pinned her.

"You should be an artist, me dear. Know that, don't you? Got it in you, straight — straight from old Bosch. Ballard's getting it all down in black and white — traced the line. Give the devil his due. Your boy's no fool."

Dale's heart raced. Hi was going to give in! She waited. His eyes were closing.

He murmured again, "You ought to be an artist," and then, "Can't be both." Dale knew what he meant.

"I can too, Hi. Bosch married, or you and I wouldn't be here." At that Hi's eyes jerked open.

"Do you want to leave me?" he asked fiercely.

"I'll come back to visit — and paint in my studio, Hi. I promise." She reached out and grasped his bony hand and held it gently. Silence. She watched, scarcely breathing. He closed his eyes again.

"Dynamite, am I? Bill's wrong," he muttered, "empty sack — can't stand upright."

"Don't say that! You're *not,* Hi! You're — you're full of beans! Why you're almost well." But even as she said it Dale's heart sank. Hi was looking confused again.

He spoke slowly, "I gave Maggie a little note — can't remember just what I said in it. Get Maggie back — we'll fix things up."

Dale didn't move. She had no body, no weight. Happiness had

129

no weight, it lifted you up, and you could float! Bill had won! Hi had given in! He was making a bargain, of course! But he liked Bill, or he never would have.

Then his words struck across her heart like a physical blow. "Get Maggie back." "The irony of it," Dale thought sadly. He had said that twice. "Get Maggie back!"

An icy stream chilled all the glow inside her, and Dale, looking down quickly, saw that Hi's eyes were closed. He was really asleep. The sedative had caught up.

Studying the old face, she saw sleep had brought to it a measure of repose and kindness. Dale rebuked herself for being surprised about the kindness. Hi *could* be kind. He'd always, or nearly always, been kind to her — except for this awful time, and she believed that even now he was relenting.

The tight bands inside her relaxed a little. Hi could be hard and selfish and stubborn. He would punish her, but not permanently. Dale came pretty close to understanding Hi's opposition to her engagement, but she couldn't account for his harshness to Bill, his unfairness. There *must* be something which neither she nor Bill knew about. But even so, she found it very hard to forgive him. She would try.

"All right, Hi," she whispered, "I'll keep on, somehow. I can't bring Maggie back, but I can bring the note, I believe." It was the note, she guessed, that Marcia had dropped and Walter had picked up. Marcia had said she'd found it among Maggie's things. She had said it wasn't important — but Marcia wouldn't know. If Walter hadn't given it to Father John, she could get it from him. If Father John had it, that would be even better. Father John could handle it.

Dale rose. She'd been kneeling beside Hi, trying to forgive him and binding up her wounds. Happiness came back more quietly, but surely. Bill *had* won. She rejoiced, looking down at the sleeping old man. "You do love me, don't you, Hi?" Stooping with a doubtful sigh, she kissed the parchment cheek lightly, and then looked toward the door.

Hi was very sound asleep. She had better go now, while she had the chance. She'd have to risk leaving Hi alone. Noiselessly she

130

crossed the room and slid like a ghost through the scarcely opened door.

She could hear her own heartbeats, that was all. Inside, the lamp was switched to low, right beside the desk and file case. Without a sound she was there. The third drawer slid out silently. Her hand thrust down quickly. Then she pulled the drawer out farther and looked very carefully between each folder, searching with frantic fingers.

But there was no little brown paper bag.

Chapter Nineteen

WHILE her heart beat a devil's tattoo, Dale tried to think, but her mind refused to accept the loss. The bag had *not* gone! It *had* to be there. She searched again, not just the third drawer, but all four of them, then conviction killed all hope, and panic followed.

"Oh God, don't let it be the lieutenant who took it!" A half sob escaped her and was quickly stifled as she stood rigidly facing the door, away from the file case, listening to footsteps. And, then, with sharp relief, quite apart from the terror which possessed her whole being, she saw Rosina.

She did not have to explain to Rosina, of course. Nevertheless, she said as steadily and casually as she could, "I slipped away from Uncle Hi for a moment, he's sound asleep. What's it, Rosina?"

"That's right, Miss Dale, you can't stay cooped up all the time — might as well be in jail — you and Mr. Bill too," she declared. Dale winced, but Rosina continued naturally and quite cheerfully, "You'll make yourself sick." Then she paused and in a different tone repeated the message she had come to deliver.

"Mrs. Rowland says for you to come down to supper *now*. I'm to stay with Mr. Hi, she says." There was resentment clearly discernible as Rosina confided, "She thinks she's running things, honey, but don't you worry — let her think so." Then soft and persuasive, "You go on, you needs your food. Mr. Hi'll be all right. I'll come for you if he so much as moves a finger."

"Where's Mr. Bill, Rosina?"

"He's gone. He and that *defective* went out the door together."
Dale hardly noticed the malapropism, which ordinarily would have
delighted her.

"Where were they going, Rosina?" she asked, her voice climbing
to a high note of alarm.

"Now don't you worry, honey, Mr. Bill's all right. He said to tell
you he was going to see his father before he comes back, and for you
not to worry about nothing."

"And where's Dr. Cotten?"

"He's gone too, Miss Dale. When Mr. Bill told him he'd given your
Uncle Hi a pill to make him sleep, like Dr. Cotten told him, then the
doctor said 'twasn't no use for him to stay either, but he'd be back
before you settled for the night."

Dale knew that Hi was safely asleep and that Rosina would be
faithfully alert. So she acquiesced and went down.

They were sitting around the supper table as if everything were
quite normal — as if they belonged there. Marcia, looking martyred
and pouring coffee into the fragile Worcester cups that Maggie had
kept under lock and key, Liza sullen, and Walter angry and aloof.
But Dale had distinctly heard him say just before she entered the
room. "No, I lost it." No one seemed to notice her presence. Their
eyes were fixed on their plates — they were half through the meal —

"Lost what?" Dale thought. But she was too dazed from the shock
of her failure to pursue the question, and her thoughts raced frantically.

"If Lt. Blackwell has the wig, Bill is lost and all I've gained from
Hi is travesty!"

She took her seat in silence, which prolonged itself until Walter,
who was the only one conventional enough to make an effort, turned
to her with a quizzical smile.

"Dale, did you know that we have a convert to the Fine Arts in
our midst?"

Dale didn't answer at first, her whole being was rebelling against
sitting here obeying orders, trying to be calm, more of a guest than
any of them at her own table, in her own home, which the Rowlands
seemed to have completely taken over.

133

She dragged her mind back to Walter's question, and answered without interest. "No. who?"

"Dr. Cotten, of all people, has become enamored of the Bosch painting. Can you stand it? The old fellow wanted to take it home with him to study, but the lieutenant wouldn't hear of it. Why I don't know, but nothing is to go out of this house!"

"What would Dr. Cotten find to study?" Dale asked, wondering. "But he can if he wishes — I don't care what the lieutenant says — Hi wouldn't mind."

"I wouldn't buck the 'lieut,' Dale. It'll just rouse his temper," Walter admonished seriously. "Besides, it's Hi's picture, you'd have to ask him first," he added, pushing back his chair briskly. "Well, we'd better be going. Are you packed up, Mother? I'll run up and get your bags."

"I'm not going home, Walter. You may carry my things back into the guest room, though. Liza and I are sleeping there — from now on."

Liza jerked her head up in surprise. "*I am not.* I am going home with Walter," she declared, her eyes appealing to him for help.

"No." Marcia's tone brooked no more discussion. "I've brought your overnight bag. There's no reason to tie Walter down," she continued virtuously. "I didn't realize that I've been imposing on him, expecting him to stay in every evening. Naturally he can't go out and leave you alone in the house. Don't be so selfish, Liza. I don't mind staying in the guest room as long as I am not alone, and there are twin beds — probably more comfortable than Maggie's hard mattress. I've hardly slept at all in there."

"Well, nobody asked you to," Dale thought, watching Walter turn frigid with anger, and then to her deep satisfaction, sweep aside his mother's pretenses.

"Can't you ever do anything, Mother, without preening your feathers and putting on a halo? Just don't use *me* to polish it up," he went on, quickly giving Marcia no time to recover. "What good you're doing Dale over here, I fail to see. *You* may have found the visit profitable," he said significantly, "and if you are still afraid of missing something you can come back every morning, after Liza is

134

in school, where she belongs." He stopped, tightening up for a finish that would curb them both. "Why should you two crowd in on Dale? Bill is right here if she needs anything. Dale can spare you. Just ask her."

Dale saw Marcia, going down for the third time, latch on to something in that instant — clearly a lifesaver. Marcia said gently, silkily, "But that's just the point, Walter, which you seem to have missed, dear. Bill *is* here — and now Maggie *isn't,* it leaves only Dale and Bill. I must think of the propriety. Since I can't be in two places at once, I'm taking the only possible course."

Walter got up looking utterly disgusted at this dished-up Victorianism and left the room. Dale was speechless. No one could beat Marcia! She'd use any weapon! Very well, let her stay. Dale gulped down her hot coffee, pushed back her chair as Walter had done, and said, without glancing at her aunt or Liza.

"I don't want anything else. Excuse me, please."

Walter was not in sight when she reached the hall, and Dale ran quickly up the stairs. She would search the study now, not just the file case — the whole room. There was no time to waste. She had very little hope but she had to try. It could be that Bill had been able to remove the wig from the drawer and, not wanting to keep it on him, had deposited it somewhere else.

She opened the study door and closed it quickly behind her. The light was on in the room and Walter was standing over by the bookcase. A minute before he had not been there. He must have been stooping, hidden from sight by Hi's big chair.

His unexpected appearance snapped her taut nerves. His smile was a little strained, but he showed no other sign of embarrassment.

"Oh, there you are," he said, not quite able to eliminate the surprise in his voice. "I wanted to talk to you, Dale."

"Did you expect to find me in the cupboard? What were you looking for?" Dale asked directly.

"Looking for?" Walter sounded puzzled.

"Yes," Dale said. "You were down behind Hi's chair and there's nothing there but the cupboard under the bookcase."

"Dale, you're a suspicious bit of goods, aren't you? But I can't say

135

I blame you for being edgy. No, I was merely looking at Hi's books, waiting for you. I dropped my glasses, it must have been just as you came in. I'm sorry I startled you."

Walter's glasses *were* in his hand, but somehow it was all too pat, and not quite convincing.

"The thing to do," Dale thought, "is to get rid of him as quickly as possible." She had to search this room. Her hands were clammy. Could Bill possibly have managed to change the hiding place for the wig, with the lieutenant right here waiting for him? She was nearly sure that Blackwell had the thing. If Dr. Cotten had seen it, he would tell her, for he would never suspect Bill of using it. If anyone *had* found it, she'd rather it be the doctor. But certainly not Walter. Could *he* have been looking for it? How would he know about it?

"I only stopped in here to speak to you when you came up," Walter said. "I wanted to talk to you alone. First to say that I'm sorry that Mother's so impossible, and that I see no reason why you should be bothered with her, or Liza either. I was trying to get them off your neck."

"Thanks for trying," Dale said shortly.

"You could help get them home, if you will back me up. Just tell them frankly you don't want them here. There's no use in being subtle or polite about it."

"If you only knew," Dale thought, "how much I want to get rid of you too!"

Then, as if reading her thoughts, Walter left her. Without another word, nor a glance in her direction, he walked away. Strange perhaps, but Dale was too relieved to have him go to resent it. She had had the impression all along that Walter was secretly pleased about something; in spite of his evident anxiety to dispose of his mother and Liza, there was a sort of suppressed excitement about him.

She tiptoed softly toward the door and closed it without a sound.

She went directly to the cupboard under the bookcase, pushing Hi's great chair aside to let the light shine fully in, and pulled open the two long low wooden doors. The cupboard was not deep, she could see quite plainly the rather untidy space all the way to the back wall. Only some wooden boxes, unpacked books; she remembered

136

when Hi had stacked them in there. An old satchel, a bundle of yellow papers, an old cane which Hi had never liked, and an empty picture frame. She was surprised that it was empty — holding only the bare stretcher — the canvas had been cut away. She remembered the picture that had been in that frame. The sad oil landscape that used to hang where the Bosch was now. She had never liked it, and she supposed that Hi had not either, since he had only saved the frame.

Dale closed the cupboard doors, dissatisfied, feeling as if she had missed something. But what? If Walter had found anything exciting, he must have taken it with him. It could have been the wig! Her heart thudded down to her toes; rather wildly she began to search.

An hour later she was convinced that the wig was not in the study. She sat tired and discouraged at Bill's desk. Her eyes were fixed upon the Bosch painting, hanging upon the pilaster directly in front of her, without seeing it. She did not notice that *Death and the Miser* was tilted at a rather rakish angle, an unnatural angle, but for a very natural reason. The picture was slightly out of line, hanging just a trifle crookedly upon the wall.

The phone beside her rang sharply, and she lifted the receiver.

"That you, Dale?" A grave quiet voice, no pet names.

"What's the matter, Bill?" she asked quickly, adding in the same breath, "I'm in the study; and it's gone, Bill. Did you take it?"

"Nope."

Her heart sank although she had not really hoped.

"Well, what's the matter?" she repeated.

"Not a thing. Who said anything was the matter?" Bill's voice was a little too bright now.

"You can't fool me, Bill Ballard, where are you? Will you please tell me in plain words."

"Sure, sure, just give me time. You're so greedy about trouble, though, honey, you just grab!"

"All right! Are you in jail? Answer me!"

"Lord, no!" Bill laughed, then spoke seriously, "I'm here at home. Didn't Rosina tell you?"

"Yes, but she also said that you left with Lt. Blackwell."

137

"And *he's* left. Just thought I'd tell you," Bill said, "that although *we* couldn't think of a thing more to tell him, he's thought of something all by himself."

"What?" Dale braced herself.

"Atta girl! It's sort of an anticlimax now, after all this buildup. Well, Our Friend has gone back to that overdose of digitalis. I fit in there like a plug in a socket — naturally. I know all about the dosage —"

"But, Bill," Dale interrupted, "you *saved* Hi. He can't think you'd try to kill Hi — and then save him!"

"Yes he can. He has a subtle brain, and a supple one. He can jump to different conclusions — if one gives way on him, he simply reaches out and hangs on to another — wonderful mental acrobatics!"

"All right, what's the other?" Dale knew that Bill was getting around to something that was going to give her a jolt. "If it's not *you* — it's an anticlimax."

"Not to me, it isn't! You're the alternative! So I just thought I'd let you in on the plot, in case the lieutenant happens by to see you.

"In this one, I'm not a thief, only a murderer. Fine! This is the way it works. We couldn't find the $25,000 so as to clear out, well heeled on our honeymoon, because Hi has hidden it too well. All right, Hi's eliminated the money, so we eliminate Hi. What's a mere $25,000 when you can get the whole works? You know you inherit, so we decide on the biggest and the best!"

"But why did we save him?" Dale persisted. "It doesn't make sense."

"Don't know — cold feet maybe. He hasn't gotten around to that yet — maybe Maggie caught on!"

"If Maggie were only here, *she'd* have him jumping — she'd tell him *she* did it, in a trance!" Dale stopped between a laugh and a sob.

"Speaking of Maggie," Bill said, then hesitated, "if you can get Marcia out of there, would you mind very much, Dale, staying in Maggie's room tonight?"

This was a serious request. Dale responded to his tone. "Not if there's a reason . . . Bill, what is it?"

"Well, you see, Dale, I haven't had a chance to talk over any-

138

thing about all this with Dad. I think I ought to — now. The doc says Hi will be all right. He'll probably go from the sedative to a perfectly natural sleep — won't stir until morning — and you could just keep your door open, on the outside chance of his waking. But I thought —"

"That Maggie's room is nearer," Dale finished for him. "Yes, of course, Bill. I'll stay there. With Marcia and Liza here — and everybody alert, I'll be perfectly safe."

"Sure you don't mind? I'll be back first thing in the morning. It will be pretty late, tonight, after a session with Dad. What about Marcia? Will she make a fuss?"

"Marcia has already moved into the guest room *with Liza!* Yes," she said lightly, answering him, "yes, she *always* has a reason, but she never gives the right one! No, I'm not scared if Dr. Cotten and you think it's all right. Better cut off, Bill. I hear someone coming. . . . Yes, I love you," she whispered, carefully placing the phone back in its cradle, with eyes fixed upon the doorknob across the room, turning silently.

Dale stiffened, afraid to move for there was no place to hide, and there wasn't time. The door opened all the way and she slumped back into her chair.

"You nearly scared me to death! Thank goodness it's you! I was just talking to Bill. I was afraid you were Lt. Blackwell."

Dr. Cotten smiled. "You startled me too," he said, coming in briskly.

"I was going to check up on Hi, but when I got this far, I thought I heard something in here."

"Well, you opened that door like a burglar. Dr. Cotten, Bill says you told him it would be all right —"

"Yes, I did, there's nothing to worry about."

"OK, but I'd rather be nearer to Hi. I'm going to sleep in Maggie's room."

The doctor looked at her, frowning a little. "Bill needs a good night, and you do too, my dear. You won't sleep a wink in Maggie's room. I *know*. Don't deny it. You get into your own bed, it's only a few steps farther — you can get to Hi — but you aren't going to need to, I tell you. Everybody is going to sleep well tonight. Come on, doctor's orders, my dear, and time you were in bed now. I'll just check up and let myself out. You don't need to come with me."

But Dale disregarded his dismissal and followed him to Hi's door. He waved her off, went in very quietly and came back promptly.

"He's fine. I'll leave his door like this — open — you can hear him turn over in bed. Are you satisfied? Now go to bed."

But Dale refused and insisted upon seeing him out, going down the stairs with him, loathe to say goodnight, even though the doctor seemed a little impatient. "Hardheaded child, don't forget your hot milk," he scolded. As she shut the front door behind him and slipped on the chain, Dale sighed. He hadn't said anything about the wig.

She waited until she heard his car start; then turned off the lights, leaving only the night light, and very slowly started back across the broad silent hall, feeling very much alone. She didn't like being alone.

"Just because Bill isn't here," she chided herself, tilting up her chin and squaring her shoulders. "OK, get going!" she said scornfully, and ran quickly up the stairs to Maggie's room.

Chapter Twenty

DALE stepped inside and stopped short. Indignation followed surprise as she looked around her. The room was a mess! It looked like a rummage sale. Marcia! With her cleaning up — or clearing out — whatever she called it! She'd emptied drawers and closet, stacked garments in separate piles: underwear, gowns, cotton housedresses. She had even hauled out Maggie's knitting bag and her bag of wool scraps with the half-finished quilt. Everything that Maggie had neatly arranged, or tucked away, was now cluttering up the chairs, the cedar chest, the bureau top, the table. Marcia had merely taken them out, spread them around, and left.

In spite of Dr. Cotten's well-meant advice, Dale had come to sleep in Maggie's room. She had promised Bill, and, she told herself, she could lie in Maggie's bed, handle Maggie's things without going to pieces. She loved everything in the room because it brought Maggie nearer.

But she hadn't expected this. Dale sighed, she was too tired to start tonight; but tomorrow all of Maggie's possessions should go right back where they had been, until such time as she could decide. She wished she'd gotten here before Marcia, but she hadn't had the time, just one day — and *what* a day!

The wool scraps, she thought, had better go back. So clearing the top of the cedar chest, she picked up the quilting bag, lifted the heavy lid to drop it in and there was the doll's trunk.

141

It was a small pink trunk that she hadn't seen or thought about for years. It was not really a trunk: it was a bank, with a lock and key. She remembered how she'd dropped her pennies in through the slot in the top and loved hearing them clink against the metal bottom. But the bank was too capacious, the bottom never seemed to get covered, and eventually she must have lost interest, because she'd forgotten all about it. Dale wasn't much of a saver, but Maggie always was — Maggie the squirrel — saving for a rainy day. How like her to have salvaged Dale's toy. Out of sentiment or thrift? What had she saved in the little pink trunk? Dale opened it.

A few photographs, pictures of Dale as a baby. One very faded, a snap of her mother holding her, and several most awful, at the age of seven or eight — front teeth missing. Shuffling through them she picked up a small gray memorandum book with neat rows of figures in columns, dates opposite. The writing was unmistakably Maggie's. This was ten years back, but as she riffled through the pages, she saw that though the months were not all listed the years came along pretty regularly. The last entry had been this very year, just last month, and opposite it the total was $1,675.25.

Dale was amazed. Maggie had saved a nice little sum, if these were her accounts, but this wasn't a bankbook, just a memorandum. She'd look at it later: it could wait, until she had time. Maggie may have left a will, she had always said that if she had anything when she died, it was to go to St. Mary's Nursery. This would help Father John a lot, but Dale didn't even know the name of Maggie's bank. Maggie had talked very little about her personal affairs, she liked her privacy — almost to the point of secrecy.

Dale closed the little trunk and put it back, saddened in spite of her brave resolutions, at the intimate touch of Maggie's simple keepsakes.

She dropped the knitting bag with the scrap bag into the chest and shut down the top. That was all she had thought about it — then.

Dale undressed quickly. She took a last peep at Hi, and leaving her door open opposite his, turned out her light. What a dreadful day it had been!

Like a tired swimmer reaching her goal, half drowned by fatigue,

142

Dale slid into bed between cool smooth sheets, scarcely causing a ripple. Then as the first deep exhaustion left her, insistent questions needled her tired mind.

"Not now," she murmured, "I can't think now."

Then her eyes flew open and her will took over; the mere act of rejection bringing her awake. Of course she could think — must think. She lay still inviting the persistent questions.

A vague idea took shape and grew from suspicion into conviction. *She knew now what Marcia had done:* the answer to Walter's question. She knew she was right, as sure as if she held a bent divining rod pointing certainly to the hidden truth. Marcia would deny it of course, virtuous and indignant; turning it into something else, something praiseworthy! Dale grew hot with indignation. "Never!" She'd never let Marcia get away with this — taking Maggie's little hoard, her life's savings — and buying a house in Westover!

But how could she prove, what was now clearly certain to her, that Marcia had taken Maggie's money from the bank — or, in fact, that it had ever been there. She had no proof.

Tingling with excitement, she reached for the lamp on the bedside table, switching the light on again. She threw back the covers with a jerk and was out of bed, and back again standing before the cedar chest. She lifted the lid quickly, and bending down for the doll trunk, she held it in her hands, this time with very different thoughts.

She examined the tiny lock: it had not been forced. But Maggie would have kept it locked. The key? She'd worry about that later. The interesting point was that Marcia had found the key, had opened the bank, and left it so deliberately. Clever of her; a locked bank with the key missing might start an inquiry, but not just a small pink trunk that was no longer used except for old snapshots.

"You overlooked things, Marcia, my dear," Dale said between her teeth. "You missed the notebook. Something must have scared you or someone interrupted before you had time to look into it! —"

Who? Could it have been the murderer coming back to Maggie's room for some reason? Who? — Always who? Like a refrain in Dale's mind. Who killed Maggie?

She took the small gray-backed book, replaced the bank, and went back to bed, tucking the record of Maggie's savings safely under her pillow. Marcia had not expected her to come in here to sleep, tonight, and find what she'd been up to. But she *had* come. Dale exulted because otherwise she might never have known. "Why," she wondered, "go to such lengths for a house in Westover?"

The reason, Dale concluded, lay deeply imbedded in meshes of selfishness, of stubborn pride and vanity. It wasn't the house itself, but what the house stood for — "My daughter's home in Westover" would do much to salve the smart, the humiliation of living, as Marcia described it, "in a decaying house in the slums." If she couldn't live in Westover herself, she wanted Mary to. Marcia had always wanted more for Mary than for Liza. Mary was pretty and attractive. Mary was a credit to her. But, Dale decided, Marcia's determination not to be thwarted, her pride and vanity were driving her too hard — Marcia was due for a fall!

Dale did not lie down again, but propped another pillow behind her, for now that she *knew,* she must build up sustaining evidence. She must go back and remember every single thing that would support her accusation.

Not too difficult. Keyed up as she was, things came racing back, clear and vivid. And Dale, remembering with insight now, understood and appreciated much that she had missed before. Her dear blunt and guileless Maggie! How wily she had been in evading Walter's questions — and how completely honest!

Only a week or two ago, Walter had been teasing her, as he often did, to start an account in the Tidewater Bank. Teasing, but partially in earnest, and curious too.

"Maggie, *when* are you going to be one of our depositors? We like nice big fat accounts. Maggie, what do you do with all your wealth? You don't spend it on finery! You have no vices! Even if my honored uncle is, as my mother claims — wrongly of course — a bit of a tightwad, you must by now, in all these years, have accumulated a fortune!"

Dale remembered that she had shaken her head, tried to warn Walter, that he was going too far — Hi was bristling. But he was enjoying himself, so he disregarded her and asked Maggie point-blank, "What bank is it in? I think it's very disloyal of you not to put your money in *my* bank, Brambleton's finest!" And Dale could see Maggie; lips shut tight, color heightened, looking straight through him. He was teasing and Maggie knew it, but she didn't like it, and she didn't mince matters.

"I don't trust these great banks," she'd said. "And I don't trust all those dandified young men behind the fancy railings either. Spend-thrifts and money-lovers, from the looks of them. How do I know that in their hearts they are honest? And I'm thinking that the more money they have to handle, the more likely it is to be sticking to somebody's fingers. But they'll not handle mine, thank you."

Walter, glancing at himself in the mirror self-consciously, had laughed and straightened his tie, and Dale remembered his answer.

"A man doesn't have to look poor to be honest," he declared. "But if such a thing did happen, the bank would make it good. *You* wouldn't lose a cent, Maggie. That's the advantage of putting your money where it's protected by large assets. Even *your* savings," and Walter had grinned, "would be a drop in the bucket to the 'Tidewater' but," and now he was really in earnest, "don't go risking them in one of these small loan affairs without knowing something about its rating."

"What I've got, Walter, and it's no fortune I'm claiming," Maggie had told him stubbornly, *"is already* in a small bank. It has no great name, I tell you that, but it's safe enough, and strong enough for my small savings. So there's an end to the matter."

Beyond that Maggie never went, and Hi, enjoying Walter's slight discomfiture, not having relished the quip about tightwads, had backed her up. "That's right, Mag. Tell Paul Pry nothing. And you, you young money-changing upstart — mind your own business."

So — Maggie's bank with no great name, had been a doll's trunk! A small bank but safe, she'd said. And it *had* been safe until Maggie wasn't here to guard it anymore. "She must have kept it locked though, and where had she kept the key? Of course she kept it locked," Dale thought, "and I've seen the key many times on a string around Maggie's neck, with her medals — nearly hidden by medals. Of course *that* was the key. And if —"

Dale got up once more. This time she went to the chest of drawers that Marcia claimed to have cleared out. "We'll see what else you found, Marcia, 'among Maggie's things' although you didn't see fit to mention this to Walter."

Dale opened one of the two small top drawers and took out a little worn cloth bag, the one that Maggie had taken to church with her, and the lieutenant had brought back yesterday. Inside it was Maggie's rosary, her eyeglass case, a crumpled handkerchief, and the police had added the string of medals taken from Maggie's poor dead neck. The little key was there too, very inconspicuous and trivial. There had seemed nothing of value in it Dale had thought, and thrust it into the drawer to take care of later along with Maggie's other possessions.

So Marcia *had* found the key and been clever enough to unlock the bank and, leaving it unlocked, put the key back.

Marcia's face wearing its innocent martyred expression came between Dale and Maggie's bag, still in her hand — and then, as if the vision had brought the reality, Dale heard Marcia's voice very plainly — and Liza's even louder, answering her. They were coming up the stairs and she suddenly remembered that the door was open. She didn't want them to know that she was here. She thought they'd gone to bed. Dale glanced at her wristwatch, then ran quickly across the room and switched off the light.

It was only ten o'clock. She had thought it was much later, but she had come straight here after Dr. Cotten had left, and before that, Liza and Marcia had gone up to the guest room. They must have come down again, and they were still quarreling, each down-talking the other. Liza was on top for the moment.

"Walter's right! Why should we stay here? You don't know what you are doing. You try to run everything and treat me like a baby."

Marcia made herself heard. "You're acting like one now." Then Liza rose above her.

"I know a lot more about a lot of things than you do. You don't

146

even know your own family or what goes on. Throwing that money away on Mary — when it could have saved Walter!"

The tragic desperate tone startled even Marcia.

"Saved Walter?" she asked, lowering her voice, but Dale could still hear clearly. "What do you mean? *Saved* Walter?"

Standing by the open door in the dark, Dale held her breath.

"Save him from — from embarrassment — from driving that awful old car!" Liza mumbled. "Shut up, Mother!" she snapped. "You've been yelling. Do you want Dale to hear you?"

Marcia's relieved voice, "Is *that* all? How very silly." She added with conviction, "Dale's in her room and asleep."

"Now," Dale decided. They were only a few feet away but they couldn't see her. "No, I'm not asleep." She raised her voice and was gratified to see them both jump. "Please be quiet, or you'll wake up Hi." Then she closed the door.

Marcia murmured something which Dale didn't hear, but she did hear the rapidly departing footsteps.

When silence, complete and unbroken, finally settled on the hall, Dale opened the door again. By some miracle they had not wakened Hi, and for the third time she went back to bed.

Her mind was still seething with retributions upon Marcia.

"You'll get that money back, Marcia, and give it to The Nursery or this will be your finish."

She wondered if circumstantial evidence could convict a person, and hoped it could. She lay back on her pillows and planned. At last came drowsiness. Half between waking and sleeping she thought of Father John. This was something for Father John — he would tell her what to do. Finally she slept.

In her dreams she heard the priest's low kind voice speaking to her through the tiny screened window in confession, "We mustn't be vengeful, my child. Our enemies are really blessings in disguise — trials that we must accept to increase our humility and our charity. Our enemies are very good for us."

And then Hi's mocking voice cut in sharply, "Life would not be worth living if we didn't keep our enemies!" His snort thinned out,

147

turning strangely into Sister Dennis' happy laugh. She dreamed of Sister Dennis, laughing, holding out the doll's trunk, those beautifully appealing eyes fixed upon her.

"How would this look in the light of eternity, Dale?"

"I don't know, Sister," Dale answered in her sleep. "I can't wait for eternity. I haven't time. I have to do something *now!*"

After that she didn't dream at all.

Chapter Twenty-One

FRIDAY night the house was very still as Dale slept, and Hi, across the hall, stirred in his sleep from time to time. In the distant guest room, Marcia also slept, but Liza tossed and fumed and dozed fitfully.

Strange surroundings, unaccustomed sounds outside, a tree branch unaccountably scraping the window, and even her mother's peaceful breathing in the twin bed next to her became irritants adding to the sum total of her wretchedness.

Loud in the silence, St. Mary's clock struck the quarter hour. And in the interval of waiting for it to strike again, Liza became aware of something different; an undertone of muffled thumps and stealthy movements. She sat up and listened, slid quietly out of bed, and tipped across the room. The noises came from the basement kitchen right below her.

This was the old wing of the house. The present guest room had once been servant's quarters. There had been a narrow ladderlike stairway leading down from the corner of this room, screened off now and never used.

Voices, whispers came up the opening and Liza leaned with an ear plastered to the plywood wall. Then she moved away.

Casting an uneasy glance at Marcia who did not move, she slipped her feet into scuffed-out moccasins, and her arms into the sleeves of her dark blue corduroy robe. She slid along with infinite care to avoid stumbling into anything. By the light, filtering in from the old-fashioned yard lamp, she succeeded in reaching the door into the hall, and crept cautiously down the back stairs to the first floor where a small passage and a few steps led to the basement.

Miraculously she made her objective. Concealed behind the open basement door which led into the kitchen, Liza was safely hidden, with an excellent opportunity to listen. The room was not too dark; here the yard lamp did better service. She might even be able to see, if she craned her neck a bit around the edge of the door.

Liza tried it, and nearly brought a termination to her so far successful sleuthing. She just managed to shut off her exclamation of surprise before it actually escaped her, and quickly jerk her head back into shadow.

She held her breath. Walter was not two feet away, scowling. "What are you doing, standing there?" The words might have been bullets killing her. Liza could not answer. Then someone *was* answering him. The voice was Nick's. Walter had not been talking to *her*. He had not even seen her!

"I'm watching this passage," Nick said. "You made fuss enough getting through that window to wake the dead."

"It's your fault," Walter snapped. "We needn't have come this way, like a pair of thugs. I could have done it much better alone, by merely staying inside."

"Fine," Nick answered. "Fine, and get away *alone* with the money. No thank you. You said you had a key to the front door, said it would be easy."

"I *have*," Walter defended himself. "I forgot the chain. Dale never puts it on. I can't think what possessed her."

"Can't think, period," Nick grumbled.

Liza was recovering. She had found a crack in the old door and also found that she could see perfectly with one eye. She saw Walter shrug.

"Stop griping," he said indifferently. "If you don't like it, get out. I can do this better alone anyway. Why should *you* be here? *I* figured this thing out. You can trust me."

"*Trust* you?" Nick's tone was very eloquent.

150

"Why not?" Walter became lofty. "I don't like your tone, Nick. You got your share of the $5,000."

"Minus the $500 to Capelli. You could have cut that down."

"For the last time, listen! One — The picture had to be paid for or — Two — Capelli would have gone to Hi, and demanded his price, $500. Three — Hi would have said he'd already paid $5,000, and produced his canceled check. The whole scheme would have blown up."

A muscle in the calf of Liza's leg suddenly cramped agonizingly. She shifted off it.

"Did you hear something?" Nick whispered.

"No," Walter said. "Come on, we're wasting time."

"Wait," Nick said stubbornly, "I'm not going until I'm sure it's safe."

"All right, three minutes by my watch, then I'm starting." Walter was cool and superior. "Why so jittery?"

"Well, why not?" Nick complained. "You gum up everything."

"Shut up," Walter said.

There was silence for half a minute, which seemed more like an hour. Then Nick, who couldn't keep still, began again.

"You *do,* and this is going to end the same way."

"What are you talking about now?" Walter asked, with exaggerated restraint.

"The job I did endorsing that check. Damn good, wasn't it? OK, I faked the signature on the picture even better. Then *you* fizzled it. Let your smart little cousin stymie you. We could have made a fortune out of that."

"Not smart, stubborn," Walter corrected. "You've got two more minutes," he said, "and you're talking too loud. Mother and Liza are still here, right over your head."

"Hell, Walter, you said you were going to get them out." Nick lowered his voice, "I'm scared of Liza. She sticks too close."

Liza moved closer to the crack. She could see them both quite well, the sneer on Walter's face. "All right, *get out!* I'll meet you at the car." And Nick's exasperation, *"Stop saying that! I'm not getting out. But don't forget, if I did, I might do a little talking."*

Walter smiled confidently. "You can't. You're up to your neck now."

Nick shook back the lock of hair that kept falling over his forehead, automatically smoothing it into place with an air of finality, and asked, "You think I can't — upset your personal affairs?"

The flash of his even white teeth did not make his smile a pleasant thing, nor his great Murillo eyes less threatening.

"All I have to do," he said slowly, "is to dial a certain number and say a few words. You're not forgetting that, are you?"

Walter pushed past him. "When this is over, I damn well am! Time's up. Come on!"

Behind the door, Liza did not breathe until the two of them had walked softly past her, the flashlight in Walter's hand pointing the way.

They reached the floor level before she stirred. Then she followed, sticking close to the wall, feeling her way with hands flat against the whitewashed bricks.

In the dim night light of the front hall, Walter paused and whispered. "Wait. I'm going to fix it so we can leave in a hurry, this way."

Nick stopped in the shadow of the broad stairway and watched Walter go quickly and silently to the front door, slip off the chain, turn the knob, and very carefully set the door an inch or two ajar. He went back, and the two, swift as running shadows, Walter leading, rounded the landing and disappeared. Liza emerged from the back wall, following like a shadow.

She did not have to pass Hi's open door nor Maggie's where Dale was, they had gone into the study. The door was not entirely closed. Liza stopped just outside. The half-closed door blocked her progress and her view. For possibly five minutes she stood. Unaccountable movements inside: a low exclamation once from Nick, quickly stifled. She moved in closer, inching along, bent forward, and gave the door a gentle push, bent forward a little more to ease into the larger space and lost her balance. Her hand went out to catch herself, the door swung inward suddenly, and there was a crash!

Sleeping more lightly now, Dale lay with the abandon of a tired child; one arm flung above her head, fingers slightly curled. She breathed evenly, quietly — then suddenly, her eyes flew open in vague alarm. She heard soft footsteps running past her door. The house was wide awake. Feet were running rapidly down the stairs. Someone was moving swiftly out in the hall. Her alarm became focused. She sprang out of bed.

Something was happening to Hi!

It was completely dark in the hall, but a faint blue light from the night bulb in Hi's room guided her. There was a hump in the center of the bed. She leaned over and touched it. He wasn't there; the covers were bunched over emptiness. She was wasting time! Her bare feet slipped across the rug, felt the cold contact of the polished floor again, and then the colder contact of the tiles in the bathroom.

She snapped on the light bracing herself for the sight of Hi stretched upon the floor as once she had seen him — blue and convulsed. He was not on the floor, not in the room. Hurry!

Back down the hall again — the light switch was the whole length of the hall ahead of her at the top of the stairs — she would reach the study first. Where were the sounds she had heard? No running feet — no one anywhere. She wanted to call out, to scream; she couldn't.

Hi's pale light was her only guide, a faint glimmer, and just beyond would be the study door. She ran, hands out before her.

"Look in the study!" The door was open space, and just inside her foot hit against something, something heavy and metallic. The pain was so intense that she stumbled, threw out her arms trying to balance. Her outstretched hands touched warm flesh, but she couldn't stop. Momentum carried her forward; she felt the impact of a human body that fell away from her, slithering down with a thud at her feet.

Even before the short gasp, half snort, half groan, Dale knew that this was Hi. Somehow she found the light and went back to the small crumpled body, dropping down upon her knees beside it.

Hi's little black eyes looked up at her, blankly. His mouth was slightly open as if he had forgotten to snap it shut again, for Hi was not laughing. There was no mirth in him now. "Because," she thought with horror, "I pushed him down — and killed him."

And then not knowing she was going to, Dale screamed, a high shrill scream. It stopped abruptly; the sound of her own voice shocked her into silence, and reaching blindly for Hi's wrist, still hoping to find a pulse, she bent down close to catch his faintest breath.

The trickle of blood snaking down behind his ear was making a dark stain on the pale rug. Hi had slumped down and fallen flat on his back on the soft rug; enough to kill him, she knew — but it would be the shock — his heart. This was a wound.

She turned his head gently sideways and saw the sticky mess, the broken skin, the blood-matted hair. How could this have happened? Until now she had not noticed the small bronze bust of Rabelais which belonged upon the bookcase, lying on the rug, in line with the door just beyond her reach.

"That was what I kicked against," she thought. Impulsively, stretching over across Hi's body, she snatched it up, and blood smeared off on her hand. She gazed at the bright red streak across her palm, wondering.

Someone was calling her. She couldn't answer. It was Marcia's irritated voice coming from the hall.

"Where are you, Dale? What's the matter? Are you crazy, yelling like that?"

Then, standing in the doorway, Marcia's eyes grew large and frightened, as she saw Dale bending over Hi. She stopped, immobilized, upon the threshold.

"For God's sake! What have you done to him?" she demanded. Dale was too distraught to resent the question. She answered simply, "I'm afraid he's dead." The words weren't real to her. "I — I thought I had killed him," she gasped.

"How did you do it? Did you hit him with that thing?" Marcia's shocked voice, avid with interest, was certainly not grief-stricken and Dale saw in Marcia's face accusation, conviction.

"No, no, I didn't! Marcia, call Dr. Cotten, quickly," she begged,

154

reaching again for Hi's hand, watching him for the faintest flicker of life.

"There must be something — whisky! It's in Hi's room, the medicine cabinet — hurry!"

Then she looked up again and saw Marcia coming slowly toward her, until she stood quite close, looking down at Hi, and her eyes were hard meeting Dale's.

"I know death when I see it. I'll have nothing to do with this," she said coldly.

The menace in her words was lost on Dale. "Stay with him, then, I'll get it," she urged and rose quickly, adding — "and Dr. Cotten."

Marcia's hand pushed her back. "Don't put on an act, Dale. I'm not a fool! Hi is dead. He doesn't need a doctor. I'll call the police."

Suddenly Dale remembered last night and her last waking thoughts about Marcia. All her antagonism came flooding back. Angrily she brushed past her aunt, ran to the desk, lifted the phone and dialed the doctor's number. She heard it ring, stop, ring, stop, repeat, repeat. She flung down the receiver and dashed out of the room.

The hall was lighted now. "Marcia must have — " she didn't complete the thought. Racing to Hi's room, she opened his medicine cabinet. A flask was on the shelf and also the digitalis bottle. She took both. When she returned, Marcia was at the desk, the phone in her hand.

She was saying with a certain eagerness. "I wouldn't tarry, officer, I'm afraid you may find murder."

Dale only half heard. She flung herself down beside the huddled body, gently eased her hand behind Hi's head raising it a little. Tipped the bottle, pouring whisky carefully into his half-open mouth. It trickled out again. Hi's head lolled back, its weight shifting in her hand. His eyes mocked her, seeming to say, "It's no use, Monkey, pull down the curtain."

When Dale put the flask down and looked around, Marcia had gone. Very gently she let Hi's head rest back upon the rug. She straightened out the little bony legs in the hideous orange and black striped pajama pants, pulled the jacket down neatly, then slowly, quietly got to her feet.

155

"Call Bill first, then Father John."

Bill's voice was very sleepy.

"It's Dale. I need you. Yes. Hi. I can't get the doctor. I'll keep on trying but it's too late, Bill. Hi is dead. All right, get here as fast as you can."

She put down the phone, her hand trembling so she had to press down hard to break the connection and pick it up again to try one more time. Then it all seemed useless. Why call Father John? Wait until morning. Why call the doctor, even? Dale took her hand away from the phone, slowly. Marcia was right. *This was murder.*

Into the stillness, filling the room with the long low wail, came the distant sound of the police siren. It came again, growing louder, nearer, as it had come when Maggie was killed.

Strange that she could not feel anything now. Maggie would say she was in a trance. Before the police came, before Lt. Blackwell got here, she'd like to find out for herself.

Why was Hi here in this room? Who had given him such a blow? Had *she* knocked him down or was he actually falling when she ran into him? She stood numbly, her eyes avoiding Hi's body, glanced farther along the floor, saw *Death and the Miser* lying there face down. Above, the wall safe denuded of its covering, looking naked on the pilaster.

Dale moved then, more quickly, and went over and picked up the small Rabelais bronze. Had the blood really come from this?

"Yes, there *were* stains on the base — the sharp corner was what had done it — made that gash behind Hi's ear.

She was standing beside the pitifully small body, with the deadly thing in her hand, when Lt. Blackwell found her. She had not heard him come. His eyes fastened upon her.

Her knees gave way, she sank down slowly, her bright head bowed over Hi's inscrutable little face. She sent him a desperate silent cry for help. But Hi stared back at her with dreadful indifference.

The lieutenant was beside her now. He was taking the bronze away from her, his hand strangely wrapped in a clean white handkerchief. She felt the strength of his arm lifting her to her feet.

156

Chapter Twenty-Two

"THIS is it," thought Dale. "This is what Father John was preparing me for days ago." But he had also given her courage to go on. The circumstantial evidence might be overwhelmingly against her, but it wasn't the end. And she could fight — now that she knew that the fall had not killed Hi, because he would never have survived that blow. Even the medical examiner, who had come with the lieutenant, had said that, after his first quick examination. *So* — it had not been the fall nor her push when she ran into the study and into him; Hi was dying *then* — on his feet. It was the blow which she had *not* given him that had killed Hi.

It was not just because she had been standing there over Hi's dead body with the weapon in her hand when Blackwell came in that made things look so bad. "He could scarcely overlook that," Dale thought miserably, "but that was only the climax." All along the case had seemed to build up against her, had pointed to her and to Bill. What good was it to say that she loved Maggie and Hi? From the police point of view, motive and opportunity were obviously there. Blackwell wouldn't be doing his job if he didn't take cognizance of the facts. It was just as Father John had said.

"It will take something very factual and definite to wipe you two out of the case." Father John never minced matters. He had talked to her frankly and very seriously about what could happen. He had said, "Blackwell is a good cop, Dale, I know he is exploring every

157

possible angle, will run down every lead that he gets. I do not think he will overlook anything. But it is best for us to face *any* possibility — squarely. No blind spots or wishful thinking. You have courage enough." Then he had made his tone quite casual. "It is possible for Blackwell to arrest on strong circumstantial evidence, on suspicion of murder. It may come to that, whether in his heart he is convinced or not, that you or Bill is guilty. If the evidence is strong enough — it would be legitimate procedure."

Now the circumstantial evidence was strong enough, Dale thought. And Marcia, she was sure, had strengthened it — telling her tales — what *she* called facts, but colored by her; so as not to wipe out suspicion of guilt, but to establish it. Her's and Bill's. No, not Bill's yet. But just how long would it take Blackwell to fasten that wig on Bill? She could hear him say — "William Nelson Ballard, I arrest you for the murder of Mary Margaret Riley."

Nevertheless, she was going to fight. As long as she knew she had not caused Hi's death, she could fight. She would stick it out now and as long as she had to. Soon Bill would come — and Dr. Cotten, if Bill had found him. She longed for Father John. He would come as soon as he knew.

Dale was sitting on the old sofa in the library. The lieutenant had brought her here after the police had swarmed into the study, the medical examiner with them. Blackwell's men, she supposed. But the one or two who were in uniform somehow made it more authentic, more frightening, black leather holsters with pistols on their hips, very businesslike, very smart. But she had heard what the medical examiner had said before she left.

The lieutenant had kept her waiting — maybe intentionally, maybe not. He had said he was going to get statements from them all — everyone in the house *now*. Bill wasn't here, but Dale knew he would get Bill later. Blackwell would get them all — everyone connected with Hi. And, she still hoped, someone who wasn't. Father John had said he was a good cop.

The lieutenant was straddling a sturdy chair he'd hauled out of the pantry — he wasn't at home on Chippendale — and he was facing her with a firm, stubborn set to his jaw, polite and unimpressed by her arguments. He had warned her that whatever she said, etc. She knew that, but she went right on telling him just the same.

She had answered his questions — where they all had been — during the evening — what they were doing — the time they'd gone to bed — every detail, as best and truthfully as he could. Her statement was there in the hands of the young detective who'd taken it all down and snapped the notebook shut just as Marcia had barged in. Without by-your-leave or with-your-leave, she had flopped weakly down upon the same sofa, as far away from Dale as she could get.

The lieutenant ignored her and Dale did too, determined to finish what she was saying, knowing full well she was being foolish. She was even more convinced now that the case against her built up from the very beginning, not from this last bit of drama, which he seemed so sure had finished it. Nevertheless, she said it all and concluded with, "Do you really think, lieutenant, that I would have arranged such a scene for your benefit, and posed with the weapon in my hand beside my uncle's body so that you could come in at exactly the right moment? I thought murderers ran away."

"Better get dressed, Miss Moncure, this isn't helping any. I have your statement. I've let you talk. I have your aunt's and Liza's. Although Liza clammed up on me. Swore she knew nothing at all. That may be so, or she's protecting someone."

Marcia stirred uneasily, "*I* didn't say Dale killed him, officer. All *I* did," Marcia turned her head slightly toward Dale, "was to tell the truth — just what I saw — what you said." Then back to Blackwell. "I won't let you put the responsibility on me!" She drooped, collapsing with little gasps, building up to a climax familiar to Dale. "I won't have anything to do with it. I think I am going to faint."

Lt. Blackwell looked disgusted. He signaled to the young detective, who put away his notes and came forward. Blackwell said, "Get Mrs. Rowland back to her room. Your daughter's there," he said, "She'll look after you."

But Marcia protested. "Not way back there, no, I won't be isolated."

Dale had forgotten Liza. She remembered now, seeing her just

159

once; they had brushed past Liza in the hall, as Lt. Blackwell was hurrying her out of the study, down to the library.

Liza had been standing near the door, looking like a sleepwalker, looking awful, in her old corduroy robe hugged tightly about her, hair streaked back from the square pale blur of her face. Then they had reached the stairs, Blackwell racing her along, and Liza had been wiped out of her mind. But now her image was back — disquieting, tense, and fearful. Impulsively Dale turned to Marcia.

"Are you afraid of Liza?" she asked.

Marcia threw her a baleful look, evading the question, "Liza? Do you think Liza would lift a finger to help me? Besides she's absolutely dazed, not really awake, *yet*. I had to shake her — sleeping like the dead. Oh Lord, I didn't mean to say that!"

Dale let it go, Marcia made her sick. All this acting. She had been perfectly calm, looking down at Hi whom she pronounced dead, quite coolly; and it came to Dale now, with conviction, that Marcia had been not only cool, but calculating. Marcia did nothing spontaneously. There was always a motive of some sort. Dale hated that kind of secret scheming. Bring things out into the open. She had not planned it, but she decided to do that now.

"You wouldn't want to go to rest in Maggie's room would you, Marcia? You finished with Maggie's room when you took Maggie's money out of that little pink bank, didn't you?"

The lieutenant became attentive. Dale waited.

Marcia looked at her for the first time directly, and with not the slightest change of expression. "I haven't the vaguest idea of what you mean. *You* were in Maggie's room tonight. I told Lt. Blackwell that you seemed to be hiding in the dark, I didn't know why."

Then she relapsed into the frightened semi-invalid again. "I'll stay here, Blackwell," actually calling him by name. "Why do you want me out of the way? What right have you to tell me where I must rest?" She turned fiercely upon the lieutenant.

Dale got up. "Let her alone, lieutenant. I'll go dress now. But *that*," she said, looking into his eyes very steadily, "does not mean I'm *going anywhere*. I just would rather have on — something better,"

160

she faltered, glancing down at the spots on her pajama top — Hi's whiskey she had spilled — and down one green silk leg to her bare foot with the angry red streak on her instep. Then with a quick lifting of her chin, she said, "When Bill and Dr. Cotten come, they'll be here soon now, they'll tell you — " she didn't finish.

She moved away from him toward the door, with head very high, seeing nothing; blinded by tears, glad the lieutenant couldn't see. Her back was straight and she hoped her trembling knees didn't betray her. She stiffened her shoulders. Not much farther to the door. Why didn't Bill come? Would he bring Father John? Was he trying to find the doctor?

Out in the hall, the officer who had not gone with Marcia was walking a little behind. So — she was a prisoner even now. Here at home, she wasn't even going to be allowed to go from room to room. Reaching her own door, she paused and the detective stepped aside with a little courteous inclination of his head — letting her pass.

Then he followed her in. She stopped. What was he going to do? Surely not stay while she dressed? He moved over to the window, looked out casually — saw the sheer drop to the street — no porch — no fire escape. He walked over to the bathroom door, looked inside — no exit. The closet next, and all there was to see. "Just to make sure you are safe, Miss Moncure," and went outside closing the door behind him quickly, but she didn't hear his footsteps retreating. No footsteps — so, he was standing right outside, waiting for her. To be sure she was safe? How dumb did they think she was? But she didn't care, nothing mattered except to get into some clothes as fast as she could and to be ready for Bill. She would *not* go before she saw Bill. The lieutenant would have to carry her.

What did one wear when one went to jail? Dale could see Hi's little black eyes screwed up — and his shoulder shaking. "Better ask Emily Post, Monkey."

"Oh, Hi, I'm going to miss you!" She grabbed the first thing off the hanger in the closet, a dark green wool. Pulled out pants and bra and slip from her bureau drawer, her stockings and girdle. Then she stopped, hesitated, and decided. She'd take a quick shower. It might be the last one she'd ever have a chance at.

161

The hot water penetrated, soothed her nerves, and the cold livened her up a bit. She didn't feel so numb; her knees were steadier.

She was nearly dressed, standing in her stocking feet, running the comb through her hair; the shower had brought back her wave — it always did — when the tap came upon her door,

"Just wondered if you're OK." The polite voice of the shy young man who had never been assigned to a job like this before. She zipped up her dress, fastened the belt, dived into the closet to the shoe rack for her soft green flats, picked up her wristwatch, and opened the door.

The lieutenant was standing outside looking impatient. He took her by the elbow and hurried her along the passage and down the wide stairway. They reached the front door and Dale was despairing when it opened violently almost knocking the lieutenant backward, and Bill burst in with Dr. Cotten just behind him.

Bill stopped as if braked. He didn't need to be told a thing. The look in his eyes, raking Lt. Blackwell, then coming back to Dale, should have warned the police officer. Dale put out her hand. For Bill's sake there mustn't be a fight.

"Where are you going, Blackwell, with Miss Moncure? The answer had better be 'Nowhere'!" and Bill took Dale's hand, holding it so tightly that it hurt.

Then the doctor moved quickly between them, putting a restraining hand on Bill's arm.

"There are better ways of handling this, Bill, of stopping it," Dr. Cotten said. "He won't get far with this." Dale liked the expression on Dr. Cotten's face too. "You're heading for a mess of trouble, Blackwell, if you take this girl out of here, I warn you. There's a penalty for false arrest."

"You don't say, doc?" Lieutenant Blackwell pushed him aside, derisively. "And there's a penalty for obstructing an officer of the law."

He jerked his head, and the uniformed policeman who had been on the door and was watching this little scene with interest, stepped forward alertly, in one quick move pushing in front of the doctor, at the same time taking a firm grip on Bill's arm, holding him back.

162

Lt. Blackwell stepped through the two feet of cleared space and Dale was lifted nearly off hers. She didn't resist, she'd better go.

Inside Lt. Blackwell's car the young detective who had guarded her — for her own good — while she dressed, sat nearest the window. Blackwell driving and Dale was tucked between. They drove in silence.

Soon the car stopped. The great square building black against the night sky towered before them. They crossed the uneven brick-paved sidewalk, poorly lighted. She stumbled and the lieutenant steadied her. She jerked her arm away.

"Don't. I'm all right. I'd rather — " He let her go. After all where could she go? The young detective was on her other side. Where they did go was into the cavernous arch flush with the street that enclosed the stone steps leading up to the great iron-grilled doors.

Lt. Blackwell was met just inside by two policeman, who had unlocked the heavy doors just as they reached the top step — magically appearing from nowhere. But when she stepped inside, Dale saw they'd come from a room a few feet away. Now they all stood in the narrow corridor.

A voice was asking, "Name?" She looked up at the officer in front of her and realized he was speaking to her. She glanced at Blackwell, who nodded at her.

"Miss Dale Moncure," he said for her.

"Occupation?" Dale wondered what.

"Artist," she said quickly. "I'm on record, Hi, as an artist in the Hall of Fame — well, one kind of fame — murder. Stop it, stop it!" This was hysteria she knew.

They were moving now with her, guiding her over to another heavy wire-screened door. The officer who had questioned her reached out with a key and unlocked it. A bare flight of concrete steps led upward, enclosed in brick walls. Slowly they climbed. On the first landing a door, like the one at the bottom. Through the grating she could see a woman in white nurses's uniform waiting in the corridor on the other side to the door. They unlocked the door and turned her over to the matron. The door was locked again. The officers went back down and the matron looked at her.

Dale was surprised to see a kind warm smile. "Don't be scared,

163

dearie, everyone is friendly here. The girls call me Hattie, and in all the fourteen years I've been here not one has given me a sassy word. I'll have to take your watch. You'll get it back when you leave," Hattie said, running her trained hands lightly and swiftly over Dale's body, even slipping her soft kid slippers off and on again so dexterously that Dale just realized that she had been searched when the matron turned and walked quietly down the dimly lighted corridor, indicating that Dale was to follow. And Dale obediently, wonderingly, fell in behind her. "Did this woman know that downstairs on the record she was charged with murder — or suspicion of murder — what was the difference?" Dale thought bitterly.

They came to an open door. Hattie put a finger to her lips for silence. The room was lined with cots, double bunks; on most of them were sleeping women. A few were empty. Slipping quietly between them, they crossed the room and paused at an open door. Dale looked inside.

"Here's the dressing room and the shower," the matron whispered, pointing with a gesture of pride. The bare utility, ugly pipes, and damp gray floor. Dale thought of her own glazed pink tiles and shower curtain.

"You want to undress, I'll get you a nightgown."

Dale shrank from the idea, recoiling from the thought of being one of them, and shook her head in quick refusal. She didn't know what she had expected — certainly not this. A cell perhaps, with bars and a cot, but at least to be alone.

"OK," Hattie was saying, "It's up to you. It's nearly morning, anyway." She turned and led the way to a single cot. "This will be yours — you better lie down." The matron turned away and went silently past the sleeping forms, that looked merely like lumps and mounds to Dale, possessed of no humanity — long and short ones — with arms flung out, arms folded — dark heads, light heads — hair trailing or short — faces just dim pale ovals. Not people, not real live people with thoughts and desires, with hopes and fears.

The cot was clean, covered with a coarse muslin sheet. Dale sat down upon it gingerly.

164

Chapter Twenty-Three

FATHER JOHN smiled back at her with understanding, as Dale asked, her voice very sprightly, "How do you like having a jailbird for a godchild?" The gladness in her eyes at sight of him did not erase the dark circles under them, the emphasis of cheekbones too deeply hollowed underneath, nor the tautened jaw line that had lost a little of its youthful curve.

"My dear, you're Dale — in or out of jail!" he quipped. "You won't be here long. Bill is getting all the machinery started. If it weren't that today is Saturday, the court closed, and Judge Spiker out of town for the weekend, it would be faster," he told her with forced cheerfulness. "The same reason holds for my not being here earlier this morning; Father Don is away. Why didn't you call me last night, Dale?"

Before answering his question, she asked eagerly, "Bill? Bill got you this morning, didn't he? I knew he would. Is Bill all right?"

"Bill," said the priest, allowing himself a gleam of amusement, "Bill is a mere shell, with a fire raging inside. He's very busy lighting other fires under lots of people: the justice of the peace, Hi's lawyers, and he'd like a conflagration with Lt. Blackwell tied to the stake."

Dale quivered, the tears starting down from her cheeks, the smile remaining.

165

They were in a small cubicle in a room on the first floor assigned to visitors. Just enough space for the two benches and table between.

"It looks like a booth in a drugstore," Dale thought with the mental vagary that seemed to possess her. "We should be having cokes." And then she answered his question:

"I didn't call you because it seemed a shame to wake you up — and useless. It was too late, Hi was dead. I think I was a little stunned. I wished, how I did wish later, that I had.

"And down here, I could have. Hattie says they let you. I could have phoned when they brought me in. But I didn't ask. I guess they thought I didn't want to call anyone. When can I see Bill?" she urged.

"I'm afraid you can't, my child. That's one reason Bill is burning up. The lieutenant refuses." Father John raised a deprecating hand. "Oh yes, he has the authority, for that and for another thing. He won't let the justice of the peace be called in to arrange your bail. 'No special treatment.' There'll be no release today.

"So we'll have to wait for Spiker, Monday: regular routine. The judge has to determine the amount, you know. But don't worry, it will be just another day, Dale. The red tape takes a little time, but Hi's lawyers will take care of you. Young Darrel in the firm is Bill's friend too. Thank goodness, Dale, they *are* who they are. Walters and Watkins, a tradition in Brambleton."

"Two more nights!" Dale shuddered. Her head began to ache. She had not gone down to breakfast.

"What have you eaten this morning?" Father John asked.

"Can you read my tummy, as well as my mind and my soul?" Dale grinned. "Hattie, the matron, was good to me. She brought me a cup of coffee."

"You eat your lunch, whether you want it or not," Father ordered. "And now let's get down to business. Tell me everything you can remember. I haven't talked to anyone yet except Bill, and only a bare outline of things then. I came right here."

"But will we have time? Will they let you stay?"

"Stay and come again when I wish. Priests are allowed that, Dale. They are liberal with the clergy. But this is Saturday. I'll have

166

confessions this afternoon, and two morning appointments, so begin, Dale. I must know all that has happened since Maggie's death. I think I know everything before that, but the lawyers don't and they will ask for every detail. This will help. There may be something which you haven't thought of, something significant."

So Dale began, and when she had finished a good half hour later there was nothing they could put a finger on and say, "This is it," but there were things to consider.

The wig in the file case. Like the cat in the well — "Who put it in? Who pulled it out?" Liza *had* been in the upstairs hall nearly bumping into her, but Dale had thought at the time that she was escaping from Marcia.

"I hope," Dale said, "that the lieutenant hasn't caught up with that yet. He'll think Bill wore it. Bill's just your size, Father — he hasn't yet, has he?"

"I don't know," Father said in answer to her jumbled question. "Bill said he had gone to the Rowlands."

"To talk to Walter?" Dale asked. "I told you how peculiar Walter was last night in the study. I wonder what he lost, if anything. Maybe the note Marcia'd found in Maggie's things. That note was meant for you Father. Did Walter bring it to you?"

The priest looked blank.

"I'll bet that's it," Dale said. She had told him of staying the night before in Maggie's room. Of finding the pink bank, empty, except for a slim gray notebook and some snapshots.

"That was her account book, and I *know* Maggie's money had been there too; Marcia took it, Father."

"Wait, Dale, wait. You don't actually know. You'll have to get further before you judge. You've nothing yet but circumstantial evidence."

"Yes — and that's enough, isn't it. It has got me here, hasn't it?"

"Tell the fingerprint men to try the pink bank, Father. Mine will be there, but underneath there may be Marcia's. And the key in Maggie's bag. I didn't touch that! That would clinch it, wouldn't it?"

"I can't tell you, Dale."

But Father John said gravely, "I am sure that Blackwell and his men do not need to be told anything. They probably know more than you do by now. Didn't you accuse Marcia of meddling in Maggie's room — even talk of taking the money, right before Blackwell?"

"Yes," admitted Dale, "I did. I wanted to face her with it unexpectedly. But, as usual, Marcia was very smooth, got out of it by accusing *me* instead."

"Don't worry, Blackwell wouldn't miss. He has, I'm sure, all of this and more, but I doubt if he'd be willing to tell *me*. Besides, I wanted your version of it," Father John said. "We must, of course, report the matter of the little account book. He'll want that, if he hasn't got it already."

"I don't know," Dale explained. "I didn't say anything about the account book before Blackwell. I didn't want Marcia to know I had it. I don't know where it is now. I left it under my pillow in Maggie's room. I just forgot about it later."

"If you think that Marcia was interrupted," asked the priest, "so that she missed the notebook, who do you think it might have been?"

"I don't know, Father." Dale's eyes widened with conjecture. "It could have been Maggie's murderer, coming to find the $25,000 — scared off when he discovered Marcia was there. But it might not have been anyone. She might just not have noticed the notebook. I was only guessing."

"You may be right. I don't believe there are two murderers. I believe that the man — because it was a man, Dale, who took my place and killed Maggie — was here again tonight to get the money. This may have been his second try. Hi heard him and went into the study. No one knows, I suppose, whether he got it or not."

"Someone else *could* have been looking for the money, Father. Marcia certainly wanted money for that house very badly."

"And she had it by then, if she took Maggie's." Father John reminded Dale.

"I can't help wondering," Dale said thoughtfully, "why Liza keeps harping on saving Walter? I know she's neurotic on the subject, makes mountains out of mole hills, ends up with such silly reasons, but just the same it must be something to set her off. She looks scared to death all of the time now."

"I doubt if it amounts to anything — something she imagines — but Blackwell isn't blind to the way anyone is acting, and you, poor child, stand way out in front of the rest. I tried to warn you, that this *could* happen to you."

"Yes," Dale said — wondering how she might have avoided it. "Thanks."

"All right, Dale, try to be patient. You won't be here long."

"Yes, Father, and I wasn't trying to incriminate anyone else — only talking to *you*."

"I understand, my child." The priest stood up reluctantly. "I have to go now. Remember, I'm praying for you."

"Father John, tell Bill please to go to see Sister Dennis," Dale said earnestly. "I know she'll be worrying. Tell her I'm all right. Tell Bill it will make me feel much better if he will just go to see her for me."

"He'll go, Dale, I'll see that he does, and I'll be back later, if I can, but don't count on it. I will come tomorrow, certainly." Father laid his hands gently upon the straight shoulders. Then, stooping, he picked up his old clerical hat from the bench. His face was set, and he left quickly.

Dale stood for a minute watching him before she felt the touch on her arm reminding her where she was. She'd almost forgotten with Father John here.

She was escorted down the hall, the doors were unlocked and locked, as the routine of last night was repeated. Upstairs, Hattie waiting; the officer returning his charge; the matron taking over. The door locked behind her again.

At lunchtime when the intercom announced it, she made herself go down. The trays were all set and waiting on the tables. They just went in and took any seat. The girl beside her, looking bored, slumped down and began eating hungrily. This surprised Dale. She raised her eyes, looking around at these women who were here, herded together, each very much alone. Here were types — some paintable — she felt a faint stirring of interest then. One, very young, across from her, beautiful really, with tilted eyes and a sullen mouth. Next to her, a stark hard face, unrevealing. And on down the line, people alive now, human, talking, eating. Some old and tired and just plain sad. The girl opposite would make an interesting model to paint. Paint! when would she be painting again — or ever *want* to paint? That was another world, too remote to imagine. She'd never paint again. "I'm sorry, Hi."

The food wasn't bad, but Dale couldn't swallow. She tried; Father John had told her that she must. The coffee helped. At last it was over. Back upstairs, back on her cot, she didn't want to talk. Some of them were — even laughing — kidding each other. Eyes rested on her and glanced away; a whispered word or two, a nod in her direction. She would not meet them. Finally she dozed; and then she was awake. Hattie was there beside her. Father John was back.

When she went down this time, Father looked tired and older. Her heart thudded.

"I didn't expect you until tomorrow. Is anything worse?" she asked before she took her seat sliding on the bench facing him, the table between.

"I'm very sorry for Liza, Dale," Father said, without preamble. "She gave Hi the overdose of digitalis." Father sat down and waited a minute for Dale to say something, then he went on. "I was just coming out of the church," he said. "She came to talk to me. I took her over to my study. She wanted me to tell you. I hardly think she would have confided in me, otherwise."

Dale simply stared. "But why?" she finally asked.

Father John reached into his pocket and brought out a square white envelope.

"You better read what she says, then I will fill in for you, since she asked me to, Dale, and I am glad she did. You have a right to know, although this doesn't clear things up. We still don't know who killed Maggie, who killed Hi. She didn't talk much afterward. She seemed to change her mind and clammed up again."

Dale took the envelope and opening it quickly, pulled out a sheet of paper, which didn't fit and had been folded crookedly.

170

"I'm sorry you're in jail because I don't think you killed Uncle Hi. I didn't either, Dale, but I am more a murderer than you are because I did put all that digitalis in Hi's medicine glass that day Maggie sent me back to take off my galoshes. It was easy, everything was right there on the shelf. Father John will tell you why I did it, I don't want to write it. Don't tell anyone *why* I did it. You can tell that I gave the overdose to Uncle Hi if you have to. I don't care what happens to me. And another thing I did that I've told Father John, I better tell you too, in case you get blamed for that — but so far I don't think anyone knows. So keep quiet about it if you can. I took some money out of Hi's wallet. You know how he always kept it full — I took it for the same reason that I gave the digitalis. But it was harder to do — watching my chance — and I couldn't take enough at a time for fear he'd miss it. I was pretty desperate, so the digitalis was the quickest way. This may sound mixed up to you, but Father John will explain. I'm sorry now, for you, Dale. You've always been nicer to me than anyone else. Walter hates me, and Nick has turned out to be horrible! I guess I'm through."

Dale folded the paper carefully, slowly, and handed it back to the priest. "How awful! Poor kid, she sounds so bitter. Why did she do it, Father?"

"Liza," said Father John, "has had a pretty rough time of it. She acted impulsively to save Walter, who is short in his accounts at the bank. Nick said several thousand, I think, and told her that Walter couldn't cover up much longer — she'd better scare up the money, or else. She thought then that Nick's only concern was Walter. . . . Saving Walter became an obsession. Nick kept pushing her right to the edge, and over she went. Saving Walter made destroying Hi seem negligible. She says she didn't even think of Hi."

Father John paused, glanced at Dale who was sitting rigid, eyes fixed upon his face unwavering. "To her, Hi was just an old man, about to die soon anyway; an obstacle between Walter and the money that meant safety. She was merely pushing the obstacle aside."

Father John went on explaining Liza, "That's what she *says* she felt; I doubt if she knows, really. Liza wouldn't analyze. Here was a chance and she took it. She's been terrified for Walter ever since — ironical, isn't it — because she's glad she didn't succeed."

"But why kill Hi?" Dale asked genuinely puzzled. "That wouldn't help her find the money."

"I don't think it was that, not the elusive $25,000. Stop a minute and think. Her mother has brought her up on the fable that Hi was depriving them all of their rightful inheritance. Not the truth, of course; for Hi was bound by his brother's will, to keep that trust fund intact as long as he lived."

"I know that. I tried once to explain it to Liza," Dale said, "but she didn't believe me, and Aunt Marcia thinks what she wants to think."

"At Hi's death, Liza knew that her mother would come into her own and could pay Walter's deficit. She thought it was the only chance, that there was no other money."

"And then," Dale said, "Marcia bought the house — Maggie's money, but Liza couldn't know that. No wonder she was wild." Remembering the recriminations outside Maggie's door. . . . Could it have been only last night?

"Marcia can pay now, and will, to save her own pride. Does she know about Walter yet?"

"No," Father John answered. "Liza said that since she'd failed, there was no use in telling her mother. She just went on trying to protect Walter, getting no thanks. Only recently has she been tormented by her own sense of guilt. Now, she says, Walter can tell Marcia."

"Walter has been cruel," Dale said vehemently.

"Walter doesn't know how much Liza knows, not all she's been doing. She didn't dare tell him." Father John smiled. "Give the devil his due."

"How did Nick know?" Dale asked.

"I have no idea. Nick isn't a very desirable character, I'm afraid."

"She says he's horrible, I wonder what he did to her. She thought she was in love with him. Do you suppose she gave him the money

172

she took, to give to Walter, and he kept it himself instead? She must have let Nick handle it, since she didn't dare do it herself. She wasn't supposed to know."

"She didn't talk about Nick." The priest shook his head regretfully. "Walter is still her obsession, in spite of what she says."

"Walter will be saved now, only because Hi is dead," Dale summed up sadly. Then her eyes became large and startled with that idea. "Father, do you think Walter — ? Could it have been Walter? I heard so many footsteps — running — where did they all go? Who were they? I told Lt. Blackwell that, but I don't suppose it helps."

"Walter says he was at home in bed. There is no proof that he wasn't. Bill is clear. Blackwell had put a tail on Bill when he went home. . . . Don't look indignant; it was a good thing he did."

"I don't see any use in telling Lt. Blackwell what Liza did, unless we have to, for Bill's sake. It isn't as if she'd killed Hi."

"That's generous of you, Dale, but . . ." Father John frowned doubtfully.

"Just let's keep it for a while," Dale said. "Liza's had a lot of grief. Why pile it on?"

"Don't get your values mixed, Dale. The truth is always important."

"What *is* the truth?" Dale asked raising questioning blue eyes to Father John's.

"Your innocence and Bill's of any complicity in these crimes," the priest said firmly. "But I'll agree to wait for a while. I can't see that that will do any harm. I'll keep this statement of Liza's." He tucked it into an inside coat pocket.

Father John stood up in the narrow space. "Now I must go, but there is one more thing. I'm sorry to have to tell you this. I said Maggie's funeral Mass today."

Dale's face changed. "Without *me!* I wanted to be there!" Her voice broke. "Who was?"

The priest looked unhappy. "I know, Dale," he spoke very softly, "but it had to be today, or wait until Monday. Too long. No funerals on Sunday. Maggie's friends were there, of course, and I was surprised to see Walter, but Walter respects the conventions. And Liza was way in the back. I did not see Marcia. Bill, of course, went. Rosina was in the front pew. Bill sent some beautiful white roses. Maggie loved them, he remembered, and so he sent them from you."

"Thursday," thought Dale. "It seems so much longer than that. Both Maggie and Hi, in these two days," she said, making no effort now to check her tears.

"Yes," Father John answered grimly. "Thursday, Maggie; Hi on Friday night. Whoever wanted that money, wanted it quickly."

"I wonder," Dale said, "if the killer is satisfied now."

After Father John had left and she was back upstairs again with the long night ahead of her, Dale decided that if the killer *was* satisfied, then it would be one of the Rowlands. They have everything to gain by Hi's death. And as for Maggie's — although none of them could have been in the confessional posing as Father John, they could have hired someone to do it. Nothing was too fantastic to imagine now. For and against, Dale's thoughts jumped. Walter was too small, and Father had insisted it was a man. Besides, Walter really had been in the bank all Thursday. Her new idea that the Rowlands might have had someone else play a part in Maggie's death put an entirely new light upon the whole thing.

Marcia and Liza might not know the right person for the job, but Walter might. She speculated about Nick. It could be Nick, but in spite of what Liza had said, she had rather liked Nick. Would Nick have struck Maggie down? And how would he know about the safe? Even Walter didn't — or she thought he didn't. The existence of the safe, she thought, had been kept secret. But someone had found it behind the picture.

The Bosch painting — down on the floor — face down, had left the safe bare and exposed. She remembered vividly the stains on the back of the old canvas, the discolorations. Had the picture fallen or been taken down in a hurry, when something had frightened the thief — or thieves? She had heard so many footsteps.

But when she had reached the study, no one was there. No one but poor little Hi. Had he been alone? There might have been someone hiding then, and slipping away after Hi fell. She had not thought

174

of that at the time, being so desperately afraid — thinking *she* had caused his death. And then Marcia had arrived.

Marcia! *Where had Marcia been?* Had she really just arrived when she came calling down the hall? Marcia could have been in the study, could have been there — and left — and come back again to accuse her; to phone the police.

Marcia had taken Maggie's money. Could she be so pushed for funds that she must bludgeon Hi for more? No. Not that way. Marcia's method would be veiled and cunning. Marcia might have given Hi the digitalis. But Liza had done that. Liza might have hit Hi in some wildly fanatical desire to rescue Walter. Liza *had* tried once to kill — later she might have tried again — succeeded. Her talk with Father John could be a very clever trick "to disarm us." Dale considered it. "I doubt if Liza is that subtle." But Liza had been outside the study door, the only person Dale had actually seen. How had she gotten there, if, as Marcia had claimed, she was dazed with sleep. Would Marcia invent an alibi for Liza? And there was Liza's note — sounding honest and tragically sincere.

It all seemed too fantastic, hopelessly confused. Yet she must try and keep on trying, if she and Bill were to be cleared. For years all of the Rowlands, even Mary, who seemed less like the others, had been looking forward to Hi's death as a sort of release; to the time when they could do and have what they wished. For years — but why now? Father John had said that? What had brought things so suddenly to a head — making Hi's death *now* so vital that murder became worth the risk?

And then, in a white light of revelation, Dale thought she saw the reason. She and Bill, ripe to be picked. There would be very little risk for the Rowlands. Marcia, Walter, and Liza all knew quite well what Lt. Blackwell with enough circumstantial evidence might do; they had helped him from the start, building up evidence against her.

This had been the ideal time — when she and Bill were wide open. They must have known the $25,000 was lost — Walter would know that Bill had gotten it from the bank. Of course he would. In spite of all the secrecy — they knew!

Tomorrow she would talk to Father John again. Her altruism was vanishing toward Liza, toward all of them. Dale felt now only a sense of outrage. If she was right, then she and Bill had been very nice puppets in a plot by all the Rowlands, or any one of them!

But Dale knew, too, that she was overwrought, perilously so, and tried for self-control. She moved her head from side to side to ease the aching. It was all she could do to stay on that narrow cot and be silent. Never, as long as she lived, would she forget this Saturday — would it ever come to an end?

Slowly the first gray light from the windows made morguelike silhouettes on the cots around her. She closed her eyes against the morbid fancy, and then from sheer exhaustion fell asleep.

Chapter Twenty-Four

THE first gray dawn of Sunday proved a sample of the day. The skies stayed gray, heavy, and humid between intervals of hard, slanting rain. If the jail had been depressing before, it was almost unbearable now to Dale, counting the hours and the minutes until Monday and release.

A break came at last, in the appearance of young Darrel, representing his firm. "Just to tell you that Mr. Watkins, who is going to handle your case, will want to see you in his office tomorrow. The afternoon will be better, as most of the morning will have gone by the time we get you out of here. You'd probably like to go home first." She would, Dale agreed.

Darrel lowered his voice, "This visit is a sort of proxy for Bill, because they can't refuse your lawyer. Bill says to tell you he will come with me tomorrow. He's out there now." Darrel's face became one broad grin. "Like a Peri outside the gates of Paradise — not my idea of the pearly gates — but Bill would rather get past them than get to heaven."

" 'Fools rush in —' Tell him to be careful," Dale said.

"He wants a firsthand report on you. How you look, how you feel. . . . It's heartbreaking, Dale," Darrel gave another wide grin, "to see St. Lawrence on the grill out there! I may call you Dale, I hope. Bill and I were in grade school together."

Dale's laugh sounded unaccustomed to her own ears. She liked

177

this Darrel, his red crew cut, his bright amber eyes, and the large mouth that had been stretched in its spacious grin since she had sat down opposite him. The cubicle seemed to be her own private conference room now.

Darrel sobered, and she liked his calm, judicious scrutiny, which was discerning and sympathetic. She found it a little too penetrating and said quickly, with a shade of embarrassment, "Tell Bill I'm fine."

The guard was approaching, coming to the door, peering in. "You have only a few more minutes, Miss Moncure, and Dr. Cotten is here."

Darrel rose, put out his hand formally. "Thanks, Miss Moncure. Mr. Watkins will contact Judge Spiker the first thing in the morning." He bowed and hurried away, a dignified attorney, swinging his briefcase.

"Doctor, lawyer, priest — " Dale enumerated, but not Bill! Darrel's visit had been immensely cheering though and, to be entirely fair, she supposed she must admit that it wasn't just Blackwell, being mean and arbitrary. Bill was under suspicion too; therefore, no collusion. And if the lieutenant booked Bill, they would put him behind bars, making a felon of him. All those confined in cells were felons, Hattie had told her; but in this jail, only men were put in cells — never women. That, Dale supposed, had kept Miss Dale Moncure — charged with suspicion of murder — out of one.

She pulled her thoughts away. Bill wasn't in here, and wasn't going to be. And she, going out tomorrow — with God's help and Hi's lawyers — would never come back!

Dale smiled a greeting as Dr. Cotten was allowed to pass the officer and come quickly toward her. If Father John had looked worn and older, the doctor looked really sick. But he waved aside her concern; disclaimed fatigue.

"I've been busy, child, busy. All yesterday, a round of cases; couldn't get here to tell you how deeply I regret this business. I tried to cope with Blackwell, but you saw how it was."

Ever since Dale could remember, Dr. Cotten had pulled her through all her ailments — but *this* he couldn't cure.

"I would have given anything to have prevented this," he said. "I was mistaken in thinking Blackwell wasn't really going to bring

178

it off. Never mind, tomorrow you will be back with us. I know the house will seem lonely without Hi, but remember, Dale, it must have happened before too long. Hi was a very sick man."

"But not like this," Dale protested. "Not — like this."

"I don't think he felt much pain, Dale. I'd doped him up, remember."

" 'A mild sedative,' Bill said. You're just trying to comfort me. Hi was awake; had come into the study. Someone hit a dreadful blow." Dale shuddered, and Dr. Cotten passed his hand wearily over his eyes.

"Still, Dale, his senses were not acute; I assure you, it was very quick — mercifully so. There was internal hemorrhage — he'd have died anyway. You must remember that. I have to hurry back to the Rowlands now. Liza — or maybe I shouldn't tell you." He stopped, his eyes brightened, Dale thought, with anger, and then he said, "Poor little fool, Liza took nearly a bottle of her mother's sleeping pills last night."

He was not really angry; this was the doctor's reaction always when truly disturbed. She remembered well how he'd frightened her when she was little, glowering down at her resentfully for being sick, then dispelling the fear, speaking so kindly, so gently.

He was whispering softly now, and glowering fiercely. "There's another thing. I had better tell you — Liza's lucky. That girl was an incipient paranoiac."

The policeman came and stood beside them. "I'm sorry the time is up, doctor."

"Leaving, officer," Dr. Cotten said. "Dale, my girl, I am doing some great things in my laboratory. Almost all last night — tonight again — and this time, I hope — "

Dale looked up at him. "I'll hear about it tomorrow, doc. . . ." He didn't seem to hear her. He was gazing over her head, rapt.

"I'm on the right track — " The officer looked at Dale, who nodded. Then, a little louder, more peremptorily, "Time's up, Dr. Cotten."

"I'm sorry," Dale said. "Thank you for coming."

"Tomorrow, Dale, tomorrow." He waved from the door, before turning into the long dim corridor.

179

Dale stood quite still, realizing belatedly what he had really told her; what he must have meant; *that Liza was dead.*

She couldn't call him back to ask him more. He had gone. Dale still could not believe that Liza had killed herself.

Much later, when Father John came, he verified it. Liza had taken her mother's sleeping pills and Marcia had found her this morning, looking peaceful at last.

She had been told; but she had been slow — too slow in grasping the fact of another tragic death. Dale wondered now; *would* Liza have become a mental case, or was the doctor, now that she was gone, making her death seem a merciful end. Dale suspected that was just what Dr. Cotten was trying to do.

But Liza's death was not a personal loss. It was a shock, making her sad, because all of the girl's life seemed now to have been sad. How little understanding and affection she had had from any of them. Dale reproached herself for not trying harder to help. But Liza had been a hard person to help, to get at — dogged and sullen — rebuffing kind intentions. And there'd been toughness in her, despite her evident misery; an ability to ride things out, which Dale had never questioned. She had been like a sturdy craft, unlovely but durable, plowing along through heavy waters. There'd never been a thought in Dale's mind of Liza's being submerged — finally and irrevocably — sunk.

Perhaps, she blamed herself, she would have been more perceptive if she had cared more, but even Liza's note had not aroused her fears. Father John was blaming himself, too. Dale suspected that between the two of them, there was more sorrow for Liza than her own family would feel. After the first shock, she doubted if they'd even miss her. Marcia had not seemed to have the least affection for her unprepossessing daughter.

"Try not to dwell on it tonight, Dale," was Father John's parting advice. She didn't *want* to think about it, and she couldn't bear the thought of another night — but she must get through the long, slow, endless hours again.

Dale had forced herself to succumb to Hattie's preferred gown. She couldn't stay in her clothes forever. But in it, she felt stripped and defenseless, and deeply humiliated, shrinking beneath the cover of thin blankets, wishing to vanish entirely.

Monday — bringing with it a nervous excitement, mounting and mounting in her; the fear that something had gone wrong; that Darrel wouldn't come; that Bill would not be with him: that Bill was ill; or that the judge had not returned and they'd refused to fix the bail.

Then, sooner than she had expected, Hattie was giving her back her watch and she was saying good-bye with a surprising rush of affection. The officers were guiding her down the stairs, being helpful, kindly. Doors were opening for her. Bill was there! Bill and Darrel. The fresh air! The bright street! She was in the car, relief rendering her inarticulate. Darrel driving; Bill with arms around her. Darrel with eyes concentrated upon nonexistent traffic problems.

At the house he let them out, breaking into that enormous grin, waving gaily — gone. She and Bill went in together.

The wide hall welcomed her with sunlight and a bouquet of yellow roses on the pier table. Rosina's smile was nearly as dazzling. Bill drew her persistently along to the library, stood still, took her coat, let it drop in a heap on the floor — drew her into his arms.

At last she pulled away from him with a smothered little laugh, and he released her. Rosina was making noises — elaborate preliminary rattling of dishes outside. And then the door swung wide and she came pushing in, a beaming smile surmounting the huge loaded tray she was carrying high with arms extended.

"Mr. Bill, just set up that card table over in the corner and you two can have your lunch right here, nice and cozy, no use bothering to go to the dining room. Miss Dale, honey, now you eat, and let me see some of them hollows fill out in your cheeks."

But as Dale drank the hot coffee and nibbled at the really tempting salad, her short moment of unclouded happiness already had begun to recede. She tried to cling to it; but looking over at Bill, who was starting on the sandwiches — food and love mixed well for Bill — Dale knew that this was just a reprieve. So much must intervene; the trial — the waiting — and what verdict?

She wanted to escape it all, to hold it at bay, or at least to circumvent it. A desperate longing for security, for their happiness together, all at once became unbearable.

"Bill," she said eagerly, "why do we have to wait? Why not go now, straight to Father John? Let him marry us now, this minute!"

Bill slowly lowered his cup. Astonishment and a look of pure delight spread over his face. Excitement flared up in his eyes, brilliant, sparkling, for a few moments, and then became subdued, diminished. The tenderness that replaced it stirred Dale more deeply. But then to her dismay, she saw negation.

He looked away from her, his mouth becoming firm, his jaws settling into that stubborn line she knew so well, and shook his head.

She couldn't believe it.

"Are you turning me down, Bill?" she asked, smiling still, clinging to a shred of humor.

"I've a long row to hoe before I can support my wife." There was no doubt about it, he meant it.

"But, Bill, not *now!* It's different now. We'll have plenty of money."

"You'll have plenty," Bill corrected her. "I know, Dale." Bill thoughtfully picked up his cup from the sandwich plate, where he had landed it, and put it back precisely into the center of its saucer. "Darrel said they'd read Hi's will. You'll have a whale of a lot, and so will Marcia." He looked up smiling, "All the Rowlands can stop bellyaching now. And what do you think? Father John gets *Death and the Miser!* Not that he wants it!" Bill laughed, "I took it over to him yesterday — thought I might as well. It's sitting on the floor of his study — face to the wall."

"Is that *all* that Hi left to Father John?" Dale asked, wonderingly, diverted in spite of herself — concerned.

"I don't know," Bill said doubtfully. "Darrel didn't tell me everything. I guess he shouldn't have told me what he did."

"Well, it won't matter," Dale said. "We'll take care of Father John and The Nursery. . . . Now you needn't try to change the subject, Bill."

But Bill was leaning forward, and Dale sensed his suppressed excitement. "We'll talk about all that later. But listen, Dale, this is important. You didn't know it, but you gave me a lead. I think it's hot. I won't tell you yet, but I'm going to follow it up right away."

Ordinarily Dale would have been impressed, excited, but now she hardly listened. Bill was fobbing her off with a red herring, evading the issue.

"Bill, it's perfectly ridiculous to talk about waiting until you can support me. The money will be *ours* — not mine. If you have to be so proud, you can pay it back to the estate, when you are rich and famous."

Bill looked at her now, miserable but unyielding. And Dale began to realize, though refusing to believe, that he really meant this utter quixotic foolishness!

She tried to be calm, searching for logic, the right words; the kind of practical talk that men would have, convincing, common sense.

"Bill, I think Hi was sorry. I was going to tell you. He was giving in — "

"I'll be damned if I'll live on Hi's money!" Bill's jaw was jutting now. "But we can fight that out later, right now I am going to concentrate on this thing I've got on to. I'd better get along."

"What's so important as our future, Bill? You're just trying to sidetrack!"

"You think this is easy? Saying 'No'?"

Dale took a firm last grip upon her self-control. "I don't blame you for being resentful, Bill. It was a dirty deal, but in the end he was sorry — he was going to make it right. I was going to tell you — but I never got the chance."

Bill looked stern now, and white. "Please, Dale, give me credit for being bigger than to hold a grudge like that. But I've always said I'm going to support — "

"Well," Dale interrupted, "can't you change? Can't you say something *else?* The money will not be Hi's."

"How does that change things?" Bill asked with such quiet, stubborn insistence that Dale wanted to burst into tears. A rising tide of fury saved her from abject weeping, and good old-fashioned temper took over now, without reason or restraint.

"Maybe it doesn't," she declared, getting to her feet, "because the real trouble isn't the money at all. That's just an excuse. The truth

183

is — that you've changed. You don't want to marry me! You don't love me any more! I should think you'd have the courage to come right out and say so!"

In some deep recess of her consciousness, Dale was appalled. Was she screaming — at *Bill* — screaming all these awful things? The last vestige of endurance had deserted her, and helplessly, disastrously, she plunged on to a shattering finish.

"If you really loved me, you wouldn't care a fig about the money. You wouldn't want to wait a minute — much less years — until you're rich — and old! All right wait! You can have a nice long wait. Forever!"

Bill listened in stunned silence; then he jumped up, his long legs tangling with the table. He came around it, knocking against it, clattering dishes, and grasped Dale by her shoulders, with both hands, and not too gently.

"Stop it, Dale! I'm going — I've got something, I tell you! When you come to your senses, I'll come back." He shook her again, and turned, pounding across the room. The library door slammed. The front door slammed. Reverberations diminished into silence. Then Dale very slowly sat down again and stared at the wrecked table.

Bill's cigarette was smoldering, burning a spot in the linen cover. She watched it burn until the hole was large and black, and the cigarette a hollow ash, lying in the midst of its own ruin.

The phone rang several times before she heard it.

Chapter Twenty-Five

WALTER'S voice was peremptory; but even in the midst of her own tumultuous emotions, Dale was conscious of anxiety and urgency in Walter.

"That you, Dale? I'm glad you're out of the hoosegow. I need you. I wish you'd come over here right away. It's important. I guess you've heard all that's been going on — all the dirt?"

Was he feeling her out? Was this a reference to himself? She doubted it and decided on caution. She said sincerely, "I've heard about Liza, Walter, and I am sorry. But I've just got home and can't come right away. I'll try to make it later."

"Later won't do. I tell you, Dale, I've got to see you at once. There's something very important for you to do, and you'll be mighty sorry if you don't. I'd take care of it myself, but I'm crippled up with a sprained ankle — damn it. Don't waste any time. I'm saying nothing more on the phone."

Dale hesitated, then asked, "Is it about Liza, something I should know?"

"Liza isn't the half of it. If you don't get here soon, it'll be too late."

"All right, I'll come."

Dale put down the phone with very mixed feelings, thinking, Walter was pretty cool — never a word of greeting — or regret — just

"Step on it!" Not even any decent feeling about Liza, poor kid. He didn't deserve, never had deserved, her utter devotion. He needn't think he would ever again have anyone to dance attendance on his every whim — but she would go and see what was so vital.

This thing of Walter's might keep her from thinking, from going back over that past half hour. She didn't want to hear her own voice yelling the things she had yelled — nor Bill's either. She tried to make her mind a blank. She succeeded only in making it a record which wouldn't turn off.

Dale raced upstairs. She'd shower and dress — fresh things from her skin out — get the taint of the jail off her body — she'd never get it out of her mind. Dale didn't try to speculate about the thing Walter was going to give her to do. No doubt it would turn out to be more important to him than to her. But she wouldn't risk turning it down. She did speculate about Walter himself.

His shortage at the bank had amazed her; she had never doubted his honesty in his relation to the bank. His self-importance, his selfishness, she knew. Dale thought of his indifference, his utter lack of feeling about Liza. "Liza isn't the half of it!" How could he!

She selected her comfortable tweeds, slipped into loafers, whipped the comb through her hair, remembering the last time she had stood before her mirror and done this very thing: the young detective outside waiting, then saying, "Are you all right, Miss Moncure?"

No, she wasn't, and might never be, Dale thought miserably, but at least for the present she could open that door and go down the hall and out of the front door without anyone's stopping her. Then desolation descended upon her. Freedom was a mockery now. Where did she want to go without Bill? She had sent him away — and she had said he could wait forever!

As she reached the foot of the stairs, she met Rosina, looking astonished, seeing her alone — leaving the house.

"Law, Miss Dale, where you goin'? Where's Mr. Bill?"

"Thanks for the nice lunch, Rosina. Mr. Bill has gone."

"Where you going, Miss Dale? What must I tell Mr. Bill when he comes back, honey?"

"I'm going over to the Rowlands, and I don't think Mr. Bill is

186

coming back any time soon, so it doesn't make any difference what you tell him."

Rosina didn't answer, and when Dale glanced back she was standing still, with a worried expression on her usually happy face, watching Dale go down the front steps.

Getting her car from the old carriage house, which Dale used as a garage, feeling the wheel under her hands and the smooth performance of the engine was purely a mechanical effort.

All down the street and for the few blocks that the car traveled toward the Rowlands, Dale watched hopefully for a glimpse of Bill. Maybe he was coming back — on his way this very minute — and she regretted leaving home. She tried to imagine what Bill was doing, where he had gone. But not in her wildest conjecture did she picture the actual fact, that Bill was at police headquarters, in close and deeply interested talk with Lt. Blackwell!

Mary opened the front door almost at the instant that Dale's hand reached for the knob. Her pretty face was subdued, and she spoke quietly. Dale felt sharply the touch of death here, in the dimly lighted hall. The scent of flowers, too sweet, almost cloying and deeply depressing, hung heavily in the air. Dale started to say something, but before she could frame a decent expression of sympathy, Marcia appeared in the doorway of the back room.

"Please come in here, Dale," she said with much of Walter's peremptory inflection, but in a tone much more coldly formal.

"Walter phoned me," Dale said, following her, "and he seemed in a hurry, Aunt Marcia, but I was coming soon, anyhow, to tell you how sorry I am about Liza."

Marcia trailed back, as successfully long-suffering as Dale had ever seen her, to her favorite old sofa, which Liza had dubbed "Marcia's Comfort Station." She reclined upon it now as she regarded Dale with unconcealed aversion.

"Liza was always utterly inconsiderate of me," she said bitterly. "And now I have to stand *this* — this disgrace — suicide! God knows why!"

Dale thought she could have told her, but why bother? It was too late now to do Liza any good. Dale stood silent, looking at her aunt,

187

and was surprised at the look of pure enmity under the scarcely restrained temper that was directed at her.

"I have to take this — this humiliation — this blot upon the family which Liza has seen fit to inflict upon me, but what I *won't* take — I want you to clearly understand — what I won't take is your effort to involve me — to incriminate me — in Hi's murder. You needn't think you can clear your skirts this way! I didn't kill Hi for money or for any other reason. No one should know that better than *you!*"

Dale felt a sudden tingle of excitement go through her — this could mean only one thing — this attack was Marcia's retaliation.

"So," she said, looking with a cool, level gaze at her aunt's face, ugly with hate and resentment, "your fingerprints *were* on the trunk — Maggie's bank."

"What if they were?" Marcia interrupted her. "Yours were there too! Of course mine were there; I have been clearing out Maggie's things — everyone knows that — but you try to make a murderer of me because of $1,600, and to save your own skin."

"$1,673.25 to be exact, but how did you know? *I* took the account book. How could you possibly know that Maggie had saved $1,600?"

Marcia, cornered for only a moment quickly recovered. "Of course, I saw the money there," she snapped. "I never denied seeing it, did I? I'm merely denying that I *took* it! *You* were skulking around in the dark. Why did you go to sleep in Maggie's room, anyway, the night that Hi was killed?" Marcia made the last part of her sentence slow and significant. "Nearer than your own room — just across the hall? Remember, you're the one charged with murder. You're only out of jail temporarily. You're in no position to make wild accusations."

"Maybe not, but I'd like to ask you one question anyway," Dale said, holding now to her self-control with steely determination.

She asked Walter's question: "Where did you get the down payment for the house in Westover?"

Marcia clamped her lips. Looking stonily at Dale, she shrugged. "You have a great deal of impertinence, Dale. Daring to ask me about my private affairs. I don't intend to be quizzed by a — a — "

"Jailbird," Dale supplied evenly.

"I had meant to stand by you, Dale. But now I'm through!"

"And I am wasting time." Dale turned to leave.

"Does she expect me to weep?" Dale thought scornfully. "What help has she given me yet?" Without actually saying so, Marcia had accused her by look and gesture and inference, even by denial — overdone. Every word she had spoken to Lt. Blackwell on Friday night had tended to implicate Dale more deeply.

And now, as Dale went slowly up the stairs to Walter's room, she changed her mind about Marcia — this Marcia — not in the help-less, feminine role she was wont to play, but as Dale had witnessed her just now. This cold, implacable Marcia was fully capable of taking up that bust of Rabelais and striking Hi down, in a chillingly deliberate decision to gain her own ends.

Chapter Twenty-Six

WALTER was impatient and fuming. He sat in his room alone, foot propped upon a stool, an ashtray at his elbow, piled with cigarette butts. As Dale entered, he was replenishing his glass from a depleted fifth of bourbon and fishing for cubes from an ice bucket on the table beside him.

"You took long enough getting here," he said, and his manner was so lofty and irritable that Dale suspected it must be deliberately exaggerated to cover his agitation. He looked below par.

Dale halted on the threshold, suddenly sorry that she had come. Why should she be here, at the beck and call of one of the Rowlands? She felt a genuine regret about Liza, but both Marcia and Walter had brushed off her sympathy. They were her relatives, not her friends. The Rowlands were for themselves, each absorbed in his own concerns. The atmosphere of this house was full of hostility toward her and Dale felt vaguely uneasy. Death and enmity hung in the air. In short, a tête-à-tête with Walter was not inviting.

While she hesitated, Walter spoke again. "Come in and shut the door. You better lock it, no use in having anyone barge in."

Dale wasn't sure that she wanted to be locked in this room with him. If not drunk now, he looked as if he soon would be. But, she told herself, there was no danger. They knew they'd get their money. Then an ugly thought flashed into her mind. "If you were dead, they would get Hi's too. If one of them *had* killed Hi, why not kill again? The first murder, they say, is always the hardest."

Then she pulled herself together, thinking that if the bandaged foot was genuine, she could handle this situation. Too much had happened to her too quickly, but where had her usual confidence, her common sense, and her humor gone to? She had lost all of them completely this morning with Bill. Never again!

Dale unconsciously straightened her shoulders, and she locked the door as Walter suggested. Then she took a seat in a chair beside his, pulled out her cigarettes, and leaned forward casually taking up his lighter from the table. He mustn't know that she was frightened. She mustn't *be* frightened.

Sitting back, she looked Walter over critically, already feeling more natural and at ease. Just her cousin, whom she'd always known, egoistical, sometimes overbearing and often irritating, but also often entertaining and pleasant. Now she knew that he was a thief, an embezzler, but he wouldn't threaten *her* for funds. He knew that his mother would and could make good his deficit now.

"Want a drink?" he asked and reached over for the bottle. Dale thought she could do with one, but she hadn't come to sit chummily and drink with Walter. She shook her head. He slopped some more liquor into his glass and met her eyes, possibly with bravado; more likely he was really indifferent to her opinion of him.

He said with perfect aplomb, "Since Liza told me she's sent you a note about the digitalis, no doubt she told you why she gave it to Hi. With her usual talent for bungling, making a martyr of herself, she's almost ruined me. All right, I can see you know about the bank, but there's a lot you don't know and I have to tell you, because of this!" He scowled at his crippled foot. "I'd take care of the job myself, otherwise."

"Where," he asked, with a change of tune, as if this question were uppermost in his mind and he couldn't wait to get to it, "where is *Death and the Miser?*"

Dale was completely surprised by the sudden change of topic and his evident anxiety. "Why?" she asked. "What's that got to do with anything?"

"It's got everything to do with everything? Where is it now?"

"Why, over at the rectory; Bill took it over there because he said Darrel said that Hi had left it to Father John."

"So he knows that? Well, you better get over there on the double quick and get it. Where did Bill put it?"

"It's in Father's study — on the floor, propped against the wall, Bill said." Dale answered almost automatically, filled with amazement at the trend of Walter's questions. "Father John doesn't really want it, Bill says."

"He better want it, if he wants $25,000. This is what you must do, Dale, since I can't. Keep Nick from getting it. Nick doesn't know where the painting is yet — that gives us some advantage — but he'll find out."

"You mean that is what it's worth? That it *is* an original?"

"God, Dale, no! I mean that the $25,000 that Hi hid, that I handed Bill, for him, at the bank, *is on the back of that picture.* That's where Hi hid it and that's where Nick will find it, before Father John does. I am damned if I am going to let that blackmailer walk off with the money — right under my nose!" Walter drained his glass and set it down with a bang.

There was only one thing that Dale was sure of in all this muddle of staggering statements: *Walter was wrong!* There was no money on the back of the Bosch painting. Hadn't she seen it flat on its face in the study? Hadn't she seen the back of the canvas old and bare of all but its stains, lying there exposed on the floor?

"No, no. If the money was ever there, it's not there now, Walter. It's gone."

"How do you know?" For a moment Walter looked alarmed, then his face cleared. "Oh, you — that's what *you* think! The old boy was smarter than that."

But Dale repeated, "There was nothing on the back of the picture — I saw it on the floor — someone had dropped it, or knocked it down and the back of the picture had nothing on it, I tell you. If twenty-five $1,000 bills had ever been stuck on it, they are gone!"

Walter looked exasperated as well as relieved. "Listen, my bright cousin, just do as I say. Get out of here now, and beat it over to

192

the rectory, before Nick gets there, if you value the money that old rascal left to Father John. *And do it now*. Bring the painting here. I'll keep on eye on it." Walter reached over and opened the table drawer. "Come, look-see, I am equipped to take care of $25,000 or any amount. Just let Nick put one foot in this door!"

Dale got up and looked into the drawer. There lay a large ugly revolver within easy reach of Walter's hand. She had no doubt it was loaded. Walter grinned as she instinctively shrank back. Less than ever did she want to stay here now, in this locked room with Walter slightly drunk, and that deadly looking gun. Then she realized that the locked door was no danger to her. The key was in the lock — all she had to do was to turn it and leave.

"Why are you sitting down again?" Walter demanded angrily. "Do I have to send you out of here with this?" His hand moved toward the drawer.

"Don't be silly," Dale said, refusing to be panicked, looking as stubborn as she could. She knew that she was necessary to Walter at this moment. "You might make me leave easily enough. I am tempted to do that now, but you can't force me over to the rectory and back, *if* your ankle is really sprained. I'm not going a step, Walter, until you explain. What has Nick to do with it? How does he know anything about the money? How do *you* know? I have told you — why won't you believe me? — that if Hi ever put the money on the back of the Bosch, someone has it already. I saw the painting the night Hi was killed, in the study, face down on the floor, before Lt. Blackwell came. He locked it in when he left. The police are still keeping the study locked. No one has been in there, until the lieutenant let Bill in to get the picture to take to Father John yesterday, and then he locked the door again.

Walter's tense impatience increased visibly. "Your curiosity may be expensive. It *may* cost Father John $25,000! Nick *may* be lifting it while we sit here wrangling."

Dale simply did not believe him; she knew she was not risking Father John's legacy. There was no legacy attached to *Death and the Miser*. She didn't understand what Walter was up to. This might be a trick, sending her on a wild-goose chase. She didn't trust Walter anymore. She would go off on no blind mission; besides, there was a lot she'd like to know. She lighted another cigarette and assumed a waiting pose. The baffled and frustrated look that Walter sent her was more convincing than anything he had yet told her, but Dale kept still, hoping that she was displaying a poker face.

"You're a stubborn little fool." Walter capitulated with bad grace. "My shortage at the bank is none of your business, but that's how Nick got mixed up in this. I lost a few times at poker, took a little to pay up, and could have put it back — but Nick caught on. One night when I was a bit high, I guess I talked too much — then I had to keep him quiet.

"The more he got the more he wanted. He even played on Liza's gullibility. The little fool had fallen for him, and he knew it. All he wanted was more money, but she thought he was helping her to save me from prison — replace the money before I was discovered. Any day it might be too late. He had her scared to a jelly. She told me this yesterday. I'll swear I didn't know it before."

Dale interrupted. "Does the bank know yet?" she asked.

"No," Walter said, "but — "

"But *how,* Walter, how have you fooled them all this time?" She assumed an exaggerated interest — but she did want all the facts she could get out of him. Her interest flattered him.

"I've got a pretty good system — overstatement of cash balance at the end of a day, and postponing the report of receipt of deposits from one day to the next. It's worked so far. Trouble is, I don't want to push my luck; and then there's Nick around my neck. Mother's got to fork up. I'm not waiting for the estate to be settled. She can borrow on her credit. She's balky but she'll do it."

"So you've told her? How did she take it?" Dale could imagine.

"Oh, she writhed and fainted in coils." Walter made a face. "But I told her to come off it, the pot was calling the kettle black — she'd rifled a bank herself."

Dale felt her heart leap. "It was Maggie's, wasn't it? She denied it, Walter."

"To you, of course, but she took it all right. I nailed her. I knew that was the down payment on the Westover house. She swears she thought it was part of Hi's $25,000 that he'd hidden, and she only borrowed it. Her collateral being the trust fund. Actually she'll get away with that too, now that Hi's dead. She can cover us both and no one the wiser." Walter grinned.

"But Nick! What about Nick?" Dale asked.

"Nick won't have any leverage after this, and I think Nick is clearing out. Scared. He'll make a try for the picture, though. You're giving him a swell chance right now — my gosh, Dale, you *must* go!"

"No." Dale sat still. "How did Nick know — or you — that Hi hid the money — if he did — on the back of the picture?"

"*I* told him." Walter hesitated, then went on. "I was pretty desperate and I guess I was pretty excited too, when I figured it out. Nick was pushing me, and I told him I'd settle up for once and for all. But he wasn't letting me do it alone." Walter paused again, arranging his thoughts. Dale wondered, if he was making all this up. But Walter went on rapidly, with no more hesitation. "He got smart and went after it himself, without me. That was the night Hi was killed, and I think either Liza or Nick must have done it, Dale. If Nick can get hold of that money, he'll clear out before the police get on to him. But I'm not sitting by letting him get away with it."

"You can always tell Lt. Blackwell," Dale suggested keeping down her excitement, afraid to hope.

"Thanks," said Walter. "We'll handle this without the lieutenant. Can't you see I'm trying to help you, Dale? Either Nick or Liza could have hit Hi after she came crashing into the study and waked him up. She told me herself that she followed Nick. Either Nick got panicky thinking Hi had seen him, or Liza, trying to give Nick a chance to get away, grabbed up that statue and whacked Hi with it."

"I don't believe Liza did it," Dale maintained. "Easy enough to put it on Liza now. She can't defend herself."

"Why'd she kill herself then?" Walter countered. "She came in here and garbled out a lot of stuff yesterday afternoon — crazy stuff about how she'd tried to save me — given Hi the digitalis for my sake. And then later, scared he'd spot my slipup at the bank and make a money motive of it, she tried to get Blackwell to concentrate on Bill. So she puts a wig in Bill's file case — damned if I know why. What good would that do me? Crazy — that is all — just plain nuts."

Dale caught her breath. Liza! So it *had* been Liza! All these disjointed things — ought to fit — she didn't know how — Liza — muddling everything — protecting Walter — implicating Bill. Liza putting the wig in the file case! But that wasn't crazy — that was pretty smart.

"Did Liza take it out again, Walter?" Dale asked.

"What? The wig? No, she said she was sorry and went back, but it was gone."

"Where were *you*, Walter, when Nick was after the picture? How did he get in? I don't believe you let him try it alone."

"You don't suppose he told me? Nick was pulling a fast one, but Liza heard him, and went to investigate, and fell up against the door — so she says — sounds typical: but she might have lied, she might have let Nick in."

Dale considered this. Liza hadn't been asleep, as Marcia had thought, or pretended to think.

"Someone put out the lights before I got there. I couldn't see and I ran into Hi." Dale checked herself, she didn't want to live it over again. "You could have been there, Walter, and Marcia too." That, she thought, would account for more of the footsteps running. "Did you kill Hi, Walter?" she asked recklessly.

"No," Walter shouted and, starting to spring up on both feet, let out a cry of anguish, and sank back again. "Go to hell!" he groaned.

"It *is* really sprained," Dale thought with satisfaction.

"I'm going now," she announced with new assurance, standing up quickly, "but not to hell, and not for the picture. I'm going to Mr. Watkins' office. I'm expected there this afternoon. I just remembered. I don't know *why* you got me here, unless you were scared, unless you thought by putting Liza and Nick on the spot you'd be safer. Hi's lawyers are going to defend me, Walter, and they're not going to miss a thing. If you're telling the truth, I'm as good as free already!"

"Sit down, Dale."

196

Dale sat, instantly, without volition. Her knees simply gave way because Walter was pointing the gun at her.

"I see I'll have to convince you this way." His face was flushed angrily. "You'll thank me for this later."

Dale wondered what he was fumbling in his pocket for. Was he drunk? How drunk? The gun stayed pretty steady in his right hand, while his left was groping toward an inside pocket.

Dale didn't move. She breathed a silent prayer, and said quietly, "You can put the gun down, Walter. I'll stay, if you've got something to show me."

Walter laid the revolver on the table. "All right, but don't try any tricks." He had succeeded in bringing out an envelope. The flap was torn open. He took from it a thin sheet of paper, airmail paper, and Dale could see the fine spidery writing as he held it up, through the nearly transparent sheet. Then she glanced down at the envelope lying before him on the table — and looked again, her eyes riveted upon it.

"That," she said in a stunned whisper, "says 'For Father John.' It's Maggie's writing." Then she exclaimed, her voice rising, unable to control her excitement. "I thought you said you'd lost it. I thought that was what you were looking for in the study."

Walter was taken completely by surprise. "What do you know about this letter?"

"I know that Marcia found it and you said you'd give it to Father John, but you didn't."

"How did you know that?" Walter asked.

"It doesn't matter, I'll tell you later, go on, Walter." Dale tried to control her impatience.

He acquiesced, also anxious to get on. "Marcia didn't find *this* letter, Dale." He held the sheet up for her to see. "She missed it entirely, because it was thin and lay flat against the envelope, I expect; or maybe she just didn't bother after she read the other, the one with the verse — 'doggerel,' she called it. But did she slip up that time!" he gloated. "I'll read that in a minute." He patted the envelope. "Hi wrote them both. First this one, dated March 8, the same day he got the $25,000 from the bank. The doggerel that

197

Marcia read he stuck in the same envelope. He gave it to Maggie, I am sure, when he thought he was dying; or he told her where it was and where the money was. She was to deliver it when he was gone. She took it and he never got it back, because he didn't know where she'd put it, and he wasn't well enough to hunt for it. I'm sure I'm right, and listen to this! Just try to laugh this off, 'Doubting Thomas.' " Walter unfolded the tissue thin sheet and read:

"Dear John —

"I'm leaving you in my will, now in the custody of Walters and Watkins, my executors — and properly worded with all the legal claptrap — my checkerboard and men, to console you for your poor and luckless checkered career — and the painting by Hieronymus Bosch, 'Death and the Miser.' I do not defend the picture, which I know you dislike — please note, that I even go so far as to point out that *behind the scene of this corruption, lies the source of all corruption.* But though you do not care for the subject, it is your job to find 'Sermons in stones — good in everything.' I have no doubt, therefore, that your Christian charity will succeed in discovering something (of which no one else is aware) to redeem the thing.

"Besides all this, I count upon the poor old guy, so beset by devils, to be a constant reminder of
                    "Your irredeemable friend,
                    Hiram Bosch."

"Don't say anything," Walter laid down the letter and took up the envelope again, extracting this time a sheet of coarse tablet paper. He unfolded it and read just three lines, which were scrawled in the center of the page.

            "Here's a clue, John, to sharpen your wits —
            The prize is here, where cloth doth bind it.
            Within the cloth, the Cloth must find it."

"Not bad! If it *is* a little obvious, remember, he had begun to

198

worry for fear the letter wasn't suggestive enough — he *wanted* Father John to find the money."

Then Walter waited while Dale still sat silent, stunned, really convinced now that Walter was right.

"Use your head, Dale. Didn't you ever hear of a false back? Some evidence of that was what I was looking for in the cupboard Friday night, not the note. I never let this envelope get out of my hands once I'd read it."

"But you said you'd lost it."

"I told Mother I'd lost it — yes. I didn't intend to turn it over to Father John — I wanted to figure it out."

"What did you find in the cupboard?" Dale asked with more respect for Walter's brains than she had ever had before.

"The empty frame and stretcher that had held the old painting — the one that Hi took down when he hung the Bosch," Walter said. "Now do you see?"

Dale saw. Hi had done a perfect job of camouflage: using the old stained back of the other picture must have solved a big problem for him. It was even approximately the same size; cutting it off the stretcher with his razor blade would have been easy. It required very little trimming to make it slip under the inside edges of the Bosch stretcher, and lie flat and smooth over twenty-five $1,000 bills. No one would even dream that it formed a double backing. The age and stains of canvas had fooled *her* completely.

Dale stood up looking at Walter with excitement. "I'll go right away," she said.

Walter was tucking the two sheets back into the envelope. With satisfied ego and triumph, he said eagerly, "I'll be waiting. Step on it, Dale — but look out for Nick. Nick will be dangerous."

Chapter Twenty-Seven

DALE was glad that she had met no one as she ran down the stairs. She wanted to get away as fast as she could. But in the car again she did not start at once. She sat thinking ruefully of Hi.

That note — how like him — inimitable, contradictory Hi! Giving a small fortune to Father John — but hiding it from him — then helping him to find it — in cryptic verse!

And again: loving her, and plunging her into unhappiness. At the last, relenting. "He didn't want to let me go, but he'd never plead," Dale thought, "he'd plan something."

Yet surely Bill was right. Hi had not designed this bitter farce primarily against them, although frustrating their love for a time had dovetailed nicely with his major plot. The plot had gone awry. Now she would never know the whole of that plan — so important to Hi that he'd let the chips fall as they may — because Hi and Maggie, the only ones who knew, were gone. No one was left.

Then Dale sat up abruptly. Someone *was* left — their murderer! And she was wasting time. No time to think now — much as she needed to. She would have to work at it while driving. She must go on.

Dale edged carefully from the curb; a car had come and parked almost on her front bumper. She maneuvered out of the narrow space. Walter had not told her the whole truth, *that* she was convinced of. When he had paused to decide just what he was going to say — and how much — she knew that he was making things the way he wanted them.

Nick, she believed, *was* after the picture, or Walter would never have sent for her, told her anything. One thing she was nearly sure of; Nick had not worked entirely on his own. Walter would not have let him get away with that, because Walter needed the money very badly.

She turned the corner and headed down Bank Street toward Holt. The rectory was not many blocks away when suddenly behind her came the wail of a siren. Dale jumped; she couldn't bear that sound. But it wasn't the police. As she pulled over to the side and stopped, the long body of the fire truck streaked past her, followed by the engine, and the fire chief's car close behind added to the din. A motorcycle policeman shot past her and forged ahead between the cars in front.

This was fine! A fire! A traffic jam! And all headed in the same direction that she was going, which meant crawling along behind, or turning off and going around, which she couldn't do now, there was no intersection for another long block. She moved out again into line, and slowly inched along.

What if Walter had tried for Hi's money before? Nick had been pushing him for a long time. Even before Maggie's cruel death, there was Liza, desperate, giving Hi the digitalis to extricate Walter. Liza again — hiding the wig — implicating Bill.

They were honking behind her now, and Dale realized she had not gone ahead with the others. Accelerating a bit, she covered the short distance and slowed again, nearly bumper to bumper. Then the jam up front brought her to a standstill. It looked as if the fire engines had stopped, but she couldn't see. Suppose it was the rectory? It couldn't be — not on this street.

Dale leaned way out over the open side of the convertible and looked. The engines had stopped, down near the next block though. They were near the corner and the hydrant was there. They were fastening the hose to it. No one would be able to pass that yet, and so she'd not be able to turn off and go around — not soon. The crowd was too thick for her to see the ground floor of the house, but the upper part was clear, the fire didn't show. Maybe it wouldn't be long.

Her mind went back to Liza as she settled back again with her hand on the wheel. Yes, Liza might have heard Walter and Nick planning. Suppose Nick had been the imposter in the confessional. Walter wouldn't fit that role at all, but Nick was the right height, and Dale suddenly realized that Nick could have done it easily. He'd know about confession; he'd been a halfway sort of Catholic — started out as one — early fallen away, but he would know enough. Walter could have heard Maggie talking of confession; Dale tried to remember. He'd been there that day, but she thought he had left before Maggie had asked; before she'd said she wanted to go for Father John's advice.

Behind her there was honking again — she wished they'd let her think . . . "Oh, all right, I'm going!" The convertible leaped forward and then had to stop again.

Walter — her mind took it up again — might not have left. He might have waited in the hall and listened; anyone could have done that. But Bill had come afterward, and she hadn't noticed.

Nick would fit, all but his hair, that shock of black hair. Dale's thoughts leaped; the wig, of course! Even Liza had thought of a wig. But if Nick had got the information from Maggie in the confessional, why had the note been so important to Walter? Perhaps Nick hadn't — perhaps Maggie had muddled it, telling it. But then, he wouldn't have killed her, not until he knew. . . .

Ahead of her the cars started moving. Dale determined not to let the irate driver squeeze past her; now she could go along at a more normal speed. They were nearing the corner, the hose must be attached. She followed in line, and then another siren wailed behind her! Over to the side again! And she could almost hear the man in the green car swearing.

Nick would not have killed Maggie — yes, he would — he *had* to — she'd followed him — recognized him!

It did hold together. Nick and Walter — Walter, the brains, still trying to find the money, and Marcia unwittingly helping him by producing Hi's note. Even if Walter wasn't actually a murderer, and

202

had never planned to kill anyone, Nick had. No wonder Nick wanted to get money — clear out. Dale made a quick shift then; there was a hole in her reasoning, because if Walter knew that Nick had killed Maggie, that would have given him the upper hand.

At this point the traffic sped up. The second siren had been another motorcycle officer coming to direct things. Now with the going smoother, Dale's thoughts moved more smoothly too. She decided she wasn't wrong after all. Walter was involved: having planned everything, he'd not want to tell. Then Marcia had come up with the note, and he'd seen a way out.

But Dale did not believe that Nick was alone in the study when Liza had bumped into the door and started all the bedlam. Any one of them — she had not yet relinquished Marcia — could have hit and killed Hi. And Walter's foot — how had he hurt it? Getting away — running. She hadn't even asked him! She believed now that Nick had killed Maggie. "Look out for Nick, Nick is dangerous," Walter had said, and then sent her off to stop him.

Nick was a killer. She was racing with a killer. Why hadn't she phoned the rectory? She could have told Father John or Father Don, Nassau even, to lock up the picture; then she'd have had time, could have gone when it was safe. No chance to phone now. Dale gripped the wheel with cold hands.

She had reached the corner. The house showed no flames and she dismissed it from her mind. She was able to detour now. Around two more blocks and she was facing the rectory. Why was she so frightened? What she had to do was very simple. Just run up and get the picture, and take it with her to the lawyers; they would put it in their safe. If both priests were out, Nassau would be in, and Nick could not be here yet. In spite of Walter's nervousness, Dale was sure Nick couldn't have located the painting so soon, if he ever could.

Both the front door, which she'd tried first, and the kitchen door were locked. She didn't ring, just in case Nick was inside; she certainly didn't want to warn him. But Dale was even more sure now; no one was in the rectory — not even Nassau, who had probably gone to the fire.

Remembering the side door then, Dale went around to the narrow little lane so close to the wall that no one used it anymore; but she often had, when a kid, short-cutting through.

The door was stuck but not locked. She pulled violently and succeeded in forcing it open enough to let herself through, easing in sideways, into darkness which was only slightly dissipated by the opening she'd scraped through.

Dale knew that she was standing on the landing at the turn of the cellar steps — up to the pantry, down to the furnace room. But suddenly, all she wanted was to turn and squeeze back out to daylight and security.

She stood wavering. "Leave now, go back home and phone," she thought. The impulse was very strong. She stood fighting her cowardice. Then very close to panic, indecision becoming unbearable, Dale moved quickly toward the steps leading straight up and grasped the handrail. She didn't look back. She couldn't have seen down into the darkness — even had she tried — not around the curved descending steps. She could not know that there was a body down there sprawled upon the floor — Nassau, who had not gone to the fire.

And so she reached the top and opened the door leading into the pantry.

From there she walked quickly and very quietly through the dining room, where the supper table was already set, a nice normal note in this strange secretive silence that possessed the house. Silence — of course. The house was empty; what did she expect? Not the infinitesimal sound that came from the second floor. It came just as she put a hand on the newel post — one foot on the first tread — starting up to Father's study, which was just above, across the hall, facing the stairway. The door was partially open; she could see the top of it, a dark angle slicing into the facing light.

The sound did not come again. She had imagined it. She held her breath and stepped up the first step, moving lightly, part of the silence. Halfway up, she paused. From the study there came faint stirrings. Someone or something was moving carefully, cautiously in there.

"Father John," Dale argued to her rising fear, "has come back

204

and is at his desk, working — he was moving a book or papers."
She so nearly called out to him that she almost choked, swallowing
back the words.

"Wait! Go and look." A few more steps up and her eyes were at
floor level, seeing only a section of the study rug. "Go closer — if it
is Nick you can creep back again — get down the stairs and outside
before he even knows you are here."

Braced by this optimism and a fair share of Hi's tenacity, plus
very real courage, Dale took the last two steps in one quick one,
and then flitted across the hall to the partially open door of Father
John's study.

Risking all for one brief moment, Dale looked inside. Father John
was not there. No one was there. Then her gaze shifted from the
desk, and she saw the bent and stooping figure, down on the floor
with his back to her. Nick had beaten her to it!

Dale's heartbeats turned into rapid hammerblows. She found it
hard to breathe — but she was as still as a cat at a hole as she
watched. Across the room she could see the edge of the stretcher
frame — the rest of the canvas back was hidden by the bulk of
his body, his wide shoulders, stooping. His head was invisible, down
out of sight as he seemed absorbed in some sort of a task. Then his
hand thrust out quickly, sideways, holding what looked like a crisp
dollar bill, and Dale's eyes followed the movement.

There on the floor lay a couple more — Hi's $1,000 bills — very
insignificant, unimpressive — those powerful slips of paper. She
scarcely glanced at them, and turned her full gaze upon the man's
back. She was frozen into unconcern about herself, her danger, her
need to retreat — before he looked around.

She remained frozen because it was too late; he was straightening
up. Dale saw his head raised above his shoulders, broad shoulders,
but she still could not move. She was trapped, trapped by shock,
temporarily paralyzed, because this was not Nick's head — this was
not Nick! The tall figure slowly unfolded, stood and suddenly
whirled around. A $1,000 treasury note fluttered down from his
loosened fingers, slowly drifted to the floor, and lay with others
scattered about his feet.

She stood motionless, vulnerable before him, and heard the words he hurled at her: a lament, furious and reproachful.

"Not you, Dale, not you! In the name of all the devils that pursue me, how did you get in here through locked doors? Why did you choose to come *now?* Or was it Hi that sent you?"

Chapter Twenty-Eight

"I DID it with mirrors," Dale answered dazedly. "How did *you*, Dr. Cotten?"

This was the strangest thing, this queer feeling of unreality which invaded her. She had concentrated so on Nick that she could not make the transition to Dr. Cotten. But there he stood, his tortured spirit demanding recognition, and what he was saying was real enough — loaded with bitterness and melodrama. She listened spellbound.

"So this is the final, the ultimate torment that Hi has inflicted upon me! Think of it, Dale!" He threw out his arms in a gesture of crucifixion. "The irony? A physician, dedicated to preserve life, repeatedly forced to destroy it!" Then, thrusting out a trembling hand, he counted off on each raised finger an appalling calendar of guilt. There was only genuine delusion, Dale felt, and enormous self-pity in the enumeration.

"An old woman, a young girl, useless and foolish, but still entitled to live; Hi himself, more deservedly, and just now an innocent Negro boy. But he might have spared me this!" And Dale, confounded by his recital, looked incredulously at his tears. "You understand that I have no choice?" She did not quite grasp his meaning, but she knew that she must handle this strange phenomenon carefully; she must break down his awful certainty of ultimate torment.

"No, doc. No, I don't understand." She challenged him courageously, "How could Hi force you? Helpless old man, ill, and now dead?" Brave words.

But the doctor coming toward her seemed to grow excessively tall, and towered before her, brooking no contradictions. She drew back but with no thought of flight, feeling as much a prisoner as if she were still in the city jail, her fascinated eyes fixed upon him as she stood rigid and listened.

"Nevertheless, he did, and *is still working against me;* by the train of events he has set in motion; by his cat-and-mouse game. Ah, how he enjoyed it! Promising — delaying — refusing! Taunting, taunting, dangling it before me, snatching it back, the money I must have; that he'd promised."

"He *is* sane," Dale thought, "terribly sane, in spite of this fanatical obsession, and is trying to shift the weight of his sins by becoming a martyr." She looked at him, hoping to see a weakening of conviction accompanying his tears. But he was trying only to make her understand, as if this would exonerate him, and lessen the struggle between them. Dale wondered how he could expect her to understand.

"The money was not for myself, Dale. For all of humanity, I needed that equipment. Only the lack of a few mechanical instruments prevented my accomplishment. I knew I could save countless lives — even those still unborn, and Hi was delaying — preventing! All I wanted was a mean paltry sum, and he withheld this gift to humanity, to tantalize me!"

"Why blame Hi?" Dale, now fully aware that here it all was, fitting together correctly at last, forced herself to rally once more to Hi's defense. "Why not blame some others? What about your Medical Society? Why must it all depend upon Hi?" she cried, rebelling at this injustice. "Hi was *not* evil. He was just an old man playing with fire perhaps, but he never intended any final lasting harm. You shall not blame him for your crimes. They are yours, not his. *I'm doing better,*" Dale thought, *"I'm defrosting."*

"He forced me, Dale."

"Hi didn't force you into Father John's confessional," she said, and then, encouraged by her own temerity, "you were there, weren't you — dressed up in a wig? Tricking Maggie. Poor trusting Maggie, with her little St. Christopher medal. You hit her when she asked for a blessing. Can you blame Hi for that?" Dale didn't wait for an answer. "Hi didn't force you to strike him down or make Liza take all those pills — God only knows *how* you did that!" She stopped for breath, shaking.

Then as if she were a child again, he silenced her with a raised hand and an obdurate look.

"I don't want you to believe that I have wished to kill anyone. Can't you see? I had to kill a few to save many. As for Liza, I gave her no pills, but a concentrated liquid dose — the same drug of course. 'A sedative,' I told her, which was the truth. She drank it down willingly. I simply pocketed a handful of pills, and left the half-empty bottle beside her bed. An easy trick." He paused and then said, "She was expendable, poor girl."

"Was she really a paranoiac?" Dale asked.

"Well, no," the doctor shrugged. "But very neurotic, and so trouble-some, putting that wig in the file case."

Dale gathered her forces again for attack. "So it was *you*, not Lt. Blackwell, who took it out. I would never have guessed it was yours. . . ."

"It was not mine, Dale, not that one. Mine I destroyed. But Liza was playing a dangerous game when she bought a wig. She went to the same shop — the only one that carries theatrical stuff. She knew what to ask for because it had to be like Father John. I couldn't let a wig come into the picture at all. Blackwell, fortunately, had not seen it. I had to confiscate it."

"Is that why you killed her?"

"No, I think she saw me Friday night when I came back for the picture. *You'd* stopped me earlier. You were in the study when I came the first time. I couldn't shake you off, so I checked on Hi, found him safely asleep, and left — but I had to come back. I had my key but the door was open this time, which put me on guard; even so, I didn't anticipate what happened."

"I put the chain on," Dale thought. "Who took it off?" But she let the doctor continue without interruption.

"As I reached the top of the stairs there was a crash and Liza, running, nearly bumped into me. She saw me whether she knew it or not; sooner or later she would remember. Hi was coming across the hall toward me — more interference. I saw the statue was on the floor. I picked it up and hit him just as he reached the study door. Happily someone turned off the lights then and feet went running down the stairs. I waited a second for clearance — and then you came. You couldn't see me in the dark, you brushed past me, and almost instantly I heard you cry out — heard Hi fall. I left quickly, the way I had come, without the money — again."

Dale was silent. How close she had come to the truth, to have missed it so completely.

"But you cannot stop me this time," the doctor exulted.

"Why couldn't you have waited? In a little while Hi would have given you the money. You know how he was."

"Because," and Dale saw that she had roused his fury again, "because by then I'd used the funds of the Medical Society — in desperation. I am the treasurer and I took them, but the money has to be replaced. They suspect. The books are to be audited."

Dale felt suddenly sick and quite rash. "So you're borrowing — in advance — like Walter, like Marcia. Thieves, all of you, thieves. Why can't you face it? Did Hi know you had stolen the money?"

"Call it stealing if you like. No, why should I tell him that?" He didn't look at her. A frown was settling on his face wiping out the bright exaltation, like a gathering storm. "I blame the Society. I blame them deeply, Dale, for refusing me repeatedly, but Hi had promised the money. Primarily I blame Hi."

Suddenly Dr. Cotten snapped back to the present. "You understand that I have no choice," he reiterated. "No one shall stop my work, not even you. I will go on. I will succeed."

All through this talk, she had watched that small thin bladed knife in his hand. He had been holding it absently. He had been using it, she supposed, to remove the covering from the back of the canvas.

Now the blade was not a tool. With a sudden frightful clarity she saw its mad potentiality.

210

He was turning it in his hand, glancing down at it, considering it. Dale watched him as if in a dream.

"My last, my personal sacrifice." The doctor's voice had become harsh and muffled. He reached for her suddenly, unexpectedly, and his arms binding, encircling iron bands, gathered her to him. She struggled helplessly as he forced her head to bend backward, tightening his hold and maneuvering her into position — turning her head.

Terror gathered all Dale's young strength then. In one last desperate frenzy of defense, she tried to push herself away from him.

There was a tremendous explosion that seemed to tear through her head, but as she sank into sudden blackness, she felt the iron bands give way.

The blackout lasted only a moment. From the floor of Father John's study she heard a confusion of sounds. Dr. Cotten's voice, unnaturally high and strident, shouted something; then immediately arms were around her again, but they couldn't be his — his voice had been distant.

Instantly she opened her eyes and saw Bill. It *would* be Bill! Now she needn't do anything . . . but Bill didn't know. She strained away from him, wildly. "Don't Bill! Don't let him get away! Stop him; Stop him!"

"Let him go," Bill said. "He won't go far, Dale. Blackwell's men are down there."

She accepted that, slowly relaxing, and let Bill's arms come around her again. Then Dale sat up taking stock of herself, her surroundings. She pushed her hair back from her forehead, and saw the gun lying on the floor like a stage prop, the second one she'd seen today, lying somewhere. Oh yes, Walter's, but this was the rectory.

"Dr. Cotten didn't have one, Bill," she said. "He was trying to do it with his knife. He was — going to cut my throat!" She clung to Bill again and was swept by a storm of weeping. Bill held her until it was over, until she was reduced to sobs, long, shuddering sobs. He tried not to think of how close she had been to death.

"That's mine, or rather Walter's," Bill explained obscurely. "If you mean the gun. I don't think I hit him. Couldn't risk hitting you. He went out that window and dropped from the balcony. They weren't expecting that. He can't get away."

"How did you get here, Bill; how did you find out? All I know is, Dr. Cotten killed them all. He told me. Oh! how horrible!"

They were sitting on the floor like a pair of kids. She was gripping his hands, an assurance against separation ever again.

Bill said, "I'll try to tell you, but there's a lot. You know, Dale, Blackwell's on our side now. Since yesterday. We got together."

"But how did he know? *We* didn't; no one did."

"It was you," Bill said. "I told you you had given me a lead, but you weren't interested then."

She shrank. She didn't want that brought up ever again. "Bill, how did you find me?" Dale asked, allowing herself a touch of feminine wile. She said softly, "It was just in the nick of time, Bill, darling, you saved me. . . ." Bill pulled her to him and this time she knew he wouldn't ever remember their quarrel.

Bill leaned over and picked up the gun. It was just possible that Dr. Cotten might come back. "We can't cover it all now, it's too much," he said. They sat close together on the floor, and Bill talked in low tones, with frequent pauses while they listened tensely for sounds from below.

"I took the gun from Walter. Rosina told me where you'd gone and I went after you. I ought to have shot Walter for sending you here, but instead I took his gun. It might be needed for Nick, but I didn't think so. I knew, you see, almost knew, it would be the doctor."

"But I don't see, Bill. I couldn't have given you a lead. I never dreamed it was he."

"You sent me to Sister Dennis!"

"Sister Dennis?" Dale raised her voice incredulously.

"Hush!" Bill warned.

"Yes, I went to see Sister Dennis. You sent me, remember? Father John told me you wanted me to go. And just before I left her, Sister said, trying to cheer us both up, 'Anyway, Bill, there's one bright spot. My prayers for Dr. Cotten have been answered.' I guess I looked surprised. 'Isn't it fine the Medical Society finally has given him the

212

money for his new apparatus?' she said. 'I've been praying for him for so long. He told me yesterday they'd OK'd it, at last. The dear man was quite overcome.' And," Bill chuckled, "so was this young man. Dale, I knew the Medical Society had put thumbs down on giving doc that money. Knew it for a fact. He wasn't a research man — a general practitioner. A man with a bee in his bonnet. Something queer. Why had he lied to Sister Dennis?

"Anything the least bit suspicious needed looking into — any old stab in the dark was worth trying — with you in that damn jail! I went right to Blackwell with it. Got quite a surprise. He already had an eye on doc. Hopkins on 'Embezzlement' told him Dr. Cotten was suspect. Hopkins was investigating for the Medical Association — missing funds. Dr. Cotten was the treasurer, you know. The Association knew he was buying a lot of new equipment for his lab. He told them Hi had given him the money, but they decided to check; called in the police — and Hopkins got the assignment. So you see, the lieutenant was *very* interested. And today Hopkins had said he was going to pick Cotten up. Blackwell comes into it now, once it ties in with the murder.

"After I talked to Blackwell, I left headquarters and rushed back to tell you. That's when Rosina sent me to the Rowlands. When I reached here, Blackwell's men had traced him, knew he was here. They didn't believe you were, though. They wouldn't let me inside. But I had to find you, so I sneaked down the lane, to the old side door. They were watching the front and the back, and had the whole square covered outside the walls. No one could get away — but I got in the same way you must have."

"That's what I did, Bill. Hush! — Who's that?"

"It's Father John! He must have been to his Monday class at the high school."

They heard his quiet, modulated voice raised, arguing, almost angrily. "But I tell you, I must find him. He may need me!"

Then the voice of one of the men, equally determined, "Stay away from him, Father! We're guarding that alley. Wait till we get him."

"That may be too late," Father John insisted stubbornly. "Get out of my way, man, I'm going out there. I'm a priest."

213

They heard footsteps running; then silence. Dale prayed aloud. "Oh God, don't let him hurt Father John."

Then a shot. A shout. Voices. Dale couldn't breathe. Then, after an eternity, they heard Father John quite distinctly, saying calmly, "I'm all right, lieutenant, just let's get him in here. It won't be long."

The lieutenant's voice then, saying, "I'm damn sorry, Father, I didn't shoot at him, I swear. That bullet must have ricocheted."

Chapter Twenty-Nine

IN THE small chapel in The Nursery Sister Dennis rose from her knees, and went into the sanctuary through the low gate in the altar rail. She removed the two prie-dieux centered before the altar, and set them back against the wall. The nuptial Mass was over. The candles had been snuffed out and the thin spirals of smoke had vanished some time ago. She went up the altar steps, moved the twin vases of pure white roses on either side of the tabernacle, a couple of inches, meticulously; and with a lovingly light touch smoothed an invisible wrinkle out of the altar cloth. She inspected the book and altar cards, saw that all was in perfect order. Then she descended the steps again slowly, stooping to pick up a couple of broken Stephanotis buds, which lay on the bottom step. She knelt once more, this time for just a few minutes, and then left, closing the chapel doors behind her.

Sister's face bloomed with happiness, as she quickened her pace and scurried with unbelievable speed down the long glistening linoleum corridor leading to the front door of The Nursery, which was open.

She passed the door of the office which was also open, glancing inside with apparent delight at the disorder — signs of festivity, used dishes and glasses sitting about on the center table — and hurried past in record-breaking antithesis to all habitual custom.

She broke into her gamin grin, as she joined Father John and the young lawyer, Darrel, out on the porch just in time to see a red-trimmed convertible round the corner, and she waved delightedly even after it had disappeared completely.

Father John was smiling too, the peaceful smile of one who knows he's done a good job, and looked at Darrel. Darrel's grin eclipsed them both.

"I'll say this for those two — when they do get started they sure move fast!"

There was a short silence, then, "It's a mystery to me," Sister Dennis said, "how she ever broke down his resistance to all that money."

Darrel turned a quizzical look upon her. "You, Sister, of all people! Stumped by a mystery?"

She looked puzzled. "I can't even guess a conundrum, Mr. Darrel — much less solve a mystery."

Darrell glanced at Father John and the priest was shaking his head, ever so slightly at Darrel, and then said loudly and firmly that he too would like to know the answer to Sister's mystery.

Darrel looked serious for a flickering second. "The answer to this one, Sister, is no mystery at all. Hi is the answer. Let's give the devil his due. Hi solved the problem! That will was a lulu, though. All the superior heads of the firm have been shaking over that will for days. Such vagaries and whims and intricacies! But let us shout praises for the way he demolished the 'Obstacle' by leaving a nice hunk of it to Bill — all for himself."

At Father John's surprised lift of eyebrows, "Didn't you know?" Darrel asked. "Oh, it isn't for free. Bill's got to sweat for it; but that's fine. That's the only way Bill would have it. He's got to finish that book, that family history that goes back to Hieronymus Bosch. Ten thousand for the work, completed and published is what the will allows."

"Vagaries," said the priest gravely, who *did* know of Hi's bequest to Dr. Cotten: two or three times the cost of the fatal equipment. Father John sighed, then brightened swiftly at the light in Sister Dennis' eyes.

"And I'm praying it will all look *wonderful* to Hi," she said with perfect conviction, "in the light of eternity."